The Diary of a Provincial Lesbian

V.G. Lee

Published 2006 by Onlywomen Press Limited, London, UK

ISBN 0–906500–86–9

British Library Cataloguing-in-Publication Data
A catalogue record for this book is available from the British Library

Typeset by RefineCatch Limited, Bungay, Suffolk, UK
Printed and bound in India by Gopsons Papers Limited

January

Georgie away working for a few more days. Am woken at five a.m. by Tilly's plaintive cry. I peer over the edge of the mattress. Tilly, (small, elderly black cat) is addressing the drawer of our divan bed – nowadays she thinks this is where I live when I'm upstairs. I pat her head and she starts back as if I've struck her with a rolled newspaper. Since going deaf everything is a surprise to her. She's become disorientated and wakes every two hours imagining it's dinner time again.

For such a frail old cat Tilly manages to beat me down the stairs. I have a bird's eye view of her hurrying along the hall and into the kitchen. Feel a pang because she used to be plump with thick soft fur. However she is still an extraordinary cat. She can say, "Hello", and "Good morning" or at least she can say, "Mellow", and "Nood norning". Were she younger and finer looking I could have carved out a career for her in advertising. As elderly cat she might be able to follow in the late Thora Hurd's footsteps advertising stair lifts and step-in baths. Small raddled feline disappears into step-in bath, "Nood norning" is heard above the sound of rushing water.

Tilly remains surprisingly athletic managing to jump from floor to chair to table, then the leap of four foot between table and work top where her empty plate waits. "Nood norning," she says cheerfully as if she's only just spotted me.

By the time I've fed Tilly, Georgie's cats, Samson and Delilah, have appeared looking bemused by the early hour. Feed them as well. Take two Neurofen. Go back to bed. Hear Tilly scrabbling in her litter tray. Put pillow over my head.

NB.1. Sometimes need to resort to two pillows over my head.

NB.2. Follow on from this reflection with further reflection that one day I will be discovered smothered by pillows over head. Who by? Probably not Georgie as she will be at a hotel in the Outer Hebrides. The front door emergency key holders. Mr. Wheeler, d.i.y. neighbour (left hand side) wanting to know if I have any wire for his Strimmer, Deirdre (right sided neighbour) wanting to know if I'm up to a full English breakfast

1

anywhere, Miriam (work colleague) wanting to know how she goes about meeting younger women. The police will be called.

"No sign of forced entry. She must have known her killer."

All key holders have watertight alibis. Deirdre telephones our local paper, the *Listening Ear*.

"I'm devastated", neighbour and close friend sobs, *"Margaret will be sorely missed. She leaves behind three motherless cats."*

Lesbian woman, (this for those reading local paper unsure what sex a lesbian might be), *found murdered. Neighbour discloses that she 'saw women coming in and out of lesbian love nest, morning, noon and night'. Multiple arrests expected.*

Radio Four: *"The sleepy seaside town of Bittlesea Bay was rocked today by the news that ..."*

Samson tentatively inserts his paw under pillow and finds my chin. Taps gently, then unsheathes claws and gives chin a playful scratch, "What the devil is that under the pillow?"

Emerge. Samson looks delighted.

"Yes?" I challenge.

"Grub up", Samson telepathises.

Look at clock. Still only five thirty-seven. Get up. Empty litter tray. Feed everybody again.

Make tea. Help myself to a chocolate digestive. Take tea back to bed. Search for *Farming Today* on the radio. Finally find a farmer using an emasculator on an unknown animal, "You need to be careful how you use it", he says to the presenter, "Remember nuts to nuts."

"I'll certainly be careful to remember that," I tell the radio and switch the farmer off.

Downstairs I hear the cat flap bang three times. Peace at last. Will sleep. Cannot sleep. Am wide awake. Get up and open the curtains. Red clouds streak the huge sky – a bad omen for the day but impressive. It is too early in the year for the sea gulls cries to be really raucous – I can only just hear them like the sound of protesters on a distant march. Down below, at the edge of the town a train trundles along taking the very first of the morning's commuters into London. Slowly Bittlesea Bay begins to waken.

Jan 5th
Georgie home tomorrow. Georgie, Georgie, Georgie! Normally

I wouldn't be so Georgie fixated but we parted on an acrimonious note. It began on the morning she was setting off to Edinburgh, when she called down to me, "Margaret, another cup of coffee wouldn't go amiss."

I experienced an increasingly familiar sensation of being a housekeeper and Georgie my employer. This was not the same sensation that Jane Eyre felt in the company of Mr. Rochester. Initial thought that I must stop wearing aprons and marigold gloves because they were becoming something of a uniform bedded down into a feeling of resentment that she would be away in Scotland on business from the 29th of December to the 7th of January. When I'd said, "But that means I won't see you over New Year," she'd replied, "But you saw me over Christmas."

Should have said immediately that surely women who were about to celebrate their tenth anniversary expected to spend all major holidays together. As always said nothing while fuming inwardly.

Made fresh coffee which in our house means *Instant* but newly boiled water.

"I could murder a couple of digestives."

Was reminded of deceased mother whose response to any childhood requests to do something had been, "What did your last servant die of? Exhaustion?"

Put several biscuits on to side of saucer. Carried coffee and biscuits upstairs. Georgie attempting to close suitcase in the middle of the landing nodded in the direction of her study desk. The words I hoped to hear were, "Thank you" or "You're an angel."

Georgie said, "You're not still sulking over me being away, are you?"

Vigorously denied sulking for any reason at all however Georgie's departure was tight lipped on both sides. Every day since have wished that Georgie was home so that any unpleasantness could be ironed out.

N.B. (Unsure of what NB stands for. Will ask Georgie on her return. Seems appropriate to diary entries). For Christmas Georgie gave me this diary – a large leather covered desk diary with four pages for each day. Also as a complementary gift, a copy of *Diary of a Provincial Lady* by E.M. Delafield, which is a gently funny book made up of articles written in the nineteen thirties about the provincial life of a married woman and her family. Georgie said, "I'm sure you could write something light and amusing – you often make me laugh."

Am going to try. Will not let Georgie read it till the end of the year. Will not even let Georgie see that I'm writing it. As I write keep before me image of next Christmas Eve, me in festive dressing gown (not yet purchased) as I appear like Eamon Andrews with my big book. Sometimes in my day-dream we sit either side of a roaring fire, sometimes Georgie sits one side of the roaring fire and I sit at her feet, but always we drink Ovaltine (our Christmas Eve night cap) as I read out hilarious Diary extracts.

Jan 6th

Visit my neighbour Deirdre which entails sliding open a section of our back fence. Deirdre is sitting at her computer, Lord Dudley next to her on the table sprawled in a cardboard box lid. (We are a cat loving street, dog lovers next street up the hill near the dog walking areas). Neither Deirdre nor Lord Dudley look up.

"She back tomorrow?" Deirdre asks, her eyes fixed on the multicoloured pattern on her computer screen.

"Yes."

"You pleased?"

"Very."

"What you doing later?"

"Cleaning."

"Fancy going to the caff?"

"Not today."

"Why not?"

"Cleaning."

I make tea in Deirdre's immaculate kitchen. Do not in any way feel like Deirdre's housekeeper. Deirdre already has a cleaner, someone to do her ironing as her partner Martin has to have two clean shirts every day and a laundry van, which is another story and proving problematic.

Sit opposite Deirdre while I drink my tea. She is an impressive woman, big, strong bodied, with a very pretty, doll-like face and masses of yellow curly hair. Small but bright blue eyes.

She is a successful packaging designer. That is what she calls herself. Or a successful woman. Or a happy woman. Or sometimes with a sensual swivel of her shoulders, "I'm just great! Stupendous! FANTASTIC".

She has advised me to also talk this way about myself.

Go home. A message from Georgie saying she can't get home till tomorrow, the roads are blocked by snow. Not to bother trying to ring back – her mobile's still not working.

Day not completely wasted. Deirdre and I go up to the Bittlesea Bay Café for a full English breakfast which lasts from eleven am till four pm. Came home, snoozed, watched the last half of an early Gregory Peck film set in Burma, finished stripping the bannister, fed the cats, emptied Tilly's litter tray. Watched forecast. As always it was wrong showing Scotland undergoing a freak spell of springlike weather. Blonde, vapid weather woman predicts: *A mild night in the northern parts of Britain*. Slept fitfully.

Jan 9th

Georgie got back yesterday looking tanned. It's amazing the difference these all over tanning booths make. There are several down here in Bittlesea Bay but yes, I appreciate that she wanted her top-up tan to be a surprise for me. She looks terrific. Out food shopping together in the supermarket caught a glimpse of us reflected in the store window and it was rather disconcerting. I mean, we've always looked quite different, but suddenly our differences seem much more marked and at odds. Georgie is tall, well built, (all the hotels she stays at have a gym), has dark hair with quite a bit of distinguished grey – in fact Georgie looks as if she might be a celebrity. I am a Margaret. I look like the worst sort of Margaret: middle height, middle build, middle coloured brown hair, middle coloured brown eyes.

To be more specific; we are a case of Piers Brosman going out with the actress Frances de la Tour. Yes, I realise Frances de la Tour is an extremely attractive woman. In just about every department she's more than a match for Piers Brosman, only physically, and I suppose I'm talking about glamour here, there'd be a disparity. And I'm definitely the Frances de la Tour character, only there's not even a hint of show bizz about me.

5

Did not discuss this with Deirdre who has adopted Martin's habit of chanting "Loser, loser," whenever somebody makes a negative statement about themselves, decided to take problem in to Miriam at work on Monday.

Jan 12th
This afternoon I walked along the sea front on my own. Georgie collating information accumulated while on business trip. It was freezing cold. The rain had turned to a fine sleet. Even so I sat on a bench and tried to pick out Beachy Head which was a faint and distant shadow. Sea a murderous grey. Watched a fishing boat tack out past the pier then change its mind and race back towards the haven of the fishing fleet end of the beach. Finally, frozen, I turned in from the sea and made my way to the Bittlesea Bay funicular railway. By the time I came out on the brow of the cliffs, the fishing boat had been dragged up onto the shingle. Stood and watched before going in the café. Inside, enveloped by muggy warmth nursed a hot chocolate and reflected on who I would like to look like given the choice; came up with a line drawing of a cowgirl.

Jan 13th
First day back at work since Christmas Eve. My boss, Tom Matthews, dropped a copy of the *Listening Ear* on my desk indicating its front page headline; *Bittlesea Bay's official lesbian community reaches double figures!*

Tom says, "They're taking over the town. First estate agents, now lesbians."

"Whatever next?" I replied. If the figures were true, Tom Matthews was employing a fifth of the lesbian population.

TM. Accountancy is a small firm. A tiny firm. There is Tom, me and Miriam who job share. I work from nine thirty to one thirty, Miriam from one to five thirty. We choose to overlap by half an hour so that we can shut the office and sit on the back step while Miriam has the last cigarette of her working afternoon and I eat my sandwiches.

Officially our job title is Accounts Typist. Unofficially we are also Secretary, Invoice Clerk, Filing Clerk, Coffee and Tea Maker and Plant Pot Waterer. In quiet moments I read female detective novels and Miriam reads science fiction.

Miriam is in her early sixties and refers to herself as a semi-retired lesbian or sometimes a very tired lesbian. Today as it was teeming we huddled in the doorway rather than our usual perch on the step. Not always easy discussing my problems even with Miriam. I'm sure she's thinking what am I bleating on about, at least I've bagged someone. Miriam appeared thoughtful and then said, "Yes, I can see it might be difficult living with a woman as damnably attractive as your Georgie – however she obviously likes the way you are or she wouldn't have stuck around all this time."

Which was surprisingly encouraging.

Miriam went on to talk about herself, announcing her new year's resolution to have a relationship with a younger woman.

"Shouldn't be too difficult as most women are younger than me," she said puffing away at her cigarette, "Pity about my body going to pot."

I insisted that what I could see of her body, (not necessary to specify neck, wrist, inch of ankles between sock and trouser leg hems), looked extremely trim. On the contrary I insisted that I was the one who had let my body go to pot.

"Yes," she agreed, "But of course you have Georgie."

Jan 14th

Miriam's mother has her third bout of flu since November. Tom Matthews always surprisingly sympathetic where Miriam's mother is concerned. I am inclined to think that Miriam uses her mother to get days off work but wouldn't dare even moot this possibility to Tom. On his desk is a photo of his own mother with her arms around him – he is about six years old and wearing a fairisle sleeveless pullover (as well as shirt, shorts, socks etc.). Tom's mother is smoking a cigarette, in fact her cigarette seems in danger of setting boy Tom's curly quiff alight. Tom often looks fondly at this photo while giving dictation.

While I'm musing on Miriam's mother and Tom's mother I spare a thought for my mother who is dead. She also smoked. Recall that when I had a splinter in my finger she sterilized the point of her darning needle by putting it into the lit end of her cigarette then used the needle to gouge out my splinter.

Tom interrupts my childhood recollections with the query,

"Are you just wool gathering Margaret or is there something constructive going on behind your dazed expression?"

Quickly respond that I am making a mental list of the gaps that need filling in the stationery cupboard.

Jan 15th

Miriam's mother near death's door. Tell Georgie over dinner. Georgie unimpressed. Says, "Miriam's mother's always at death's door. I bet you a fiver that she'll be right as rain by next week."

"Not this time. Tom's penciled question marks through the last half of next week in case he has to go to the funeral."

Jan 17th

Last night we had a dinner party. My old friend Laura came down from London without Pam, her latest flame. There was also Simone and Nicole who are more Georgie's friends, and Deirdre and Martin. Simone and Deirdre both wore long glittery scarves. Simone wore hers knotted warmly round her neck, implying a case of laryngitis, Deirdre had hers theatrically thrown about her voluptuous shoulders. Deirdre is more my friend, but Martin is nobody's friend. He says *People, when you get to know them, tend to be a disappointment.* Considering his views he is always surprisingly good company at social events providing there is an endless source of alcohol.

I cooked sea bass, bought locally, with parsley sauce. Noticed Deirdre and Martin weren't too keen and had a sudden recollection of Deirdre telling me on Jan the first that their new years resolution was to start the Atkins Diet but it was to be top secret till they were ready to amaze their friends by their astonishing weight loss. Caught Deirdre's eye and instantly knew that they'd eaten their usual steak and salad before they'd come out. Deirdre knew I knew and looked defensive, which meant her blue eyes got watery.

Was it a good evening? I think so. Martin told a funny story about Mussolini who is one of his heroes. Martin's heroes aren't everyone's heroes. Fortunately he does draw the line at Hitler. Then Nic and Simone did an hour on their upvc windows and Laura gave a demonstration of how to correctly dance the tango using the broom for a partner. Returned it to the cupboard saying, "You haven't half got a lot of cleaning equipment in there. All Pam's got is a brush and pan."

Deirdre looked appalled, "What about a hoover? We couldn't live without our Dyson, could we Martin?"

"Indeed *we* couldn't."

This was meant to be humorously sarcastic as it's touch and go whether Martin even knows where the Dyson lives. Or perhaps he thinks that's the name of the person who irons his shirts. *Dyson, when you hang my shirts up could you colour match them to my fresh underpants?*

"Pam's got floor boards. She just brushes the bits into the cracks between," Laura said blithely checking her jaw line in the mirror over the fireplace.

"Eeugh!" Deirdre resolves never to visit Laura and Pam's flat were she to be invited.

Georgie says, "Is this talk about cleaning very interesting? Margaret, the music's stopped. Put something lively on."

Riffle through our collection of cd's. Consider putting on the late Kathleen Ferrier warbling *What is life to me without thee, what is life if thou art dead?* Instead find Emmylou Harris who everyone, except Deirdre who hates music, will like.

True to form Deirdre first asks for the music to be turned down, then appeals plaintively, "Haven't you got any background music? Must there always be singing? What happened to good old peace and quiet?"

Georgie, Martin, and Nic retire to the front room to talk about work. Georgie designs lighting systems for the leisure industry as in clubs and casinos, Martin designs music systems for a similar market, Nic took a course in home electrics, so they have much to discuss. Which leaves me, Simone, Deirdre and Laura. For five minutes conversation is sporadic and then we hit on why can't Laura be satisfied with any of her girl friends. This pleases Laura who loves the opportunity to talk about herself, pleases Simone who likes hearing about trials, tribulations or serious illness, pleases Deirdre as she loves giving advice, pleases me because I can relax and stop worrying that the evening has been a failure and it is probably my fault.

Later, as we're getting ready for bed, Georgie reveals that she can take or leave Deirdre and Laura.

"They're self satisfied and empty headed," she says.

I don't immediately defend my friends because yes, they are both the above but also funny, affectionate and resourceful. As usual say nothing. No actually I say "You may be right", but pull my face into an unattractive apologetic grimace. Which seems as if I'm apologizing to Georgie for the quality of my friends. I should be apologizing to Deirdre and Laura.

Snuggled up in bed with the light out I say, "What about Martin?"

Georgie makes an irritable movement of her shoulders, "He's all right. At least he has something sensible to say."

Georgie falls asleep while I am still trying to remember one sensible thing I've said that evening.

Jan 19th
Came home via supermarket. Bought six tins of cat food, three bottles of cat milk plus bag of cat litter for Tilly who now prefers to use the indoor facilities. Staggered up the steep incline that is our street, momentarily wondering how people like Sir Edmund Hilary had managed to climb Mount Everest even with bearers bearing shopping?

Miriam's mother has made a miraculous recovery. Tom treats us to chocolate eclairs at lunch time by way of celebration. Miriam visibly moved by Tom's thoughtfulness.

Owe Georgie a fiver.

Jan 22nd
Bought copy of the *Listening Ear* and yes, they've printed my letter. But not all of it. They've left out the opening paragraph welcoming the influx of ten lesbians to Bittlesea Bay and only printed the section about the need for more dog toilets and calls for increased vigilance by dog wardens and the non-dog owning public. Glad I didn't use my real name. Signed myself A. Oakley as in Annie Oakley. Spent two hours writing a letter of complaint to the local about discriminatory editing of readers' letters. *Does the Listening Ear have a problem with the burgeoning lesbian community?*

Jan 24th
Receive e-mail this morning from old school friend Tabby,

saying she is visiting another old school friend, Nina, who lives in Tunbridge Wells and wonders if she could break her journey at my house. Problem: the last time I saw Tabby was at my engagement party to Ronald twenty five years ago. Although we have kept in touch via Christmas cards and the odd e-mail she has no idea that my proclivities came to their senses soon after. Show Tabby's e-mail to Georgie. She says, "You haven't seen her in a quarter of a century, why would you want to see her now?"

Which suddenly makes me insist that it is of vital importance that I do see her now.

"But why?"

"Because longevity in relationships is priceless!" I almost shout.

Georgie gives me a steady look and then goes upstairs to her office in the box room. I hear the door close. March up stairs, fling open box room door and demand, "Well shall I or shan't I?"

She looks up from her laptop as if within the last minute she's completely forgotten my existence. "Whatever", she says.

"What exactly does 'whatever' mean?"

"Whatever you want to do, just do it but let me get on. I've several important calls to make."

Do not like being dismissed so important calls can be made, however try to imagine myself to be Rose from *Upstairs, Downstairs* and bob a curtsey before saying, "Would you like a coffee while you make your calls, ma'am?"

"No thank you."

Georgie is not amused or has never in the distant past watched *Upstairs, Downstairs*.

"Are you saying 'no thank you', because you're annoyed with me?"

"No."

"Look, I know you want a coffee. You always have a coffee about now."

"Very well, I'll have a coffee."

Unhappy with Georgie's resigned tone but take her a coffee. She thanks me without looking up. Wonder if there is any significance about coffee. Is coffee – Georgie drinking it and me making it, making us both irritable?

Answer: inconclusive. I e-mail Tabby:

Dear Tabby, change this to *Hi Tabby*, which looks more casual but not as casual as *Yo Tabby*. *It would be lovely to see you again after such a long time. I didn't marry Ronald, I fell in love with his sister would you believe? To cut a long story short I now live with Georgie, also a woman but not Ronald's sister although she remains a good friend.*

Tabby replies within the hour:

See you around five pm. on Tuesday 27th.

Meet Miriam in *The Corner Coffee Shop*. We order two Coffee Ice *Magnifico's*. Our mugs contain a small amount of cold coffee topped with three inches of ice cream and pink marshmallow, a chocolate flake sticking out of each summit. Miriam and I often discuss diets, usually Deirdre and Martin's diets. Today, guiltily we do not discuss diets, we just luxuriate. I tell Miriam about the forthcoming visit of old school friend and she reveals that she still lives with her mother.

"Do you get on with your mother?" I ask cautiously, knowing mothers can be tricky subjects.

"She's a feisty old lady," Miriam says which tells me little. Was the sort of description I'd give of my own mother when first discussing her, only moving on later to "She's a miserable old bat."

Almost immediately Miriam moves on saying, "She can be cantankerous."

"In what way?", I arrange my features into a diplomatic expression before biting off a chunk of chocolate flake.

Miriam looks evasive. The tip of her nose pinkens and she pulls a tissue from her anorak pocket.

"So this is where the two of you hide out!" Our shoulders are gripped and both our faces plunged into ice cream. We come up spluttering.

"Sorry," Tom Matthews says, "Mind if I squat?" and he pulls up a chair looking eagerly at Miriam then me, then back to Miriam.

I say, "Just talking about mothers."

He strokes his long chin, "Can't live with them, can't live without them," he says.

"Well you have to, if they die," I say cheerfully. Realise that the early evening *Corner Coffee Shop* crowd, amused by the spectacle of two women doused in cream, are now listening to our conversation. Many, possibly mothers, are frowning in my direction.

"My old mum's a jewel," Tom says, "I'd be devastated if anything happened to her."

"Me too," says Miriam who I've obviously completely misunderstood. I push aside Coffee Ice *Magnifico* and stand up. Say, "Better see about Georgie's tea."

"Georgie?" Tom queries, "Your fellah? Your better half?"

"My partner."

Leave. As I pass the *Coffee Shop's* window I see that Tom has commandeered my *Magnifico* and is talking to Miriam. Cannot see Miriam's face.

Jan 27th

Central heating radiator in guest bedroom not working so get Georgie to bring early model, electric fan heater down from loft. This causes much swearing and ill natured thumping as fan heater, a relic from Georgie's bed-sit days has hidden itself away in the twenty fourth of twenty four cardboard boxes.

Downstairs in kitchen I prepare my four cheese lasagna, which invariably results in dinner guest later experiencing either horrific or erotic nightmares. Adorn table with left over Christmas crackers, Christmas paper serviettes, Christmas red and gold candles.

"Ridiculous," Georgie says on her way through to the sitting room, "It looks as if you've got Cardinal Wolsey coming to dinner. I need a drink."

"Of course you do," I say soothingly. Pour both of us double strength gin and tonics with moon and star shaped ice cubes. Carry them into sitting room. In doorway regret non removal of Marigold gloves.

"Cheers," I shout gaily.

"Cheers," she mutters grimly. Takes mouthful then looks suspiciously at glass, "Go easy on the gin next time."

Work out that Tabby's train was due in ten minutes ago which means her taxi should be arriving at any moment. Take off apron, rubber gloves, switch on porch light, Vivaldi's Four Seasons. Don't personally care for the classics but every birthday am bought a classical CD by Georgie's parents. This my own fault as on first introduction I'd enthused over their extensive collection and said that my one ambition was to turn the back bedroom into a classical music library.

Take Georgie in a refill, have one for myself. Light candles. Set Four Seasons back to the beginning. Georgie appears in kitchen doorway looking more relaxed, "You are a fraud," she says, "You just want to impress this woman."

"Well why not?"

We have one of those rare split seconds of total communion and then the phone rings. It is Tabby saying there are no taxis at the station, it is pitch black and she's being watched by several sinister looking men. I say, "Don't worry, we'll collect you. Be there in five minutes."

Georgie stares at me with stunned annoyance.

"Margaret I can't possibly drive, I'm well over the limit."

"I'll drive."

"You're well over the limit."

"It wouldn't matter if I lose my license – I hardly use the car."

"I'll bloody drive."

In silence we drive to the station. From the tense line of Georgie's jaw I can tell she's absolutely furious. We pull into the station forecourt, pass a line of four waiting taxis. Immediately recognise Tabby, her sergeant major posture hasn't changed at all. The six metal buttons of her double breasted military style winter coat looks as if they'd been regularly spit and polished. Know then that I am mad to have invited her. A door in my memory has swung open. I'm remembering the young Tabby, remembering that I didn't like her, remembering that nobody liked her apart from another girl called Nina, whom nobody liked either.

I hurry forwards. Kiss her cheek. She rears back as if I've made a pass at her, "Have you been drinking?" are her first words of greeting.

"Only a small g & t. We didn't expect to be driving this evening."

"I don't know whether I should let myself get in a car with the two of you in this state."

We stand silently. "Oh very well. I expect taxis down here don't come cheap."

14

She marches ahead of me towards the car. Gets in next to Georgie. I slip into the back seat.

Tabby's visit abominable. Appeared insulted by crackers, picked at lasagna, while clasping her stomach with spare hand, drank only tap water, disliked central heating, also fan heaters. Said fan heaters were death traps. Introduced her to Samson, Delilah and Tilly in certain knowledge that pets can often be excellent bonding agents.

"Do you have any pets?" I ask.

"I prefer people," Tabby replies grimly.

From nervousness I squeak, "As pets?"

Later when Georgie has retired to bed with trumped up migraine Tabby says, "That was a nasty trick, dumping Ronald for his sister. There was nothing wrong with Ronald. I wouldn't have said 'no' to Ronald."

"As I mentioned in my e-mail I fell in love with his sister."

"Well where is she?"

"As I mentioned in my e-mail I'm now with Georgie."

"First you fall in love with Ronald, then his sister, now Georgie, who's next? You were like that at school – no staying power. We always had to bring in a substitute for the second half of a hockey match."

Show Tabby to her room. Offer her a choice of novels.

"I don't think so," she says with a shudder as if I've offered her pornography instead of an Anita Brookner, a Margaret Drabble, and a Pat Barker. Marches into guest room saying, "Now for a start we'll have this off," and unplugs the fan heater. Shuts bedroom door firmly in my face.

Would like to discuss the Tabby phenomena with Georgie but she is feigning deep and satisfying sleep. Query: why did Tabby agree to stay if she so disliked and disapproved of me? Tossed and turned for some time. It's not pleasant to be disliked and disapproved of in one's own house by guests. Not what one expects.

Finally Georgie switches side lamp on and sits up.

"I know what you're fretting about but listen and then go to sleep. Your mate Tabby will be just as dreadful to her friend

15

Nina tomorrow. She can't help being dreadful. It's her nature and not anything personal about you. Ok?"

"How do you know?"

"Because I just do know. You act. I think. Sometimes that works in your favour, this time it didn't. Now can we get some shut-eye?"

We settle down, Georgie lying on her back, me tucked under her arm, my head resting on her shoulder, "Sorry about Tabby," I whisper.

"We'll laugh about this tomorrow."

With relief we waved Tabby off to the station in a taxi the next afternoon and then we did laugh.

February

Feb 1st

A word about the Bittlesea Bay Café which is one of my favourite places. It looks out over green hills dotted with patches of gorse that by mid-March become vivid splashes of yellow – also out over the sea front and the sea. There's a terrace balcony where we sit when the weather's ok, the home made cakes are delicious, gâteaux divided into generous wedges, huge cream teas from Easter Bank Holiday onwards. A nice touch are the large metal water bowls left out for all visiting dogs. Dogs are allowed in the café provided they stick to the smoking area.

Georgie says it's not very clean which I dispute. She has a habit of running her hand across unfamiliar table tops and sometimes being unpleasantly surprised by what adheres. No matter, I love it. Deirdre loves it. She says, "Unbeatable," smacking her lips as if the café's a mouth watering plate of food, "Where else could you find such a view?"

Which is very loyal of her as she's traveled to India, Australia, Greece, Holland, Italy, Canada and Cornwall and must have found an equally fabulous view in at least one of those exotic places!

This afternoon, by the time I arrived Deirdre is already

ensconced. As always she looks almost larger than life, wearing a cream and pale pink patterned trouser suit, her stylish raffia handbag colour matched to ensemble by way of attached cream and pink silk roses. Also pink scarf, pink lipstick and pink cheeks. Outside it's six degrees centigrade, inside and Deirdre's dressed for a summer wedding.

"I'll be mum," she says as I strip off my fleece, woolen waistcoat, hat, scarf, gloves.

Cheerfully we remark on how this is the first time that the metal tea pot has poured without soaking the tablecloth, however the metal milk jug more than makes up for this and we mop up the mess with two paper serviettes.

"Wow! Is this fantastic or is this fantastic?!", exclaims Deidre taking in the view of anorakhed dog walkers battling against the wind. Her gaze pans back to my carrier bags, "Been shopping?"

"Just the Hospice shop."

She leans forward and says soto vocé, "Would they have any really old, antique fabrics in a place like that? You know, the sort of stuff that's worth a fortune but the old dears that run the place haven't got a clue."

Deirdre as a successful designer with accounts at Debenhams and John Lewis has never been near a charity shop. She did once come with me to a boot fair out in the countryside, again in the hope of purchasing quantities of antique fabric and was appalled at what she saw as the poverty of stalls and stall holders.

"Eeuw?" she'd squealed standing on the edge of the field and looking shocked, "So depressing."

I looked across the table into her eager face, "I don't think so."

"What about knitwear? Really old pure wool, cashmere, textural weaves? Texture. Quality antique texture – that's what I'm after."

Severely I say, "Deirdre this is a poor area. Who'd have cashmere and antique textural weaves to send to charity shops?"

"Rich old biddies fallen on hard times."

"Now that's enough."

"But just suppose there was something like that, what sort of money are we talking?"

17

"Two pounds fifty upwards."

Deirdre sits sharply back in her chair, "That much? I'd have thought they'd be asking twenty pence an article, fifty pence max."

"You'd have thought wrong. They have to make a profit."

"I don't see why charities should be making profits out of other people."

I sigh. Deirdre and I don't always understand each other. Live in very different worlds with some overlap which finds us meeting up at least once a week and in between discussing life and its variables on the telephone.

"How's Martin?" I ask to change the subject.

Apart from the odd occasion when Martin regales us with his humorous Mussolini anecdotes, he is a semi-recluse. As a rule he comes out after dark usually when everyone else is going to bed. If spotted by me, unexpectedly during daylight hours, he holds up his hand to shield his face as if I am a member of the paparazzi and have been camped outside his house for several weeks to get that one shot of Martin making for his car.

"I have no idea," she says stiffly, "Can we change the subject?"

We move on to the subject of where ice cream vans go in winter.

Feb 3rd

Receive e-mail from Tabby thanking us for a lovely evening and offering to put us up if we are ever passing through Daventry, although she'll warn us now that she only has a studio flat so we'd have to bring sleeping bags and sleep on the kitchen floor. Nina sends her best wishes.

Feb 6th

Re. Hospice Shop, by strange coincidence Deirdre is not the only person interested in it. This morning as I passed on the way to work, as per usual I peered in (to snaffle bargains one must be vigilant). Shop doesn't open till ten a.m. but there's generally some member of staff milling around inside sorting through the bags of stuff left on the door step during the night. Today was not unusual, a member of staff milled and that member of staff was ... Miriam!

18

"That can't be Miriam," I said to myself knowing full well that it was.

She saw me peering, grinned rather self consciously then mouthed, "We're closed," and directed me to the 'CLOSED' sign on the door. Mouthed back, "I'm well aware of that. See you later."

Found myself in bad temper and envious state. Considered the Hospice Shop very much my own personal terrain. Had bought many almost fashionable items there, taken them home – washed, fabric conditioned, ironed, mended, shortened, lengthened and added to. I may not have Deirdre's fashionista style or Georgie's cosmopolitan casual but I'd managed pretty well so far. Often Miriam had said over something refurbished during the weekend, "That's new. It really suits you."

And I'd smiled demurely (which I appreciate is not a pleasant or genuine way to smile), and said a simple, "Thank you. Er … London," or "Present from Georgie – she knows what I like."

Now I was scuppered. From now on Miriam would recognise my purchases. I'd shop in fear that one day I'd find her lurking behind the Hospice sales desk instead of her rightful afternoon place behind her desk at T.M. Accountancy. *"Good heavens Margaret, do I see something off the 'Every Item a £1' rail in your hand?"*

And she would get first pick of the bargains, the twice worn tweed jacket, the Gap jeans that someone had grown out of, almost new men's shirts, the hooded fleeces. Mentally I ticked my wardrobe off in my head. That was it. All over for me. By the time I'd reached work I'd built up quite a Miriam antagonism.

"What a face," Tom Matthews said.

One o'clock on the dot Miriam came in carrying two sacks of clothing. Did not wish to speak to her – ever again. Drops bags behind her desk, takes cigarettes and lighter from her rucksack, says, "Aren't you coming for my ciggy break – it's stopped raining?"

I humph and sigh. Take out wrapped sandwich which suddenly seems a despicable, measly sandwich and why don't I buy grander sandwich from Marks and Spencer instead of always this insipid, handmade apology?

Stand on step, say, "Actually it hasn't stopped raining."

Miriam shrugs, "Nothing to speak of. I suppose you're wondering what I was doing in the Hospice Shop."

I feign surprise, "Not at all."

"Well, what else can I do, Margaret?" Her voice is dismal. She puffs grey smoke up at the grey sky. My animosity is momentarily stopped in its tracks.

"I don't understand."

"How am I ever going to meet anybody? There's nowhere in this town. When mother goes I'll be just another lonely, aging woman. I won't even have a past worth looking back on."

"But why a job at a charity shop?"

"*You* go there."

Quelled my instant denial. Swallowed and nodded.

She continued, "I've noticed quite a few younger lesbians going in there. I'm not talking really young, more your age. Attainable lesbians. So I thought, give it a try Miriam. Nothing ventured etcetera. What do you think?"

I agreed. Got home late because Miriam insisted on showing me all the clothes she'd bought. Very nice. Saw several articles that I would have bought myself. Tom came in and said, *this is not a glorified dress shop* and *I hope that lot's been fumigated.*

That evening wished Georgie was at home to discuss: my meanness of spirit, Miriam's desperation.

Sat Feb 7th

Nic dropped Thompson and Morgan seed catalogue through our letterbox while I was out at the Post Office photographic booth taking my picture for a new passport. Had spent ten pounds fifty on three attempts. First attempt so pale that I looked as if my face was made of ectoplasm and it was peering out from the 'other side', second attempt and I'm leaning forward, mouth open in the middle of exclamation of "Oh blow it," as flash goes off in my face. Third try which had to be final as I had no money left, I look like an embittered woman who after leaving booth intends to walk into the sea with a hundredweight of stones in her pockets.

Attached to seed catalogue was a purple post-it note saying, "Margaret. Maybe we can reconnoiter in the next few days?"

(Nic's partner Simone has no interest in gardening except for her annual demand for "Colour! Anything but green. We're surrounded by green and I hate it! I'm a hot pink woman!")

Look up "reconnoiter". As I thought – to *survey or inspect an enemy's position*.

Nic and I have surveyed the enemy's position for the past three years which means the gardens in our neighbourhood. Nic's ambition is for her garden to win the golden trowel in the Bittlesea Bay Best in Bloom Competition. It is automatically assumed that I will be happy with a Certificate of Distinction. So far Nic's won the bronze trowel and an Order of Merit for her patio planters.

However, this year I have different ideas. I don't want to enter the competition or spend the summer watering, weeding and worrying. With the help of Deirdre's woman gardener I'm going to turn my hillside garden into a wildflower meadow.

Georgie coming in from an overnight stay at a Travel Inn in Hemel Hempstead sees Nic's note and catalogue on the kitchen table and says, "It's great the way she always includes you. Any chance of a coffee?"

Fill kettle mulling over the fact that my loved one's inability to make herself a cup of coffee is becoming an issue. Wish there was a pleasant way to respond, "You know where the kettle is."

Georgie takes her coffee and a Mars Bar up to her office. I take out secret pad of graph paper and secret paperback on how to create your own meadow. Also various colour pencils. Begin sketching.

Feb 9th

Travel up on the train to London to visit Laura who is in hospital for a minor operation. Twenty years ago Laura and I worked for *Marks and Spencer*. She was in charge of 'men's socks', I was 'leisure wear'. It was a happy time only ever spoilt when our conversation was interrupted by customers or a supervisor.

Some days earlier when I'd told Deirdre about the possibility of my hospital visit she'd said with narrowed eyes and an accusatory note to her voice, "You've had rather a lot to do with the sick and dying over the last year or so, haven't you?" as if I was someone with a passion for hanging about hospitals waiting for people to die.

Defensively I'd countered, "They often need to talk and I'm a good listener. I'm patient, punctual, bring in a variety of useful and imaginative gifts ..."

I'd lost her. She stretched her plump arms above her head and cried, "Oh why can't we all accept death with good grace and just shuffle off when our time comes? Ill people give me the heebie-jeebies, they're totally self absorbed."

"They have to be. They're going through a grueling personal experience."

Deirdre slapped her forehead – a sign of some flash of insight she's about to share with me. "I think at least eighty five percent of ill people, maybe ninety five percent, bring illness on themselves by being self absorbed in the first place."

"I don't think so."

"I know so." Goes on to list everyone she knows who's died or nearly died, finding instances of self absorption in every case.

On train I work on A. Oakley's latest letter to the *Listening Ear*. Subject: what constitutes a successful public lavatory? I itemize, availability, cleanliness, privacy. Man sauntering through ladies facilities wielding mop and bucket, shouting, "anyone need a new roll?" is untenable. Have any other readers suffered a similar experience?

Feb 10th
Laura survives operation. Nurse telephones to say, Laura doing fine but has over taxed her vocal chords. It seems that Laura has a low pain threshold. Actually nurse says in caustic tone, "Laura has a low discomfort threshold."

Buy book of wild flowers. Begin studying kerbside flora. See daisies, buttercups and dandelions. Cheerful, brightens up the pavement but hardly exciting.

Feb 11th
Nic telephones to ask whether I've chosen what I want from

her catalogue. Say "Yes." She says, she and Simone will collect catalogue and my order after dinner this evening.

I retrieve catalogue from paper recycling box and search through for some plant that might possibly suit my hillside meadow. Choose Lady Slipper Orchid, a lily called a Sea Daffodil which seems appropriate to the seaside and also a new variety of Comfrey guaranteed not to become invasive. Go upstairs to back bedroom and role play in front of the full length mirror how I'm going to tell Nic I will not be joining her in the competition this year.

Ploy 1: the dishonest play for sympathy:

Nic, vis a vis the competition I don't feel well enough to tackle it this year. Hand loiters around breast bone to signify unspecified weakness.

Whatever's the matter with you?

Pause. Too tempting of fate for me to imply anything serious in breast bone area, *My right foot's not what it was.*

Nic looks bewildered. Simone and Georgie will cease their own conversation and start listening.

Ploy 2: the dishonest play for sympathy and understanding:

If you don't mind Nic, I'll give the comp. a miss – I'd rather like the summer to take time out for reflection.

On what?

I did lose my parents recently.

Surely that was five or six years ago.

And then the guinea pig died.

Did it?

And Samson massacring the little Blue Tit family nesting in the back wall, last spring.

Did he?

As Deirdre next door says, I've had a lot to cope with in the way of the ill and dying.

Have you?

At which point Georgie intervenes, *Take no notice Nic. Of course she's doing the competition. She's like this every year, imagines she's not up to it.*

They arrived at eight thirty. All four of us sat down at the kitchen table. Nic, Simone and Georgie were in splendid moods. Georgie loves having her friends dropping in. She becomes warm, generous and ... happy. Perhaps we should live in a commune. Gave Nic back her catalogue with my order.

Nic observes, "Not very impressive Margaret. You mustn't be so timid with your garden. Just because you've got a one in three slope doesn't mean you can't be adventurous. It's a matter of compensating for sun burn, poor irrigation, clay soil, etcetera. I'll add on a few more. Now when are we off to size up the enemy? Sort out the wheat from the chaff, their weaknesses and their strengths. Yes, top me up Georgie. I love a good drop of red."

Georgie tops up all our glasses. I lean forward, my arms folded on the table in front of me in what I see as a relaxed pose, "The thing is Nic ..."

Simone yawns, looks at her watch, our clock, "Someone tell me what the correct time is please?"

"Eight forty five," says Nic, "So pick an afternoon. I'm all yours."

"But the thing is Nic ..."

Georgie interrupts, "The thing is Nic, the bloke next door has asked her to join his Neighbourhood Watch Scheme a couple of afternoons a week, Margaret doesn't feel she can put in the required amount of time with the gardening."

Stunned I manage to nod my head, "I really can't this year, Nic. Any watering or weeding you need help with ..."

"And even that may be a problem. You know, I need the car for work and it's a good two mile walk to your house," Georgie says.

Nic beams, "I quite understand. No problem. To be honest I rather fancy having a shot at the prize on my own this year. I feel lucky. Got the bronze. Been there, done that. I say skip silver, go for gold. Mind over matter. I'm visualizing that golden trowel mounted on a dark oak plaque above the lounge fireplace."

Later when they've gone home I ask Georgie how she knew I didn't want to enter the competition. She said, "I heard you practicing your speech in the back bedroom. Why didn't you tell me you didn't want to do it?"

"I thought you'd be annoyed. Nic is your best friend."

"Nic's quite capable of winning her golden trowel without

24

any help from you. Just one thing, I wasn't lying about the bloke next door and the Neighbourhood Watch. He's popping in next Tuesday about five o'clock to speak to you. You don't have to say 'yes'. You can say 'no'."

But could I?

Feb 12th

Georgie off to Argyllshire this morning. As always when setting off to vistas new, she was remarkably cheerful. She says that it wouldn't do for both of us to get miserable and someone in the family has to maintain a stiff upper lip.

Feb 14th

A splendid day! Got up and fed the cats. All in good humour even Tilly who allowed me to rub the top of her head with my chin after her usual, "Nood norning". "Nood norning Tilly," I said. Must watch this. Could become an embarrassing habit. 'Nood norning' is becoming second nature to say while "Good morning" is starting to sound like a greeting in a foreign language. Made cup of tea and allowed myself as it was a rather special Saturday to add two chocolate bourbon biscuits. Took this back to bed. Ate both bourbons before tea cool enough to drink. Allowed myself two further bourbons. Opened the bedroom curtains and lay in bed listening for the postman. Ours is a quiet street apart from the seagull cries and I can hear the postman when he is several houses away. He whistles old tunes made famous by singers like Connie Francis and Pat Boone which I imagine could be very irritating for his partner (if he has one) but is useful for alerting those lying expectantly in bed to his proximity.

This morning he was whistling *San Antonio Rose*. Mum used to have this on an LP by Bob Wills and the Texas Playboys. A very long time ago. I know not how I remembered so much information, I just did. Perhaps some early babyhood memory of mum dancing round the sitting room on her own.

Up my front steps the postman clumped. *Clump, clump, clump! Clatter!* went the letterbox, followed by a soft thud as the post landed on our patterned coir door mat.

Listened for his retreating *clump, clump, clump.* (Once several years ago I whizzed down to collect the post wearing only bra

25

and pants. Met postman's startled eyes peering through letterbox at me. Disembodied voice says, "This one won't fit through the box, what shall I do?" "Just leave it on the step please," I'd called out before darting hunched into the sitting room. Letterbox clattering shut. Was mortified. Heard postman's exclamation, "Blimey! She's a big girl!"

Bills, bank statements, a jiffy bag, but yes, there it was. Georgie had remembered – my Valentine's Day card. Took card and jiffy bag back to bed. Opened card – two ducks sitting next to each other on a squashy red sofa kissing with open beaks. Words: *We'll always be quacking good friends* and inside, *Love Georgie*. In the jiffy bag was a CD of the soundtrack from La Moulin Rouge which she'd forgotten that she'd liked more than me. I know I shall grow to like it.

Not worth sending Georgie anything and anyway I don't exactly know where she is. "Moving around Argyllshire," she'd said vaguely, "so pretty much incommunicado which doesn't mean that you're not in my thoughts, Margaret."

N.B. Did say jokingly, "Might be worth buying a pied a terre in Scotland, you're up there such a lot."

Georgie said, "That might not be such a bad idea." Of course she was also joking.

Her Valentine Card from me is waiting on her desk. I opted for grey kittens cuddling over a ball of wool. I wrote, "Mew, mew, mew – I love you," which sounds embarrassingly sentimental but I do believe in a long term relationship, it pays to work at keeping that romantic spark alive.

Also I've bought her a white shirt from *Thomas Pink*, slightly fitted styling. Next month, March 20th, first day of spring, is our anniversary. I visualize Georgie wearing a pair of black high waisted, flamenco style trousers and this shirt. Collar open, sleeves turned back from her wrists. "Ho-lay!"

Think back to our first ever meeting, Georgie on one bench me on another, Brighton sea front, March 20th 1994. I'd said, "Do you think that seagull's in difficulty?" and she'd answered, "It's not a seagull it's a paper bag," and we'd both started laughing. At that time Georgie lived in Brighton, I was there on a week's holiday getting over the breakup of a four week relationship. Georgie was with someone but that was almost over although it took her nearly a year to get completely disentangled and move in with me. She has a heart as soft as butter.

Later in the morning took my card and CD in to show Deirdre. Deirdre very sniffy about the CD.

"Not my type of music," she said.

Did not say, "Deirdre, what is your type of music?" Instead asked cheerfully after Martin's Valentine gift.

"We don't bother. It's not *our* scene. It's all commercial, mass produced sentimentality," Deirdre said disparagingly. "We bought Lord Dudley a card though, and a new velvet collar, some expensive cat treats and a Percy Pig cuddly toy to keep him company in his basket at night. We love Lord Dudley."

"I know you do." I said as Lord Dudley entered on cue looking every inch the handsomest cat in the street, the blue of his new collar setting off the bright yellow-green of his eyes.

Very sunny in the afternoon. Almost like spring. Noticed first green points of the daffodil leaves poking through the mud. Deirdre and I walked along the sea front, then ventured onto the pebble beach. Sat on Marks & Spencer carrier bags brought for that very purpose and studied the sea. Deirdre said, "Can we see France from here?"

I said, "I certainly can't. Without my glasses on I can hardly see you."

"I think I can see France."

"I don't think you can. On the map we're round a corner, so that a bit of land blocks our vision of France."

"Maps are often wrong. They were drawn by humans and humans are fallible."

Couldn't argue with that. Very mellow. Georgie back tomorrow. Planning a dinner of *Chicken a L'Orange*, roast and boiled spuds, beans and cauliflower cheese.

Feb 17th
Well no I couldn't say 'no' to Mr. Wheeler, neighbour and Neighbourhood Watch representative. Actually not actually neighbourhood watch, it is Mr. Wheeler's own invention Wheeler's Watch. There are two other watchers: Mrs. Mugsby and Mrs. Ballantyne. Mr. Wheeler says they're a pair of nosey

parkers so he's putting their nosey parkerness to good use. Wonder how he's classified me?

I hadn't seen Mr. Wheeler for some weeks. Usually whenever I'm out in our garden, he is out in his with an eloquent supply of advice on what I should do about our fencing, our brick path, our drain covers. There was no Mrs. Wheeler. She'd died before we'd come to live next door. Deirdre who's lived in her house for fifteen years says that in those days Mr. Wheeler wasn't so interfering, in fact when she'd seen them out together it had made her feel quite 'goo-ey', as they'd seemed genuinely fond of each other.

"Not that any of us know what goes on behind closed doors," she'd added cryptically.

Georgie retired to her office at five to five telling me *I was on my own* and *the best of british*, Mr. Wheeler climbed up our steps at five p.m. sharp. It was a cold day so I asked him in. He agreed to stand on the front door mat and no further. Glanced suspiciously at the pictures on our hall wall as if they might contain scenes of an erotic lesbian nature.

"How are you Mr. Wheeler, I haven't seen you in weeks. Been away?"

I waited with my head on one side and an encouraging smile.

"As a matter of fact I've been the victim of a hit and run incident."

"That's dreadful."

"Yes. I came out of the supermarket, was carrying my bags to the car when I was knocked over. A silver Toyota shot out of a parking space and hit me."

"And they didn't stop?"

"*They* stopped just long enough to gather up my bags of shopping. That's what *they* were after – all my stuff for the weekend including a turkey and a shoulder of lamb."

"They must have been very hungry to attempt something so drastic."

"I can see I've got a woolly headed liberal in you – there is no such thing as a hungry Toyota driver. You get hungry, you sell the car, you become a cab driver, you don't run over pensioners."

"Of course not. Disgraceful. Incomprehensible."

Mr. Wheeler shook his leaflets at me, "Nothing incomprehensible about unmitigated wickedness. There you go again making excuses when I'm the poor bugger who's been used and abused. Who's making excuses for me?"

Insisted that I quite understood, that I should have stopped at disgraceful, and what did he want me to do because nothing was too arduous if it meant such hooliganism, sorry unmitigated wickedness could be stamped out.

He handed me one of his pieces of paper, "This is a map of your area. Two hours an afternoon, twice a week – just keep walking and watching. Not too much to ask of an able bodied person, is it?"

I agreed that it wasn't. Saw Mr. Wheeler back down our steps. Suddenly had a thought and called out, "Have you asked Deirdre at number forty-two? She's very able bodied."

"She refused. Said if anyone tried it on with her, she'd knock them into the middle of next week." For the first time a small admiring smile crossed Mr. Wheeler's face.

Feb 20th

Miriam reports that she is certainly meeting women but no one whom she's really clicked with as yet. Says she is trying to perfect a light, slightly flirtatious note. Blushes and corrects herself, is trying to perfect more the possibility of her tone becoming flirtatious should an opportunity arise. Unfortunately has been gently reprimanded by Mrs. Ferguson the manageress, for being over zealous with the younger women customers.

"Let them fend for themselves. Don't hover. They don't want us old ladies fussing over them."

Miriam privately most offended as Mrs. Ferguson must be twenty years older than herself which she knows shouldn't be an issue, because aren't we all women and why should she expect a woman twenty years her junior to look at her, Miriam, when she's dismissing Mrs. Ferguson who admittedly is happily married and wouldn't be interested in Miriam anyway? Also Mrs. Ferguson has advised her against smiling at the customers, and also to keep chit-chat to a minimum.

Went in myself this afternoon on the way home from work to buy a Denby ware plate I'd seen in the window. Also a chrome tray. Also a picture of swans in flight. Also a leather waistcoat that might suit Laura if she lost two stone. Knew Mrs. Ferguson by sight from my frequent visits to the Hospice Shop so made straight for her with proposed purchases.

She said, "Swan pictures are so uplifting even when the swans are indistinct," and I agreed.

Said, "You're right, you can't have too many swan pictures or trays either. Trays have so many uses."

Mrs. Ferguson had nothing to say regarding trays. Decided not to elaborate. As she wrapped the plate, first in newspaper, then in a very old and creased Safeways carrier bag I said, "Is the lady with the pepper and salt coloured hair in today?" knowing full well that I'd left Miriam back at the office up to her elbows in the filing cabinet drawer.

"She only works here in the mornings," Mrs. Ferguson replied.

"What a pity. Lovely woman. Invariably knows what suits me. Worth her weight in gold."

Feb 21st

Deirdre asks me to pop in and witness Martin, the boy genius who's been on a wine tasting afternoon. Martin lies on the settee wearing his dressing gown by way of a smoking jacket, a crystal glass of red wine resting perilously on his stomach.

"The chap running the course says Martin has *the nose*," enthuses Deirdre.

"I have the nose," Martin echoes twitching his nostrils. He raises his head, raises his glass to *the nose*, "Ah the aroma of fresh raspberries with the underlying tang of summer in Provence."

"What are you drinking?" I ask.

"Diet Coke. I've had a bucketful of vin extraordinaire, the nose and the gut need time to recoup."

Feb 23rd

Monday, one p.m. Miriam arrives in the office in a state of wild excitement. Apparently on Friday a woman went into the Hospice Shop, bought a plate and then asked after her. Referred to her as *a lovely woman* and said that she, Miriam, was *worth her weight in gold*.

Miriam ebullient. "What do you think? Have I hit pay dirt at last?"

Privately find this a rather offensive phrase but in no position to criticize Miriam. Reply weakly, "Whether you have or haven't, it's very positive news."

"Mrs. Ferguson said the woman comes in the shop almost every week *and* she's spotted her peering in the window countless times. The next time she sees her, if I'm there she'll point her out to me."

"What did Mrs. Ferguson say the woman looked like?"

"Quite ordinary but so what? I'm not looking for Marilyn Monroe."

I realise that from now on I'll have to take a completely different route back and forth from work and that for ever more the Hospice Shop is barred to me. Miriam continues burbling on, "I think I'm in love. I'm so happy. This is the best day of my life."

"But you don't even know the woman."

"I feel as if I do. She's ordinary. I love ordinary. I'm not going to tell mum, not until we're going out. Don't you say anything, although I don't mind if you mention it to your close friends but I don't want this getting out on the Bittlesea lesbian grape vine …"

Return home by new and dismal route. With sinking heart I remember that this is my first Wheeler's Watch afternoon. Droop indoors. House very quiet. Cats all asleep by individual central heating radiators. Note from Georgie to say she'll be back around nine but not to bother about food as she's eating with a client. Go upstairs. Put on my Wheeler's Watch sash over my winter coat and pin my Wheeler's Watch badge to the lapel. Also belt on my small standard issue, waist satchel containing a torch (even though it's broad daylight), a whistle, note book, pen.

N.B. Must acknowledge that Mr. Wheeler has put a lot of time and energy into this scheme although I believe Mrs. Mugsby, his Number Two, performed the needlework.

Feel extremely bulky. Outside it's started to rain but Mr. Wheeler has told me on the telephone the night before that rain must not be used as an excuse for failing in my civic duty. Find unflattering hat. Leave house comparing Georgie's jet setting life of Scottish jaunts and dinner with clients to mine.

See Mr. Wheeler standing in his bay window. He nods to me in stern approval as if he's my commanding officer and I'm a raw recruit which of course I am.

Go over in my head the Wheeler's Watch instructions. I'm to watch out for people and vehicles behaving suspiciously, for excessive smoke issuing from buildings, screams, raised voices, dogs barking, cats and babies crying. Also have been told to make myself conspicuous, as my very presence marching up and down the roads of my *watch*, will act as a deterrent.

See nothing and nobody. Everybody is indoors waiting for the rain to stop. There is just me. However do begin to enjoy myself in a strange way. Quite pleasant to have a bona fide reason for staring into the front windows and gardens of complete strangers. Peering into their cars. Flashing my torch unnecessarily into alley ways.

Finally meet an old neighbour from when I was single and lived two roads away from where I live now, name of Sylvia Preston. Elderly widow. Good cake maker. She asks me in for tea and good cake. Drapes my coat over a clothes horse in front of her roaring fire. Sits me down in an armchair on one side of the hearth, sits herself down on the other side. She tells me that my old house has gone to rack and ruin. There have been a succession of owners, each worse than the last. The present incumbents are strangers to soap and water and play their music morning, noon and night. They are worth keeping an eye on.

She then takes me on a tour of her house showing off the many improvements her son-in-law has made, but of course she says, *he has his eye on the main chance*, i.e. her early demise because her *heart's not the heart of a twenty year old*.

I finally leave, promising to look in again. Bump into a soaking wet Mr. Wheeler who has been secretly trailing me. Accusingly he says, "You've been in that house for twenty seven minutes."

"She was furnishing me with insider information," I say and his eyes widen in disbelief.

Feb 24th
Many responses to my letter re. successful public lavatories. Mrs. Adele Fisher writes, *personally I find the presence of a suitable*

man in the ladies toilet reassuring. I feel no embarrassment at the offer of a toilet roll from the male sex only gratitude.

Letter from Mr. E.Stanley saying that male lavatory attendants in female lavatories were due to the council's lunatic, politically correct, everyone's the same, policy and that he would personally ensure that Mrs. Stanley no longer used the Bittlesea Bay facilities. E-mail from someone called *Grey Beagle* to say, *Hey babe, the guy has to make a living. Cut him a little slack!* E-mail from Suzie B saying, *Saucy so-and-so. Is lavatory attendant up for grabs? Which particular toilet can I find him in?*

Finally letter from a Martin J. Storm complaining that such a trivial letter had been printed in the first place. *The man is employed by the council. He is not an ogre. It's a 'public' lavatory not the Savoy. How often does A. Oakley use this facility or is she just one of the band of trouble making, nitpicking females that bedevil this town?*

Note from the Editor to say that this line of correspondence had gone far enough.

Feb 25th
No time to discuss progress in Miriam's love life at lunchtime as Georgie and I were driving up to London to have drinks at the Glass Bar at Euston Station then dinner with her parents at a restaurant in Islington.

I'd never been to the Glass Bar before although Georgie is a regular, being in London more often, meeting up with work connections. Was amazed and charmed. Resembled Doctor Who's tardis – tiny on the outside, spacious within – enough room for several settees, armchairs, coffee tables and masses of women. Would have liked to go over the room with a tape measure and then compared inside measurement with outside measurement. Said as much to Georgie.

Georgie immediately welcomed as if she's an old and dear friend of everybody. I stood behind her, my smile about level with her shoulder. Suddenly felt I had a deeper understanding of what HRH, Prince Philip might have gone through. Obviously many of his ill-judged remarks were a form of attention seeking.

"This is Margaret," Georgie finally remembered me,

"Margaret, meet Rosemary, Sandra, Abi, Chris, Tanya, Lizzie, Jo Anne …"

"Nello", I said. Damn! Made ready to recount amusing story of Tilly's extraordinary vocabulary but nobody had noticed, although fleeting frown flew across beloved's brow.

As always when I came into London with Georgie to meet her friends I regretted my choice of clothes. Suddenly my charity shop refurbishments looked exactly that. My wide, flapping trousers which I'd seen as boho-chic looked ridiculous, everyone else wore boot leg jeans, the collar of my shirt was unfashionably huge and there wasn't a patterned shirt in the room never mind a pattern of gaily wrapped toffees. How did I invariably get everything so wrong?

"Hi, what do you do?" I asked Lizzie or maybe Sandra.

"I'm a choreographer – modern ballet and jazz dance."

Swallowed 'Crikey' and 'Well I never', said instead, "So how do you know Georgie?"

"She designed the lighting for our company's last production, *Women on Women want Women on Women*. Georgie's brilliant! How do you know her?"

"I'm her partner. We've been together nearly ten years. Anniversary next month."

"Great," making 'great' sound somehow like 'dreary'. "Better get a drink. You're ok, aren't you?," she nodded towards my almost empty glass.

"Yes. Fine. This is more than a sufficiency," kicked myself in the leg, hard.

Sandra or Lizzie disappeared into crowd around the bar. Could see Georgie at the crowd's centre. Sighed. Drooped. Slumped. Suddenly my glass was whisked out of my hand and replaced with a full one.

I stared into a rather somber face. Tanned but not like Georgie's tanning booth tan. Tanned like someone gets when they work outdoors. The woman must have been at least ten years my junior. She was my height, brown hair cut short, steady brown eyes. Nothing really distinctive about her and yet the thought sped across my mind that she was quite unique. Not in an immediate physical attraction way, just an observation, a first impression. And I knew absolutely that this first impression was true.

"Thank you," I said, "I'm Margaret."

"I know. I heard someone introduce you. I'm –", but she got no further, another woman grabbed hold of her hand and pulled her across the room, "Bye," she called out, "Take care."

Which was nice. Which for a little while transformed the evening. Met up with Georgie's parents. Georgie adores them. I'd adore them if they'd adore me. They quite like me but ideally they want a much grander partner for their only daughter. I don't mind. Or I didn't mind. My happiness held right up till we left the restaurant. We stood on the pavement saying our goodbyes, buttoning up coats, kissing cheeks.

The parents looked fondly at me as if I was at least an endearing puppy. One with high spirits and boundless, bounding good nature. I didn't mind that either.

I said, "Now don't forget, put aside Saturday March the 20th. You can stay over. There won't be masses of guests, just close friends and family."

Georgie's mother said, "Any particular celebration?"

Georgie said, "Don't worry ma, nothing definite."

"But of course it's definite," I said, "Or have you got some secret, romantic plan tucked up your sleeve? Can you believe it, a decade together and still deliriously happy."

Couldn't stop burbling. Ma and Pa-in-law were looking uneasy, sending enquiring glances to Georgie, Georgie shaking her head at them and narrowing her eyes. Something was very wrong. I shut up.

Georgie said, "We'll have to see."

In silence we walked to where our car was parked. In silence we drove for nearly an hour. Georgie switched the radio on once, Eric Clapton singing about his darling looking wonderful that evening. She switched it off.

Georgie broke the silence. She said in a quiet, cold voice, "I wish you hadn't gone on like that. Why must you always pre-empt a situation?"

Had no answer as not aware that I pre-empted situations.

"All I'm saying," she continued, "is it's not such a great idea making a fuss over one day in the calendar and anyway purely logistically, it's not going to work out."

"Why are you talking to me as if I'm a client and you're

36

explaining a hitch in a business project?" I asked keeping my voice mild.

"I'm trying to bring you down to earth, that's all."

"No, that isn't it. You're trying to tell me something unpleasant but wrapping it up in cold words."

"Better than turning everything into a bouncing, desperate cheerfulness," she said, "With you everything has to be a joke or ... a whimper."

Only I could know the effort it would take for Georgie to be so cruel. She wasn't, isn't a cruel woman. These words of hers weren't carelessly said.

Feb 27th
Sorry diary, no bouncing, desperate cheerfulness today.

What I mustn't do is think that Georgie has stopped loving me. She says she loves me as much as ever but now it is a different love – as deep and long lasting but missing out on the excitement and maybe that will prove all we need to last out our lifetime. But only maybe.

Georgie has suggested and I've agreed to a trial separation of two months. She says she expects our time apart will revitalize our relationship. She is actually going to rent a flat off a friend in Edinburgh as that seems to be where most of her work is at the moment.

It will do us good, she says, to re-assess where we are going, where we want to go. *Don't be surprised*, she says with a wry smile, *if I come high tailing back to you within a fortnight*.

I have to believe that at the end of two months Georgie will return. Not to the same old Margaret of the apron and mari-gold gloves, I'll try to be a new, exciting Margaret. I'll do what it takes even if it means me sitting every morning in front of the mirror and reciting Deirdre's mantra, "I am fantastic. I am a sensual, sexual woman. I like what I see."

Sunday Feb 29th
Georgie left this morning. Took Samson and Delilah with her. It is impossible to recite Deirdre's mantra. I am not fantastic. I am not a sensual, sexual woman. I do not like what I see.

March

March 10th
Back with diary. However nothing worth noting has happened in my life over the last ten days. No word from Georgie.

March 12th
Wake up with a start. Tilly lying next to me also is awake. What is that noise? Surely not skateboarders trying to avoid the daytime traffic? (Our house is on the very summit of a hill and the centre of the road is popular with skateboarders, roller skaters, battery powered scooters and unicyclists). The noise continues. It comes from nearer the house. Surely not Mr. Wheeler busy on some nocturnal d.i.y. job. Still sounds too near. It's as if somebody is repeatedly rattling the side gate into the back garden. Get up. Find torch and lean out of bedroom window. Shine torch on back gate and area in front of the house. Nothing. No one. Noise stops for a few seconds and then continues.

I feel uneasy. Tilly looks uneasy. Put on dressing gown saying reassuringly, "You stay where you are, Tilly." Secretly hope Tilly will accompany me. She stays, her green eyes wide and anxious. "Don't worry, mummy sort it out." I reach for my antique ski pole, an irresistible buy from a Methodist Jumble Sale circa 1984.

Go downstairs and through house switching on lights and singing the old Sandie Shaw hit, *I walk along the city streets you used to walk along with me ...*

Upsetting lyrics in the circumstances but the only song immediately suggesting itself. By the time I reach the kitchen my eyes are watering and I desperately need to blow my nose.

And as I walk recalling just how much in love we used to be ...

Tear off a piece of towel roll. Stop singing. Cautiously and silently open the kitchen window which looks over the back garden side of the gate. Blow nose loudly.

Stunned silence then the scramble of something or someone completely invisible frantically breaching the fence between my garden and Mr. Wheeler's. The sky is filled with the cries of

38

disturbed sea gulls. Close window. Warm some milk. Sit at kitchen table.

But how can I forget you when there is always something there to remind me ...?

Of course am reminded of Georgie in her charcoal coloured toweling dressing gown, how she would be either telephoning the police or shrugging her shoulders and saying, "Don't worry, it was probably just a rat." How I'd never felt frightened of anything when she was with me. How she'd reassure me as we made our way back up to bed, "Margaret, we're quite safe. The two of us are big strapping women. We're more than a match for burglars or rats."

And I might say, "What if it's a ghost?"

And she'd reply, "It won't be."

Took my glass of milk upstairs. Tilly fast asleep. I slept. In the morning woke to find my brain supplying more Sandie Shaw.

I was born to love you and I will never be free ...

I didn't want to be free of Georgie.

Thought about checking the back garden but incident of strangely rattling gate seems dim and distant memory put next to pain of song words.

March 13th

Deirdre unveils plans for her new garden layout. Quite a presentation. I am invited and also her other neighbours, two elderly sisters Vera and Morag. Deirdre had made cakes, wedges of sponge covered in pink icing and acid green hundreds and thousands. She wore a peachy pink chiffon kaftan with matching bracelets, a pink feather in her hair. We were asked to sit down around the dining room table, asked what we wanted in the way of tea, coffee or fruit juice. Handed a small plate each with a pink paper serviette and told to 'Please get stuck into the cakes." Our mouths full, Deirdre began. She welcomed our attendance as if we'd come from at least as far away as an adjoining county, she told us that she felt it 'absolutely crucial to keep her neighbours on side'.

Vera and Morag nodded while also looking mystified.

"As you can see," Deirdre said pointing with a plastic ruler at the plan laid out on the table, "What is now lawn and cuoy

carp pool will become a decked terrace with seating for six persons in an ornamental gazebo."

We nodded our approval. No, our admiration.

"My entire new garden will be fenced in with willow panels painted alternate shades of sea green and sky blue, obviously to mirror the effect of sea and sky."

Morag asked, "How tall will the fence be?'

"Brave woman!", I thought and nodded more approval and admiration.

Deirdre tapped her perfect white teeth with the ruler and avoided Morag's eyes, "Six foot give or take a foot or three."

"So it could reach nine foot?"

"That is a possibility."

"We can't have that," Vera gently murmured to Morag.

"No we can't have that," said Morag firmly.

Deirdre's face and body seems to dilate with pent up emotion – she hates her ambitions to be curtailed.

"It probably won't be quite nine foot," she snaps.

"Better to know the exact height before the fence goes up. Nothing worse than neighborly disputes. What do you think Margaret?" Vera peers round the side of her larger sister.

Deirdre fixes me with a 'Back me up here' look.

Personally, at that moment I couldn't care less if Deirdre built a life size model of the Taj Mahal in her back garden but Vera and Morag didn't seem two women who could easily stand up for themselves whereas Deirdre ... did.

"Legally I don't think you can put up a fence over six foot without planning permission."

Deirdre looks annoyed, anxious and betrayed, "I don't believe it."

"I think you'll find I'm right."

The sisters look relieved. Vera says to Morag, "We don't object to six foot do we Morag?"

"But I object to six foot," expostulates Deirdre, "I'll still be able to see your washing line and your prop," she shudders.

"Surely that's not so bad?" I ask reasonably.

She turns her back on the sisters and mouths, "and their pants."

Have discussed Deirdre's neighbours' pants before. Have stood in her back bedroom and surreptitiously viewed these pants. The sisters take a voluminous size and they wear and wash in bulk – most drying days there's a line full of faded, large knickers flapping cheerfully in the breeze.

"Now Deirdre," I appeal gently.

"Oh for goodness sake, ok. Six foot but will you two promise not to set your prop at such a high setting. Would you accept a whirly line if I paid for it?"

Sisters look at each other, appalled at offer of whirly line.

"Oh no Deirdre, a woman in the local paper was almost garroted by her whirly line. And anyway you don't get a good air supply filtering between your washed items."

"Ever considered a tumble dryer?" Deirdre asks silkily.

"Never!" the sisters say.

March 15th

All systems go next door. Deirdre is not a woman to hang about. Woman gardener arrived in a dilapidated lorry with two others and a cement mixer. As yet can't pick her out as they are all swathed in concealing outdoor clothes. Weather quite mild yet they look ready to attempt Mont Blanc.

The fences on both sides of Deirdre's garden are down and Martin's taken the car and retired to the *Corner Coffee Shop*.

NB. Martin. Increasingly he can be found at the *Corner Coffee Shop*, Deirdre says. He says she and Lord Dudley are disrupting his home life with their various projects all of which require complete freedom from any sound or movement Martin might need to make. Do not believe that Martin blames Lord Dudley – this is just Deirdre making out she has the majority vote in the house.

In the *Corner Coffee Shop*, Martin's set up an office space for himself in an alcove at the back. The staff are very good natured about this, in fact they seem pleased to have Martin monopolizing a four person table with his laptop, mobile, ashtray and half hourly intake of cappuccino and Danish pastry. It is almost as if he was Ernest Hemingway working on *For Whom the Bell Tolls*.

A couple of times I've popped in with Miriam. I am determined not to treat Martin as if he is Ernest Hemingway so call out, "Hello there, Martin". He ignores me or looks about the room as if expecting some other chap to respond.

Deirdre says when her new garden is well on its way to completion she'll send the gardener over to discuss mine with me.

"What's the woman's name?" I asked.

"I've no idea. I call her *pet.*"

March 16th

Not much going on in my life at the minute. Not sleeping very well and when I do sleep there seem to be noises at the back of my dreams. Apart from work I'm sticking close to home. Tilly is all the company I need. She's getting very frail. Yesterday she didn't make the jump between the table and the work top. Landed quite badly but got up and went to try again. I picked her up and set her back down next to her plate. There is nothing of her but skin and bone. It breaks my heart.

March 17th

Laura rang this evening while I was eating.

"But it's only seven o'clock. In London nobody eats before eight, more like nine," she says.

I reply, that everybody in Bittlesea Bay is asleep by nine and they need a couple of hours first to watch the local news and weather forecast on television while their food digests.

She says, "Ok, you eat – I'll talk. First I'm no longer with Pam, I'm with Iris. Iris has a better figure – you know me, I've always been a breast woman."

I swallow a piece of mushroom omelette and say, "I knew no such thing. Aren't you being rather superficial? Isn't Pam upset?"

"No, Pam's relieved. She says I was much too much of a good thing which is rather complimentary. Now I like Iris a lot. You might not like Iris so I'm going to keep her under wraps for a month or two. Shall I just say she's controlling in the nicest possible way," Laura pauses as if some pleasant controlling memory has occurred to her.

We don't talk much about me but that's ok as I haven't really anything I want to say.

In bed I think about Laura and how all her many emotional

43

dramas seem to wash over her and leave no mark. I imagine her heart, pink, healthy, unblemished.

March 18th
Life seems unutterably dreary! This evening met Miriam from work and went with her to visit her mother. They have a sea front flat, unfortunately a basement flat. The sea isn't visible only shoes and ankles as pedestrians pass by on the pavement outside. However I exclaim enthusiastically at the sea's proximity. *Only a stone's throw* I say, *how wonderful, lucky you!*

Expect to meet very old lady wrapped in shawls and genteely irritable. But no Miriam's mother looks about the same age as Miriam, maybe even a year or two younger. She is smart, petite and wears a skirt and matching boxy jacket with a large spray broach of turquoise brilliants on her lapel. She looks ready for a royal garden party right down to her shoes which are navy blue and cream with a small heel. Am amazed!

"How do you do, Mrs. Mason," and we shake hands. Her fingers feel like a cluster of brittle twigs. Thinks; Miriam must have taken after her father as she is quite a reassuringly hefty woman.

I am led into a room off a dark hall. It is like stepping back decades and reminds me of my grandmother's house only furnished more lavishly. There is a comfortable three piece suite and many occasional tables. Everywhere I look are pieces of crochet: chair backs, arm rests, doilies, crocheted rugs, even crochet framed in ebony and hung on the walls. While Miriam and her mother sort out sherry and nibbles from a large sideboard I dawdle from item of crochet to item of crochet making admiring noises.

"This is beautiful, breathtaking, what workmanship, hugely accomplished." I draw the line at the 'earth shatteringly stupendous', teetering on the tip of my tongue.

"Miriam's a clever little puss," Miriam's mother says fondly. Miriam, looking nothing like a 'little puss', grimaces.

"Miriam did all this?" I exclaim looking at Miriam in a new light. Unsure at that moment whether a good light or a bad light.

"It passes an evening," Miriam says with an apologetic shrug.

44

She and I take an armchair each while Miriam's mother puts her feet up, crossing one neat, nyloned ankle over the other.

"Cheers," she says holding up her crystal schooner, "Miriam, offer Margaret the Bombay Mix."

I take a handful of Bombay Mix and try not to drop them on the immaculate pink carpet.

"Cheers," I say.

"Cheers," Miriam says. She looks suddenly dispirited. Her mother peers hopefully from me to Miriam as if we are bright young things who must have tales of debutante parties and dancing till dawn to relate. Cannot immediately summon up a single subject that might be interesting. Ask myself what I know about crochet and the answer is *nothing*. Ask myself if I know anything about related subjects: knitting, dress making, tatting. Finally say loudly, "Do you remember french knitting?"

Miriam and her mother look blank.

"You knocked four small nails into the top of a cotton reel, then wound wool round the nails, then over and eventually a long snake of french knitting came out through the cotton reel hole. People made bedside mats. I made a table mat."

"Did you? Did it take long?"

"About a fortnight."

Silence as they both digest taking a fortnight to produce a table mat then Miriam says energetically, "What books are you reading at present?"

My mind scurries over the books on my bedside table. Decide that *Creating a Meadow Garden* is of no interest while *Lesbians sighted at nine o'clock – a World War II romance* inappropriate for sherry with Miriam's mother so reply, "*Annie Oakley, the Woman behind the Buckskins*".

"That sounds exciting", says Miriam's mother, "I used to love those cowboy series in the fifties and sixties. Do you remember Range Rider – I think he wore buckskins – or fringed leathers?"

Miriam frantic – imagining I am about to disclose something about Annie Oakley that might shock her mother. She taps her nose, blinks her eyes and doubles up with a coughing fit. Finally splutters out, "I've almost finished *The Testament of Youth*. Vera Britain was an extraordinary woman."

I agree that she was, particularly portrayed by Cheryl Campbell in the television series.

Miriam's mother looks misty eyed, "Ah youth," she says, "*Fair and shining youth. That age might take the things youth needed not!* Dear William Wordsworth."

Miriam and I nod our agreement that William Wordsworth was indeed a dear man. I stay for another hour that seems like three. Miriam sees me out. "Come again," Miriam's mother calls from the sitting room.

At the front door Miriam says, "Thanks for coming. Evenings with mum can get bloody lonely."

"My pleasure. Your mother is charming." Note: must find a way of either being truthful without upsetting anyone or being untruthful without upsetting myself.

"Is she?" Miriam looks doubtful.

Walk home with what seems like a gale force wind behind me. However, reaching the foot of my hill I find that instead of having to toil up as I usually do I sink back into the wind as if it's another armchair and amazingly the wind does all the work, carrying me up the steep incline and depositing me at my front gate. I'm cold but it is an exhilarating experience that quite erases the depression lingering from the Miriam and mother part of the evening.

March 19th
I haven't seen Nic and Simone since Georgie left. Don't know whether to telephone them or not. Are they avoiding me? Do they know something I don't?

March 20th
Not a lot could possibly happen today as I am determined to stay indoors with the blinds down to block out the light and also to discourage visitors. Nothing in the post from Georgie. In ten years this is the first time she's missed an anniversary. Have taken my diary back to bed and am determined to keep writing! About anything! Except …

Vis a vis seagulls; once March is reached they wake up at odd hours throughout the night particularly if the lifeboat boom goes off down on the sea front which it invariably does once a fortnight at two a.m. Then the entire gull population takes to the night sky, vocally and aerially (if there is such a word). Their cries monopolize the dawn chorus. I lie in bed and for some unfathomable reason imagine the seagulls have instead become a million penguins. The gradual build up of their voices seems genial and stationery; penguin bodies still, penguin heads swiveling, "Morning neighbour, mum, dad, brother, sister ... chimney, window ledge, trellis, black, white and ginger cat ..." they have a word with everything and everyone, yet nobody wants a word with them. Sometimes I can hardly hear the interviewer on 'Farming Today' trying to encourage a shy farmer's wife into an effusion over her home made cheeses for the squall of seagulls/penguins. In the autumn they quieten down. An almost eerie silence falls over Bittlesea Bay lasting till now. All those seagull/penguin families have taken themselves off to the beach for the winter, riding the waves, big brown feathered babies 'peep-peeping' hopefully at their parents but by then they're almost on their own.

Eventually got up, had bath, took telephone call from Laura who suddenly can see no point in her life, past, present or future and has a hangover due to drinking three pints of cider and a bottle of wine. Pause for her to light a cigarette and me to replenish my chamomile tea then she asks, "From what I've told you about Iris, do you think she has a sense of humour?"

In no mood for kindly prevarication reply, "No, not in the slightest."

Laura seems surprised.

Checked emails. Thirty three. Thirty from internet book group. Don't know how they find time to read so many books plus write reviews. I open only emails with exciting titles such as 'Piracy and sodomy on the high seas'. Also an email about achieving beautiful nails, an offer from Tesco.com offering vouchers if I buy a fridge freezer or plasma television from their electrical department and a message from Friends Reunited asking if I'd like to renew my subscription. *There are school friends waiting to speak to you!* Very disappointed. Nothing from Georgie. Could easily have cried but tell myself that thirty three dud emails is a small disappointment compared to troubles overseas or being called Jack Straw and always needing to swallow repeatedly when being interviewed.

Laura rang again to say she felt a little better and had eaten a cheese and chutney sandwich. She broached the topic of nobody she knew owning up to a liking for Branston Chutney. I said, "Everybody's a food snob these days."

Laura said, "Iris has taken against Chardonnay."

"Why?"

"She says she much prefers Sauvignon Blanc. What do you think?"

"She's talking out of her hat."

"Iris doesn't wear a hat, she has a kagool with a hood," Laura informs me good naturedly. She continues for another five minutes extolling Iris's virtues, finally I cut in, "Do you know what day this is?"

Laura pauses then says, "Yes of course I do, that's why I rang. I thought I'd distract you."

I swallow, "Well you have a bit. Thank you."

Then Deirdre takes over. Arrives with sandwiches and insists I come with her up onto the cliffs. We sit on a bench for almost an hour looking out to sea. It feels almost warm. Down below us beach enthusiasts run about with bare legs and fleeces. Sandwiches delicious. Also a flask of very sweet hot chocolate.

"By the bye," Deirdre says, "My gardener bod can't consider your garden till the beginning of April."

"Did you tell her about my steep slope?"

Deirdre looks thoughtful then says, "I said, as you can see it's in quite a state. I may have said, "Rather you than me.""

"Thanks."

Onwards to meet Martin in the foyer of the Odeon to see the afternoon showing of *Terminator 3*.

Came out. Deirdre announced, "That's the best film I've seen in a long time."

Can't quite agree but say nothing. Martin also says nothing. Deirdre looks a little anxious adding, "Although I don't think a lorry with a crane on it could travel that fast – do you?"

"Possibly," I said one eye on Martin. Still no reaction. "Coffee at the *Corner Coffee* – my treat?" I ask.

Corner Coffee Shop quite busy with late afternoon shoppers. Send Deirdre and Martin off to bag table and I queue up for Martin's cappuccino, a *Coffee ice Magnifico* for me and Deirdre's passion fruit and orange juice which as expected the *Corner Coffee* doesn't stock. The *Corner Coffee Shop* of Bittlesea Bay Town Centre is not an establishment catering for the passion fruit crowd. Deirdre is visibly disappointed with plain orange juice and eyes my *Magnifico* with ill concealed envy.

Martin is still saying nothing about the film but has found a copy of the Daily Mail and is now displaying fury over the front page article claiming, 'The Atkins Diet' is dangerous.

"Of course it's a plot by the processed food manufacturers because for the first time their profits are actually under threat." He's looking truculently at me.

"There's two sides to every debate," I diplomatically reply.

"Not this one," Martin thunders.

"Three sides?"

He gives me a stern look spoilt by his newly acquired cappuccino froth mustache, "The Atkins Diet is the only diet that works for life. LIFE. It is a way of life which means these bastards," he stabs a nicotined index finger at a photograph of George Best pictured taking a liquid breakfast of white wine, "will be out of a job."

"Further up Martin," Deirdre says.

"What?!" Martin roars. He glares at Deirdre as if he's suddenly seen her in a new and unpleasant light, "What?!" he roars again.

"You're pointing at George Best."

"Exactly my point. This rag of a newspaper, stinks. Why can't they leave him to drink himself to death in peace?"

"Especially with his new liver. That should last at least twenty years," offers Deirdre.

"I don't know about that," I say, "and to be honest vis a vis the Atkins Diet, I realise it works but not everybody would thrive on such a drastic mix of food."

Which is the wrong thing to say because Martin and Deirdre have now been on and off the Atkins Diet for almost three months. I could see that were I not a woman Martin would have liked to take me by the scruff of the neck and eject me from the *Corner Coffee Shop*. Instead he fixes me with a steely glare and rasps, "If it was good enough for our hunter gatherer ancestors it's fucking good enough for me."

Silence falls on our table. Again I bite back my words concerning our gorilla ancestry and their love of vegetation. Deirdre looks almost tearful, "We're each in control of our own destinies," she says, blinking rapidly. Seeing Deirdre upset, we quieten down. The unpleasant moment passes and we agree that the Daily Mail is an unspeakable paper before dividing it up between the three of us to read quietly. After half an hour of peace, Martin looks at his watch and says, "Does anyone fancy going back in the Odeon and watching *Mission Impossible 2*?"

This time when we emerge from the cinema it is eight thirty. We buy two take-away pizzas and eat them in my kitchen washed down with red wine. I'm in bed by ten. And so my anniversary passes.

March 22nd

Woken just after two by blood chilling sounds – like cats fighting only more savage and louder. In between the cries, the sound of manic scrabbling at the back gate. Where was Tilly? No time to reason that Tilly didn't go outside anymore, because in my mind's eye I saw poor Tilly dangling from the slavering jaws of a dog fox, her own small cry overwhelmed.

Shot out of bed. Also no time to locate ski pole but did grab torch. Raced downstairs almost tripping over Tilly sitting crouched on the bottom stair. Switched on hall light and examined her. Very frightened, start of nervous incontinence cycle imminent if I didn't put a stop to the dreadful screeching coming from outside.

Rushed through house and unlocked the back door. The dreadful crying ceased but the scrabbling noise became more frantic. I rounded the side of the house and shone my torch. It was a badger. In my opinion, and having only ever seen a badger in the distance or on television, this was the biggest badger ever, a giant of the species. We were about twelve foot apart. Badger looked over his shoulder at me, (no particular reason for assigning male gender to Brock). His eyes caught in the torch beam glinted – insanely?

What did I know of badgers? Only the bit on the Archers

where Phil and David Archer go on about badgers giving their dairy herd T.B. Now why did I think I'd also heard that enraged badgers charge humans when cornered and were capable of leaping more than five foot in the air and fastening their teeth into that person's throat? Horrid image of me staggering back into the kitchen trying to dislodge furious and possibly rabid badger.

Headline in *Listening Ear*, "Plucky lone woman slaughtered by renegade badger!"

"Calm down badger," I ordered which had no effect at all.

I picked up a plastic flower pot and tossed it at him. It glanced lightly off his back. Immediately he turned and rushed towards me. I screamed, stepped back, dropped torch, panicked. Badger every bit as terrified swerved to his left into an alcove between the shed and our fire log store. I picked up the torch and switched it off.

His head was pressed against the fence in the theory that if he couldn't see me, I couldn't see him. I noticed a patch of white against the black of his dusty fur coat. He trembled as I gingerly tip-toed past. Pulled the top and bottom, back gate bolts, lifted the latch, wedged the gate open with a piece of wood. Retreated back to the corner of the house and waited.

Took two minutes for badger to find his courage – peel away from the fence and trot through the open gate.

March 23rd
This afternoon found myself dwelling on animals, wild and domestic. Am I starting to feel more of a rapport with my furred and feathered friends than with human-kind? Would not like to think that were true but when recounting badger tale to Miriam at lunch found myself referring to Mr. Badger quite easily as if describing Mr. Wheeler trying to escape from my garden. Then went on to a rambling story about how Mr. and Mrs. Golden Eagle couldn't have baby eagles because their eggs were infertile due to farmers' blanket use of TNT sprays.

Miriam looking very puzzled, "I thought farmers couldn't use TNT anymore."

"Oh no they can't. This is Mr. and Mrs. Golden Eagle circa 1970."

"Oh," says Miriam, "So we're not talking recent history?"

51

Going home I realised that in the past week alone I'd also told Miriam about Tilly's ability to talk, about a duck and two ducklings Georgie stopped the car for last spring, that seagulls could be trained to lower their voices by the firm repetition of "That's quite enough," and my aunt's minah bird that swore. Aunt and minah bird dead at least fifteen years.

March 24th

Miriam querying my badger story. Says she repeated story to naturalist family friend who'd said, "What was badger doing off beaten track?" If badgers 'beaten track' was now outside my kitchen window surely I would be woken every night from now on. Had I? Admitted I hadn't. Put forward my own theory that badger had somehow fallen off 'beaten track' and into my garden by accident. "From a helicopter?" Miriam quipped. And now I continued firmly, liberated badger had returned to wherever his 'beaten track' was and would be more careful in the future.

March 25th

Reported back to Mr. Wheeler; one flat left empty with fan light window open in Crawford Road, one lost dog – black and white, answers to the name of Findlay, one estate agent's board sited at a hazardous angle over the pavement.

"Nothing else to report Margaret? Are you keeping an eye on front garden dustbins for multiple empty bottles and lager cans?"

"Yes Mr. Wheeler. Saw none."

"Any leafleting needed re. the dog?"

"Taken care of by owner."

"Should I get onto the estate agent?"

"Done it".."

"Excellent Margaret. You're proving an asset to the Watch. Now what about that open window? Perhaps give the police a bell – don't want squatters moving in, do we?"

Agree that we don't. Realised that I was standing to attention, hand positioned on breast as if I was carrying a musket. *Present arms, Margaret. Stand at ease.* Made my body relax, slumped shoulders.

I was in Mr. Wheeler's kitchen. It was old fashioned but

clean and very tidy. On the dresser was a silver framed photograph of Mr. Wheeler and his wife, possibly the same age as I am now. I looked away.

"Cup of tea?"

"Better get on."

Mr. Wheeler ignored this and put a light under the kettle, "I'd like you to hang on for a moment. Just a quick word although I dare say it's none of my business. Sit yourself down."

Pulled out kitchen chair. Red plastic seat which reminded me of my childhood kitchen furniture only we'd had turquoise blue plastic seats. Hoped Mr. Wheeler wasn't going to give me a lecture on wasn't it time I stopped this lesbian nonsense and became a pillar of the community? Watched him make tea in a pot with tea leaves. He let it brew. Put a chrome tea strainer and a sugar basin decorated with pink flowers on the table. Cups, saucers, teapot, milk jug, sugar basin – they all matched. Pretty and feminine. Reminders of his beloved wife.

"Biscuit?"

"Thank you."

Custard creams.

Mr. Wheeler pulled up the chair opposite and poured the tea.

"Now I'm not one to interfere – or perhaps I am."

He didn't smile. First I shook my head then I nodded. He continued, "I've noticed your ... pal, hasn't been about recently."

"No."

"And you've been looking ruddy miserable."

Said nothing to that.

"Would I be right in thinking the two of you have had a falling out?"

I sighed deeply. How would Deirdre handle Mr. Wheeler? *I don't discuss my personal life with neighbours Mr. Wheeler. Could cause bad blood if there was a reconciliation. Neighbours taking sides – Martin says that's how wars are caused.*

But I'm not Deirdre, I'm Margaret and I've grown to like Mr. Wheeler which makes me interpret what could be nosiness for concern, so I say, "We're having a trial separation till the end of April. Hopefully after that we'll get back to normal."

53

"Hmm," he said, "And what if you don't?"

"I *will* be ruddy miserable."

"Can I give you some advice?"

"As long as you don't mind if I don't take it."

"Fair enough," he stood up and walked over to the dresser, picked up the photograph, "My wife didn't die, you know. Everybody in this road thought she did because that's what I told them. We kept ourselves to ourselves pretty much so nobody expected to go to funerals and anyway people have their own lives to live. Actually she left me. Is still alive. Lives in Doncaster with a chap called Trevor. My son says he's not a bad bloke. What I wanted to tell you was that I wasted years hoping she'd come back. Years." He looked at me, a deep frown on his face as if he was trying not to get upset, "Even now, if she walked through the front door I'd be so darn pleased. But the waiting hasn't been worth the candle."

"But Mr. Wheeler, Georgie's only been gone a few weeks – I couldn't just start re-arranging my life – if she doesn't come back I'd be devastated for a very long time if not forever."

I gulped hot tea, my eyelids blinking rapidly. He put the frame down and came back to the table.

"Of course you'd be devastated, what I'm saying is don't let whatever happens, good, bad, or tragic flatten you. Flatten *you* Margaret, the stuff inside that makes *you* tick! You have to consider yourself because nobody else will. Take it or leave it. I hope your Georgie does come back and you both live happily ever after."

He looked as if he might say something more but he didn't.

Finished my tea, admired the african violets on his window-sill all the while thinking, *Mr. Wheeler's got a bloody cheek, who does he think he is*, but not really annoyed. I recognised a gem of truth in what he'd said. I thought of that awful word Georgie had used, 'whimper'. I didn't want to be a Margaret always desperate for her approval.

On the doorstep he held out his hand and I shook it. Went home.

March 26th

This afternoon Deirdre arrives while I'm in the middle of planting up my seed trays. For meadow project am propagat-

54

ing sweet peas, fox gloves, cornflowers, stocks and antirrhinums. Deirdre settles herself on my carrier bag of recycled
egg cartons but doesn't seem to notice.

"I'd make the tea myself but I'm knackered," she says.

"Why's that?," I ask, absorbed in scattering minute
antirrhinum seeds over moist compost.

"My garden of course. The jewel in my crown. Been on my
feet all morning organizing Janice."

"Janice?"

"The gardener. Can't make up my mind whether I like her or
not. She asked me not to call her 'pet'. Didn't ask pleasantly
mind you, asked with attitude. Sullen. Yes, sullen sums her up.
Garden looks fantastic though. Fan-bloody-tastic! I just wish I
had the time to enjoy it but I'm up in London early evening.
That's why I'm dressed like this."

"Oh." Study Deirdre's outfit. She's wearing a grey pashmina
over a green tweed trouser suit, a purple velour hat, the brim
pinned to the crown by a splendid dirk broach of silver and
amethyst.

"I think I look very Liberty's crossed with Harvey Nichols.
What do you think?"

"You look splendid and very rich."

She beamed and rubbed her hands together, "Good. Rich,
that's how I want to look – I'm doing dinner with a connection
who's gi-normous in food labeling. Are you going to make that
tea or am I going to die of thirst?"

Put kettle on. Rummage for Deirdre's Earl Grey tea, my
Peppermint tea.

"No milk," she shouts, "I'm avoiding dairy. Got cake?"

"Can you eat cake on Atkins?"

"I'm off Atkins for the day, I'll do double Atkins tomorrow."

We drink tea. Deirdre scrutinizes my seed trays and says, "Is
all this fuss really necessary?" She waves her hand at the trays,
plastic pots, small sack of peat free compost, packets of seeds,
roll of kitchen foil, milk bottle full of water and atomizer,
"Surely it's easier to buy full grown? You can't turn round for
trays of annuals in every single shop. Even the pub on the
corner's got a plant stand outside."

"I like growing from seed."

"Well if you've got time on your hands …"

I change the subject bringing it back to her, "So, the Atkins Diet is a movable feast at the moment?"

"Sort of. I absolutely agree with Martin that Atkins is a diet for life only neither of us can resist white bread and chips. So weekdays, (apart from today) it's Atkins, weekends it's Atkins plus bread and chips."

"Have you lost any weight?"

"Gained two pounds," she mumbles.

"How many?"

"Gained four pounds – but can lose that almost over night if I'm really stringent. Extraordinary but I feel that I know Atkins very well. Almost as if he's the butler, no as if he's our dietitian and close personal friend."

"Like Dyson?"

"Exactly."

"Any particular reason for today's visit?" I cut open my packet of corn flower seeds.

"Yes. I'm having a grand open garden soirée next Sunday, weather permitting. One till three. Janice will be there so it's not like you'll be on your own as far as the 'L' word goes."

"What makes you think she's a lesbian?"

Deirdre flinches. She does not like to call a spade a spade or even a lesbian a lesbian.

"I heard her talking to the two women who helped her. And there was horsing around and bodily contact – straight women don't behave like that with each other. So you'll come?"

"Sounds good," I say, heart sinking.

March 29th

Miriam subdued. Feel I should offer to visit her and her mother again but think at the moment I would rather walk under a bus. Compromise with myself by asking how her love life is, any news from the Hospice Shop?

She shakes her head sadly, "Not a sniff. Not a dicky bird. All the young lesbians have gone to ground including my lone admirer. We do get a few in around my age but I find women my age so depressing. They ask for things like well worn in, wide fitting shoes to accommodate their bunions. How gross is that?"

I agree that is pretty gross but say, "Surely some of them are presentable. After all you did say you'd settle for ordinary?"

Scathingly, as if I am an infant, she says, "Margaret, there's ordinary and ordinary. I'm desperate but not that desperate."

Leave work. Sun shining. Suddenly decide to take old route home past the Hospice Shop. I will at least cheer Miriam up. Hospice Shop heaving. Good weather has brought everyone out in search of spring outfits. Fight for right to riffle through size fourteens. Finally seize a scarlet jacket and on the trouser carousel find a pair of smart black trousers, the original swing ticket hanging from the label. Push my way through scrum to reach Mrs. Ferguson manning the till. She stares hard at me before saying, "That will be four pounds fifty."

Give her a fiver and as she hands me my change she says, "We haven't seen you in lately."

"Mother's been poorly," I lie. Mother has been dead nearly five years and wouldn't have minded, her motto being *If you're going to tell a lie tell an elaborate one*, "Can't desert mum now she's on her last legs."

"Oh dear, is she very bad?"

"Fraid so. A matter of waiting."

"How old is the poor woman?"

Judged Mrs. Ferguson to be in her eighties – wouldn't like her to think she's close in age to fictional dying mother so say, "Ninety seven."

"That's a very good age! You must have been a late baby?"

"I was a very late baby. The only child with a white haired mum. Didn't matter to me. Loved every white hair on her head," stopped myself from adding, "and eyebrows."

Felt ridiculously cheerful. As I opened the door, called out, "And do say hello to my pepper and salt woman. What's her name?"

"Miriam. You wouldn't like to leave a telephone number? I think Miriam would like a word. I can heartily recommend Miriam as an excellent co-worker and I believe she has a warm and faithful heart."

"If you don't mind I won't at the present time. There's a long haul ahead of me with mum but do tell Miriam that I often recall her cheery face."

Thinks: that should raise Miriam's spirits for a while without offering any immediate expectations. Leave jacket and trousers in dry cleaners, continued onwards till I came to the sea front. Walked as far as pier where I bought six scented candles and a set of sea shell wind chimes. Walked back. Took funicular up cliff to *Bittlesea Bay Cafe*.

Greeted warmly by waitress, "What you again?"

Took slab of fruit cake out onto terrace. Sat on metal chair with feet resting on railing. Sea almost blue. Sun almost warm. Me almost ok.

April

April 1st

This afternoon met elderly woman in street who tells me to keep up the good work and where is my bucket? Reply that I don't have a bucket. She hands me a pound coin and asks, "Do I get a sticker?"

Realise she's taken in my Wheeler's Watch sash and assumed I'm collecting for charity. Explain who and what I am and try to return her pound.

She shakes her head and says, "Get yourself a cup of tea, you look perished."

I am perished. From my front window I mistook brilliant sunshine for a summer's day of at least sixty four degrees fahrenheit, whatever that might be in centigrade.

Decide to head for the supermarket café for my cup of tea and as I hurry along spend time counting in my head all the various cafés and tea shops at my disposal: supermarket, Bittlesea Bay Clifftop, Corner Coffee, Debenhams (magnificent sea view but disinterested staff), British Home Stores, Marks and Spencer, Littlewoods, various Italian restaurants ... lose count. As I cross the supermarket car park, I recognise Nic and Simone pushing two full trollies towards me. At the same moment they recognise me. Simone's trolley attempts to veer off between two closely parked cars while Nic's trolley hesitates.

"Stop!", I command, the authority of my voice surprising

them and me. They stop as do several other shoppers with and without trolleys. Nic and Simone exchange urgent looks with each other which I know so well. That mutual telepathy running between the long term couple enabling them to arrive at an official line on an embarrassing situation without actual words being exchanged. Once upon a time Georgie and I had it.

I beam at them. A mega-sized reassuring beam. In return they send me relieved, self conscious grins. I hurry up to them and lean across their piled high trolleys to kiss their cheeks.

"How lovely to see you both." And it is lovely. I'm genuinely pleased to see them, and in pain too, because they are familiar and linked to Georgie. I know I must not show them how upset I am, how hurt and frightened. I must put them at ease, as I can do so well, with warm and self deprecating humour. I draw inspiration from their shopping, two sacks of peat, trays of petunias, lobelia, alyssum, geraniums, four wicker hanging baskets already planted up, a box of Miracle-Gro.

I manage a boisterous, "Aha, gardener par excellence! Forging ahead of the competition! All systems go!"

They both nod. Simone wheels her trolley back into tandem and looks fondly at Nic, "She's done amazing things in that garden. I mean it's only April the first and already it's a blaze of colour. We've got red, yellow, blue and pink. Every shade of pink I could ask for."

"That's terrific."

Nic shrugs, "Just daffs and tulips. Early days. How about you?"

"Deirdre's gardener is going to help me dig up the back and turn it into a meadow."

They both look perplexed.

"Wildflowers. Bird, bee and insect habitat." I explain.

It slips out of Nic's mouth, "Whatever does Georgie think?" Her cheeks turn scarlet, "Oh, I'm sorry," she says.

"That's ok. Haven't had a chance to tell Georgie my plans. We'll talk when she comes home at the end of the month."

"Of course you will," Simone says, "We intended to pop in but what with Nic's competition and our holiday in Tenerife the days have just rushed by."

"No problem. I've been pretty busy myself, catching up with friends and family."

"I think you're being very brave," Simone says squeezing my arm and fixing me with her most sincere gaze.

"Am I?"

"Georgie wants her head examined."

I try a laugh, not much more than a 'ha-ha' but good natured rather than embittered, "Georgie is her own woman. I'm not holding anyone to me by force. I'm sure we'll work out a solution and in the meantime I've got to get on with my life."

"Good for you," says Nic, "Look we'll definitely telephone. I want your advice about the back bed – it's got to have 'in-your-face-drama' and you've an eye for the right specimen plant."

They agree I must come over. I agree with them – I must come over. All sorts of phrases fill my head and almost spill out; *don't worry about me, I'm not a pining woman, where is Georgie?, not jealous, will she come back? absolutely fine on my own, so much more the real me, have you spoken to her? why is she doing this, what did I do wrong?*

Say goodbyes. I saunter away from them and into the supermarket toilet where I study myself in the chipped mirror. Inside I feel as if I'm teetering on a cliff edge, convinced I'm about to crash onto the rocks below. I decide not to bother with cups of tea, instead I'll do my shopping for the weekend. Use the pound coin to get a trolley. Another image intrudes. There is Georgie and there I am, the one pushing the trolley into this very supermarket. Georgie says, "Margaret, you and the trolley wait here in the dairy section while I scoot round and get what we need."

Off Georgie scoots leaving me with the responsibility of the trolley and the limited vista of milk, cheese and spreads, or yoghurt, cream, créme fraiche.

I am in turmoil.

April 2nd

Miriam complaining about her mother again. Says mother has trouble recalling long words which is especially irritating as mother is an anagram fanatic. Miriam feels unhealthy interest in anagrams has lead to this problem in the first place. Mother calls out, "I see three syllables. I see an *m* and the vowels *a* and *u*. Complete word sounds like 'mubala'."

Mother spends a vocal entire evening trying to work out alternative for 'mubala'. Just before going off to bed she shouts, "I've got it. Laundromat."

Miriam remonstrates, "Laundromat sounds nothing like 'mubala'."

"Three syllables, an *m, a* and a *u*. Laundromat – mubala. Very similar."

April 3rd

Because tomorrow is Deirdre's soirée I decide to visit my local hairdresser, *Hair Today, Shorn Tomorrow*. Michelle does my hair. She is half my age and has no interest in me whatsoever, never asking me what I might be doing at the weekend as she assumes that women over forty do nothing. Same applies re. holidays. In fact she hardly even takes an interest in my hair, able to cut it quite well while keeping an eye out for anyone she knows going past the shop window. Sometimes she'll remember I'm there and say, "Ok?" to a section of the mirror about a foot above my head and I'll reply, "Fine," with a conciliatory raising of my eyebrows.

Today, I take my seat in my usual ripped black leatherette chair adjacent to the magazine rack. Michele approaches wearing an expression of resigned boredom. We both stare at my reflection. Dispiritedly she pulls a strand of hair each side of my face down as far as it will go and says, "Same as usual?" and changes her chewing gum from left side of her mouth to right.

I say, "I'd like a feathery trim plus white blonde and aubergine highlights."

Michelle looks puzzled, "Aubergine?" she repeats.

"Red. Dark red. And white blonde."

"What about another copper tint?"

"No thank you."

She steps back. Fills her cheeks with air and gently puffs it out before saying, "I really don't think your face can take it."

Which against my will makes me laugh, "I'll be the judge of that," I say.

Two and a half hours later and I'm done. Michelle has given me her full attention throughout. I look ... extraordinary. I don't look like Margaret anymore. Although Michelle has been rendered speechless I can tell she's impressed because she's looking at me with something approaching interest.

"Going anywhere nice?" she finally asks me.

"A soirée," I tell her.'

"With your boyfriend?"

"Definitely not."

In the evening, Laura rings to say that she and Iris have booked a walking weekend for the end of April. She's bought walking boots, a special stick and an inflatable tent.

"But you don't like walking," I remonstrate, "you've always said, if it's not within fifty yards of a parking space it's not worth seeing."

Laura is silent for a moment then she says, as if after deep consideration, that she thinks I may have misunderstood her completely throughout our twenty five year friendship, "I've never fought shy of walking," she says.

"That's a very strange phrase; you've never fought shy of walking. What does it mean?"

"What it says. I've never fought shy of walking, you've just never been around ..."

"While you were not fighting your non-existent shyness of walking?"

"Exactly. And anyway if I'm capable of dancing for two hours non-stop I can certainly do walking. What have you been up to today?"

"I've had my hair dyed white blonde and aubergine."

"Sounds like a raspberry ripple."

"It looks nothing like a raspberry ripple. What colour is Iris's hair?"

"It feels like silk."

"Yes, but what colour is it?"

"Muddy brown."

April 4th

Dress with care for Deirdre's soirée. Wear olive green combat trousers, black cotton shirt with a Nehru collar which I leave unbuttoned. In fact I leave several buttons unbuttoned. Consider pinning back one side of the Nehru collar with a cameo broach my aunt left me but decide there's no point in a Nehru collar if I make it into half a revere. Deirdre telephones while I'm getting ready to say, did I know it had rained earlier and if I didn't know, she was letting me know so that I could bring a pair of slippers because as we'd all be walking round her garden she didn't want the lounge carpet ruined by muddy shoes. (Not that there is any mud in Deirdre's garden.) She'd already rung a number of guests and had sent Martin out to *Shoe Fayre* to stock up on cheap fluffy slippers for those guests uncontactable.

I ask her, "Won't your male guests object to fluffy slippers?"

"There aren't any male guests. There's just Martin and Lord Dudley."

Put slippers, a pair of rather smart, fleece lined bootees in an appropriate carrier bag. Would not sully Deirdre and Martin's stylish home with Tesco or Safeways carrier bags. Dithered between Ottakars and Debenhams, came down in favour of Ottakars as would rather other guests saw me as a bookish woman than a Debenhams woman.

Get wine from fridge. As I'm leaving the telephone rings and the answer phone intercepts the call. Stand in the kitchen doorway listening but it's only Laura wondering what I'm doing over Easter.

The rain has stopped. The sun shines. The day is springlike. I knock on Deirdre's front door as the movable fence has been replaced by an unmovable willow counterpart. Martin lets me in. His expression is grim.

"I'm letting you in," he says, "but that's my lot. I'll be incommunicado at the *Corner Coffee Shop*. Why does she have to do this?"

He doesn't wait for my reply, just grabs his jacket and hurries past me and out of the front door. In the other direction through the open back door I can see Deirdre and several women. Deirdre is wearing an astonishing outfit, a trouser suit in blue and grey camouflage material, charcoal grey designer wellington boots, her bouncy yellow curls tied back with a blue bandanna. I realise that she's trying to give a 'hands-on' impression to her visitors.

"I swear to god carrying those sacks of cobbles nearly did for

63

me," she's saying, pressing one hand into the small of her back. Careful deconstruction of her sentence proves she isn't exactly lying, only I as the nosy neighbour watching from the back bedroom know the truth, possibly Morag and Vera as two more nosy neighbours watching from their back bedroom window, and Janice the gardener who'd carried the sacks of cobbles – but she hasn't arrived yet.

"You've done a fabulous job," a woman in black silk is saying.

Deirdre spots me hovering in the kitchen doorway and hurries forward with an insincere smile of pleasure. Up close and her lips and eyes narrow, "Where's Martin?" she hisses.

"Gone," I say.

"The bloody ... bloody ..." and then her smile is back in place, "Why Dorothea," she purrs, "and little Sasha and Freya. Leave your slippers by the back door, Margaret. Good god, your hair! Janice – my support, my angel. Margaret point Janice in the direction of spare slippers, so she's prepared."

Janice is wearing Doc Martins with purple laces. Also jeans and a checked, fleece shirt. She looks annoyed or, as Deirdre would say, she looks sullen. Also familiar but I put this down to the fact that she's been just out of focus but in and around Deirdre's garden for almost ten days.

"Hello Janice," I say brightly, "Deirdre wants anyone going in the garden to change into slippers on their way back indoors." I point to the pink and white fluffy slippers lined up next to Lord Dudley's litter tray, "I've brought my own ubiquitous bootees."

Thinks: why must I always sound like a gung-ho games mistress?

"No way am I wearing slippers," Janice says emphatically, "I'd rather go home now."

"But Deirdre's garden is all your handiwork and your design. You might get new customers."

"I thought you were my new customer."

"I won't be an impressive customer like Deirdre. My needs are fairly straightforward," which for some reason makes me redden and stare out past Janice's left ear.

"Yeah. Well. One job at a time," she says gruffly, "I think I like your hair -- peony coloured," and then she's gone, marching out into Deirdre's garden. The small crowd parts and Janice disappears into their midst. I hear Deirdre yelling, "She's a star, an absolute star."

Make conversation with Dorothea. Also a Phillida and her teenage son, Sherman. Muse that decades earlier Dorothea may well have been just Dot and Phillida, Phylis. Cannot think what a Sherman would have been called.

"And you are?" Dorothea asks after ten minutes vibrant conversation.

"Margaret. I live next door," wave vaguely in the direction of my garden.

"No, I meant what do you do?"

"I'm an accounts typist."

"Really? Is that rewarding work?"

"Extremely," I enthuse, "Never a dull moment."

Catch Janice's eye. She is propped against one pillar of the gazebo and I do believe she's trying not to smile. Have recurrence of the certainty that I know Janice from somewhere else but am distracted by Vera and Morag's washing line slowly coming into view over the top of Deirdre's fence. As there is no breeze their twelve pairs of pants hang lifeless and faded. Deirdre who is talking animatedly to Phillida continues to talk but her eyes harden, narrow and glitter.

April 6th

My garden has a terrace and then the aforementioned steep slope. This year it is a mass of weeds as if the previous autumn I'd gone out with a large packet marked "Invasive weeds and many others" and scattered the seeds everywhere. There must be at least twenty different varieties of weed and yet not one looked like a wild flower suitable for my wild flower meadow. Janice arrived as I stood in contemplation. I begin briskly, "My plan is to turn this," wave of hand in direction of slope, "into a wild flower meadow. I can afford five hundred pounds."

Which wasn't true. I could afford two hundred and fifty pounds but suddenly such an amount to someone who'd transformed Deirdre's garden into a Chelsea Flower Show contender seemed laughable.

Janice folds her arms and purses her lips.

65

"You really need a rotavator which would be an extra sixty quid."

"In that case I can't afford it," I say firmly.

She kicks one of my few remaining perfectly good plants, "Plant stock's tired."

"It's the best I can do. I'm growing quite a few seedlings," I then wave vaguely towards the kitchen window. Janice doesn't bother to look.

"Better get started then," she says.

"So five hundred's ok?"

"If that's all you've got, it will have to be."

Janice refuses to look me in the eye, just keeps swinging her foot at my innocent plant. (There's something so familiar about her.) Go indoors and try to think who I know who looks sullen. Nobody apart from Martin.

At ten thirty I take her out a mug of tea and two chocolate digestives. She says, "God my back's killing me," and takes her refreshments over to the bench. From time to time during the four hours she's working I take out tea and biscuits. Not much seems to have been done. She tells me: I have a fine view, that she can't stand couch grass, that there are blue tits nesting in the back wall and if they don't look out a cat will get their babies. I tell her that this was what happened last year, how Samson and Delilah sat on that very bench and watched and waited. Went into some detail. Thought I made the story exciting, yet poignant, while avoiding sentimentality. When I'd finished she asked, "Who are Samson and Delilah?"

"Georgie's cats," I said, "They're not here at the moment." I change the subject by apologizing profusely for the couch grass.

She shrugs, "Not your fault," which is true, "it's just a bastard to get out. Strong root system," casts a faraway look over my hillside, "Mind you, it's probably underpinning the whole slope. Once it's shifted, the first heavy rain and you'll probably have the whole back garden whooshing into your kitchen."

"Surely not?"

"Could happen."

I'm relieved when Janice goes home, saying she'll be back in a fortnight. I'm relieved that it doesn't look like rain.

April 8th
Deirdre complaining that next door neighbours Vera and
Morag have turned their hose on seagull couple nesting on *her*,
(Deirdre's) extension. She is in half a mind to report them to
the RSPCA. Point out to Deirdre that hose spray very small
beer where seagulls are concerned. Deirdre unconvinced.

April 9th. Good Friday
Am invited to Deirdre and Martin's for dinner. Deirdre has
'dressed' the table as opposed to laying it. This Easter she's
gone for a sumptuous royal blue and gold theme. Wonder why
it is that Deirdre's use of the paper doily looks eccentrically
stylish? Another nice touch is Lord Dudley in his box lid on the
end of the table. As it's Easter they've bought him a plastic egg
to play with. Every now and then Lord Dudley gets absolutely
livid with this new toy and tosses it out of the box lid. When it
lands in my plate Deirdre and Martin are enchanted as if
they've been training Lord Dudley to enact this very deed for
some time.

Not entirely Atkins today. There are potatoes; golden
roasted and mash. Deirdre is an excellent cook. Roast pork
with all the trimmings for dinner. A nice touch is the small
dish of delicious pork crackling set between Martin and myself.
Deirdre admits to overdosing on pork crackling while in the
kitchen.

However Martin not as enthusiastic as expected, recounting
harrowing details of how the roots of his teeth have had to be
filled due to receding gums. Have never heard of roots being
filled. Martin bares his teeth at us. I don't bother to find my
glasses as would rather not see his filled roots. I say, "Dear me,"
and begin chomping my way through the lion's share of crackling. Deirdre says to Martin, "Ok darling, gnashers away now."

We all retire to lounge area, a sofa each for them, Martin
pulls up an armchair for me and puts it between the two sofas. I
feel like a compere on a panel game, say jovially, "Now Couple
Number One, what is the capital of British Honduras?"

Decide I've had too much to drink. Make my excuses and
leave them eating Dairy Box and watching *Nightmare on Elm
Street*.

April 10th

Arrive at Laura's late Saturday afternoon. She is cutting up a carrot and four celery sticks into very small segments to poke into the cream cheese and chive dip.

"There's crisps as well. And stuffed pasta. Don't know what it's stuffed with – I've thrown the packaging away."

"Very acceptable," I say.

Laura lives in a one bedroom, garden flat in North London with two inscrutable cats, Bill and Ben. Bill is the original watching-paint-dry cat. He spends hours staring at the wall or the table leg. He is tabby and lozenge shaped and the best way to hold him is as if he were a bagpipe.

Pasta and dip simple but delicious. After dinner Laura attempts to re-create her and Iris's dancing triumph of the previous weekend.

"Use your imagination," she says, "Iris is my height only more womanly shaped – she's wearing a green satin dress and headband. And one, two, three, one two three ... We dance together like birds of a feather."

Refrain from pedantry as to whether birds dance or not. Laura dips an imaginary Iris so that her hair, if it is more than four inches long, skims the beech effect laminated floor. Laura looks up triumphantly at an invisible audience and smiles.

"Hooray!" I shout.

She clicks her heels and executes a neat bow. If Iris was with her, Laura would have let her crumple into a heap at her feet while she enjoyed the many imagined accolades.

Can see Laura would like to re-create this scene several more times so indicate that my wine glass is empty. While she opens another bottle I try to teach Bill and Ben, initially to sit but as they do little else but sit change my tack and try to teach them to stand. Both cats look blank.

Over fresh drink ask Laura what she thinks of my hair?

"It's different."

Ask Laura if she thinks Georgie misses me?

"Who knows?"

Give up on me and ask Laura what Iris is up to?

"Working."

"At Easter?"

"She never stops. She's brilliant at whatever she does."

"What does she do?"
"No idea."

April 12th
Got home around mid-day. Whenever I've been away recently, even if it's only out shopping down to the town I can't help a feeling of anticipation creeping in as I run up the six steps leading to my front door. I expect letters even when there's no post, or a note, or a message on my answer phone. Something, anything from Georgie. And now Easter has come and gone, and it's our first Easter apart and of course – there's no something, no anything, just nothing.

As I'm carrying my case upstairs the phone rings. Rush downstairs knowing it will only be Deirdre.

"Goody-goody, you're back. Fancy a run out somewhere?", Deirdre asks.

No, no, no. I don't want to run anywhere.

"Perhaps tea at the café?" I suggest.

"I could murder a cake," Deirdre says, "Only we're not eating cakes." This is more of a question than a mission statement issued on behalf of herself and Martin.

"Well I'm definitely not eating cake," I say firmly.

"We could still meet up."

"Yes lets."

"What about a visit to Sissinghurst? Vita Sackville West did the garden, she's one of yours isn't she?" Deirdre asks.

"Deirdre it won't be brilliant there at this time of the year."

"How about Charleston? Vanessa Bell. I hear her fellah was a gay boy. I wouldn't stand for Martin playing around like that, I'd … chop off his balls."

Even over the telephone Deirdre reminds me of a skittish Shetland pony.

I say, "I'd love to go to Charleston but not today. Let's meet for tea and compare diaries."

Didn't know if Deirdre had a diary. She'd told me that her memory's phenomenal and she doesn't need to write things down. Can't stand reading either. Says, *I have a go at a book but after a page or three I think, 'what's he droning on about? Get to the point, mate.'.*

"But it's Bank Holiday, what about a picnic in the car. We could park in the carpark and look out at the sea?"

"No."

She moots the possibility of a barbecue later if the sun comes out, tea and cake in Debenhams which is no longer her sort of store apart from their John Rocha towels and bedding.

I respond by being vague hoping that Deirdre will get the message that all I want is to be left alone. She doesn't. Finally cite Kipling's 'the cat that walked by itself'.

After a pause for reflection she replied, "Lord Dudley can be a solitary cat but generally he can't get enough of me and Martin's company."

"What I mean is I'm a solitary cat."

I can almost hear her wrinkling her nose as if I'd announced, "I'm a groovy chick."

"In what way?"

"Sometimes I rather like my own company."

"Oh me too," her voice becomes dreamy, "I love staring up at the night sky imagining all those planets ..." tails off as her imagination fails to provide an answer as to what all those planets might be doing.

April 19th

Janice the gardener arrives at ten a.m. Comes in round the back and taps on my kitchen window. I open the door and say, "Tea, coffee?"

"Tea," she says. When I turn round from plugging in the kettle I find Janice sitting at the kitchen table studying my television guide.

"Just seeing what's on," she says, turning the pages. I notice her fingers are stained green. Is this a gardening marketing ploy? *Yes, I truly have got green fingers. No really.*

Make tea and bring it and biscuits to Janice. Sit down opposite. Some green and blue in the crease of her chin and the fine lines each side of her nose.

Janice looks up and catches my curious stare.

"Face painting," she says reaching for a biscuit.

"Oh," I say, "Do you have children?"

"No. Why should I?" she says truculently.

70

Suddenly feel as if a huge chasm has opened up between me and Janice. There must be about ten years difference in our ages yet she is making me feel like her grandmother.

I try an impatient, worldly sigh, "Isn't face painting generally associated with children?"

"No."

"Well it is to me."

She shrugs, "We had a druid party at the weekend."

Note the 'we'. "Was it fun?" which seemed an inadequate question.

"Yeah, it was. So, what's on the agenda for this morning or should I go my own sweet way?"

In businesslike fashion I pick up my cup and march out into garden. Cannot imagine that Janice was as (offensively) laid back with Deirdre as she seems to be with me. For some reason my face including my ears feel hot. I'm certain they're scarlet. Climb steps to the gravelled terrace and look up at the sloping area. A fair bit of heavy digging still to do. After several minutes Janice follows me up, no doubt having first made notes for her following week's television viewing. I say firmly, "You've still got quite a bit of digging to do."

"That's a killer on my back."

"I'm sorry about that, but it was a killer on my back."

"You can understand my point of view then."

"Janice if you don't want to do the job ..."

"I just don't want to do that bit of the job ..."

"But I can manage most of the other bits. I didn't need any help with them."

"What if you helped me?"

"But I'm paying you to do the job."

She shrugged, "I better get on with it then. I can't afford to lose the money."

Which was awful. I couldn't afford to pay the money. But could I afford it, more or less, than Janice could afford to lose it? In the past Georgie paid for food and many of the bills because she earnt vastly more than me but I'd had no money from her the whole time she'd been away. Janice walked dispiritedly down the steps, left her mug on the window sill and went round to the shed. I looked at my watch. I looked at the slope. It was steep. And yes, if I had a bad back, then why

71

shouldn't she have one as well particularly after lifting all Deirdre's sacks of cobble stones?

"Get out both the forks," I shouted down to her.

She looked over her shoulder, "Why?"

"Because ... because it's my garden and I want to be a part of turning that bloody slope into something fabulous."

April 21st

Miriam very low. Has recently given up smoking, day before yesterday in fact. This lunchtime stood on back step of TM Accountancy for ten minutes without saying anything. I tried. Described plans for my hillside meadow in unnecessary detail. Finally Miriam cut loudly across my description saying, "It's no good. I'm not interested. Your hillside meadow could be swept out to sea for all I care. The only words in my head are, I WANT A CIGARETTE NOW! If I can't smoke, my life is not worth living."

"Then smoke."

"I can't," she wailed; "Mrs. Ferguson and my mother have rightly pointed out that I'm ruining my complexion and my voice is at least three octaves lower than it should be."

Am amazed that Miriam worries about loss of complexion and personally rather envy her low voice. Wonder how many cigarettes would I have to smoke to lower my voice three octaves.

Miriam leaves me on the step and goes back to her desk where I hear her unwrapping another piece of Nicorette chewing gum.

Also a smoking ban in place at *Corner Coffee Shop*. Martin has been under siege. For several days *Coffee Shop* staff made allowance for him to continue smoking unobtrusively, keeping his cigarette concealed beneath the table top. Manageress arrives back from skiing holiday and says regretfully this can't go on. Concealed cigarette is an increased fire hazard. It's on the cards, (what cards?) that either the table top will ignite or Martin's trousers will.

Deirdre told me that Martin was 'incandescent'. He'd penned a letter to the *Listening Ear*, copies to a government health minister whose name has gone completely out of her head. Talks of taking this issue to the highest court in the land.

Expect fuss to die down shortly but then see Martin's polemic in the newspaper, headline: *Small town – small minds*, and outlined in red to denote fury of writer. Realise Deirdre's Martin is *Martin J. Storm* of the ladies toilets correspondence. This inspires me to post off an immediate response, my headline, *Victory for Planet Clean Air!*. As always sign myself A. Oakley but on a whim add, Fire and Pollution Prevention Officer.

In meantime spot Martin standing in seedy outside niche between Smiths and the *Corner Coffee Shop*, puffing his cigarette and looking bitter.

Sunday April 24th
The *Bittlesea Bay Café* is packed with tourists all bearing bulging rucksacks. Deirdre wants them banned. (The rucksacks not the tourists although she's not too keen on them either.) She says individual rucksacks take up as much space as a child or a small adult. Do not point out that Deirdre with her flowing scarves, various draperies, handbag, key purse and huge sheaf of hair takes up as much space as three medium sized adults.

N.B. Do not spend all my life shuttling between cafés although on re-reading previous entries it seems I do.

"He's coping ... I think," she says responding to my inquiry about Martin's smoking ban, "However more to the point I'm worried about Lord Dudley," she looks worriedly towards the sea.

"Why?"

"I think he's got ear mites."

"Not a big problem – better take him to the vet."

"Yes, but say I take him to the vet and the vet finds cancer or diabetes – I'm in to the tune of minimum, three hundred pounds and a lot of heartache – then at the end of all that Lord Dudley still dies," her pink lipsticked lower lip trembles, blue eyes fill with tears.

"We're only talking ear mites Deirdre."

"Could be cancer of the ear."

"Is he off his food?"

"No way."

"Has he stopped sitting in his box lid?"

She smiles maternally, "Bless him, he loves that box lid."

"Then if it's anything, it's ear mites."

"He's had such a hard life, poor lamb."

"Rubbish," I say brusquely. Lord Dudley is nothing like a lamb. He's a spoilt fluffy cat with one or two winning ways including using Martin and Deirdre's white leather sofas as scratching posts. Deirdre has taped sheets of cardboard around the corners of each sofa so that now they look as if they're still in the process of being unpacked.

"You've changed," she says reproachfully, "Once upon a time you'd have been as worried as I am about Lord Dudley."

"Deirdre, how would you be feeling if Martin left you for two months?"

"Relieved. No really, I'd make the most of my time alone. Put a positive slant on the situation. Tell myself, 'hey dude, time waits for no man.' Woman in your case. Tell me," she hunches forward across the table and lowers her voice, "why doesn't your lot take more care of themselves? I'm talking cosmetically here. I've read about 'lipstick lesbians' but I never see any."

"You probably do see them but they look just, well almost the same as you."

Deirdre sits back in her chair, appalled, "I hope not. No offense but I wouldn't want to be mistaken for a lipstick lezzer. You know, certain things go with that territory and I'm not in the market for suck it and see."

She waves her hands as if drying nail polish. As always find it difficult to be offended by Deirdre being offensive. An almost biblical phrase pops into my head, *She knows not what she says.*

"Can we leave this discussion for another time, Deirdre?"

"Whatever. Only throwing ideas up in the air, crunching the numbers, moving the goal posts. Keep your wig on."

Have to laugh – or I'd cry.

April 25th

Antirrhinums are all up and jostling each other. Ditto corn flowers and fox gloves although these are straggly. Have twenty two tomato plants, at least as many courgettes and my sunflowers are a foot high and beginning to block out the light from the bathroom window. Oh yes, sweet corn also going great guns. Only fear is that I've planted everything at least a month too early. Janice said, "Pity you don't have a greenhouse but then where would you put it?" Told her "Non-supportive remarks don't help!"

However, as I trawled round Woolworth's I spot the very last plastic mini-greenhouse in the store. Trudge home up hill as the funicular railway (my usual route back from Woolworth's) is not working as staff are having a training day behind locked doors. This happens at least once a month. Laughter and the clink of glasses can be heard as I stagger past carrying greenhouse.

Set it up and manage to fit tomatoes and sweet corn inside. Wrestle paste table from shed and put that in spare room. Clear all my windowsills of seedlings so house looks half respectable in preparation of Georgie's longed for return at end of month. (Still no word, she always leaves things to the last minute.)

Spare room now looks a green and rather intimidating place to enter. Will have to enter it though as it also houses Tilly's litter tray.

Laura rang from somewhere in the Cotswolds, "Iris recommends a covered litter tray."

"Does she?"

"She reckons they're more hygienic."

"Are they?"

"You can get special liners for them."

"Can you?"

"You're a bit anti-Iris aren't you?"

"No, I'm anti-Iris's recommendations. How's the walking?"

"Great!", Laura says. In the background I can hear Bonnie Tyler singing.

"Where are you?"

"Pub. Look got to go. Iris alert."

Nic telephones to confirm a date in May for afternoon tea. I tell her about my plastic mini-greenhouse. She tells me about her large glass greenhouse. Apparently, she has already produced a courgette the size of her thumb and she's watching it with interest.

I ask her what else she's growing?

"The works," she replies.

She tells me a tale of how years ago, about three girlfriends before she met Simone, she went out with a woman called Stevie. They shared an allotment. When they split up, Stevie got custody of the allotment and Nic was almost more heart-broken about losing the allotment than losing Stevie. I agree that losing an allotment could be very painful.

Nic finishes off with, "Heard anything?"

"Not yet. Any day now."

"That's the spirit."

Somewhere in the room with her I hear Simone saying, "Did you say it?"

"Say what?" I ask.

"We both wanted to say that although we know it's going to be ok, whatever happens we're here for you as well. You're a good mate, Margaret."

Am touched.

April 26th

Miriam still low. Says it makes her sick, her mother is spending all her pension on new clothes. Says mother is having a late life crisis. Says life at present, what with not smoking and feckless mother, is hellish. Reveals that our boss Tom Matthews has been a tower of strength.

"Because Margaret, you've not really been there for me," she says reproachfully, which is true but in the circumstances unfair.

Consider Miriam's unfairness while walking home. Reach conclusion that my cheerful, jokey exterior is perhaps too convincing but what can I do? Surely not in my best interests to walk round with a face similar to Miriam's. I can almost guarantee that Miriam's sour expression will not attract the younger women she so hankers after.

I am unhappy. Of course I'm unhappy but I can't give in to it. Think irrelevantly about Tom Matthews being *a tower of strength* which reminds me of Frankie Vaughan who'd had a hit with *A Tower of Strength*. He'd been mum's favourite singer till Frank Ifield came along with *I Remember You* and an ability to yodel, notwithstanding an extremely wide neck, oily hair and voice. Bring myself back to Tom Matthews and how little I know about him and that perhaps Miriam now knows more than I do and does that worry me? "Not really," I tell myself as I mount our front steps.

Unlock front door. Door pushes against that morning's post.

Bank statement, double glazing offer, also a small light blue envelope. My heart is truly in my mouth as I recognise Georgie's sprawling handwriting. Carry letter into kitchen. Stroke Tilly who is lying fast asleep on the kitchen table. Tilly looks up sharply, forever surprised that it's me and not the grim reaper.

Georgie's letter more frustrating than disappointing. Not really a letter at all, only a few lines.

"Dear Margaret, if it's ok I'd like to see you on Saturday. If this is a problem you can leave a message at this number. Should arrive around one. Love Georgie."

No address. Edinburgh postmark. I read and re-read the words. Try to imbue *Dear Margaret*, and *love Georgie* with romantic meaning. Concentrate on *love Georgie*. Far more promising than say, *yours sincerely, Georgie*, or *yours faithfully, G. Truman*. Allow myself a flicker of hope. After two glasses of wine, flicker becomes a flame.

April 28th

Buy exquisite pale green duvet set in Debenhams, buy pink broiderie anglaise pyjamas in Marks and Spencer, also an organic chicken, vegetables and fresh cream based pudding. Go back for flowers: lilies and tulips. Go back, (ridiculous I know) for toilet rolls with silver fleur de lis pattern.

Stagger up my road under weight of full rucksack, also carry many carrier bags. For once don't feel like beast of burden. Feel: happy. HAPPY. **HAPPY!** Maybe misguidedly happy but can't help it. I overflow with optimism. Am convinced that it is not possible for Georgie to just stop loving me. She will have missed me like hell. I imagine how pleased I'd be to see me after an absence of nearly two months. Considered how many lovable qualities I possessed. Lovable. I am not the same as Deirdre in the successful, sensual, sexual departments but yes, I believe I am lovable. I can endear myself. Count many people I have endeared myself to during lifetime. Run out of fingers.

Self-congratulation cut short by sight of Janice's white lorry parked outside the house. This is not a Janice day. A Janice day is Tuesday. Realise that Janice hadn't come on Tuesday. I had been so wound up with thoughts of an imminent Georgie I hadn't noticed.

Janice has constructed a precarious bridge of scaffolding

planks from my top step to the back of her lorry. She's using this bridge to run her wheel barrow back and forth. And here was Janice, wheelbarrow loaded with weeds and shrub clippings. Note that even in repose Janice looks sullen. She sees me and pauses, deserts barrow and jumps nimbly down onto the pavement. Sort of lopes towards me. I've never consciously noticed a woman loping and somewhere inside my head I register that loping is attractive – an at ease with own body and self image way of getting about. Without any salutation Janice grabs my carrier bags, "You should get a cab when you're this loaded," she growls, "Ridiculous!"

I grin foolishly, "Thank you Janice," I say.

Feel like Deirdre at her explosive best. I tell Janice, "Brilliant news, my partner Georgie's coming home the day after tomorrow," I'm hurrying to keep up with her.

"Big deal," Janice says.

"It's a big deal for me."

"Big deal," Janice says.

Ignore this and say, "Look Janice is it ok if I don't help you today? I'll do my share in the week and I promise that the next time you come I'll be out there."

"What if there isn't a next time?"

"You wouldn't leave me in the lurch, would you?"

"Might do."

Decide this is Janice attempting humour so ignore it. We edge past her wooden bridge and up the steps. She waits while I open the door then dumps carrier bags on doormat.

"Better get on," she says.

I go through the house like a whirlwind. Throw open windows. Down below see Janice labouring away. She's taken off her fleece. Under it she wears a white singlet. Only April but she's already tanned. Her muscles ripple pleasingly. Find I'm still smiling. Thinks: No bad thing for Georgie to find there's a Janice tilling our soil. Make her realise that I'm not the type of woman to let the grass grow under my feet. On the contrary, all grass (particularly couch) now in back of Janice's lorry.

Shake duster out of bedroom window, "You're doing a grand job," I shout. She turns her back on me and continues digging.

Next door, Deirdre comes out through her patio doors and surveys her decking, hands on hips. She calls out to Martin who's lurking inside, "Oh do come in the garden – it's a fantastic day. We could have lunch in the gazebo."

Hear Martin's barked reply, "No way!"

Deirdre sees me, "What can you do with him? You don't fancy lunch in my gazebo, do you?"

"Sorry Deirdre, Georgie's back day after tomorrow."

Deirdre raises her eyebrows and says, "Thank god that woman finally smelt the coffee."

I have no idea what Deirdre means but this is one of her frequently used phrases. It has superseded last month's frequently used phrase about her and Martin *not singing from the same hymn sheet*. Query: Are Deirdre's many phrases common parlance and she more tuned in to the zeitgeist than I am?

Think again: actually reference to Georgie smelling the coffee quite apposite. Have read in *Listening Ear's* property section that permeating home with aroma of fresh ground coffee, newly baked bread and orange peel seduces reluctant buyers. No oranges and have never baked bread before so could seem a. contrived or b. go horribly wrong. But coffee – yes. Smother memories of our issues around coffee and rummage in back of kitchen cupboard for percolator, unused Christmas gift circa 1999 plus pack of fresh coffee that came with it. Coffee now five years old so not so fresh, decide on trial run with Janice. Janice leans on fork and says, "Don't drink the stuff. Causes headaches and is addictive."

"Smells good."

She sniffs it and almost smiles, "Yes it does," she hands the mug back to me, "but I like tea."

April 29th

Went to bed early in anticipation. Read a chapter of my book about Augusta, Byron's half-sister, which sends me off to sleep within ten minutes. Am woken by telephone ringing downstairs. Switch on bedside lamp. Clock says one thirty. Tilly lying next to me looks surprised then expectant. Is it breakfast time already?

"It's not breakfast time," I say but she scrambles off the bed and waits in the doorway looking as if she should be wearing an old threadbare dressing gown and hair curlers.

"Tilly it's not breakfast time — now get out of my way, you daft cat."

Hurry downstairs. Pick up receiver, "Hello."

Whispering.

"What?"

Louder whispering.

"Can you speak up? Is that you Georgie?"

I just about make out, "No it's me."

Of course it's Laura.

"Do you know what time it is?" I say.

"Half past one."

"I mean what do you want?"

"Just to talk."

"Can't you talk to Iris?"

"She's asleep. Margaret, I hate this camping lark. I want to go home."

"Well go home in the morning."

"I'm not allowed to. Iris says we came away to refresh our relationship and by god that's what we're going to do."

"That sounds romantic."

"It's not funny."

"I'm not laughing. Look you must make the best of it. You can't stay in the Cotswolds forever. There must be work Iris needs to do in London?"

"Not till next Monday."

"There you are then. It's Friday already."

"I've never been so miserable in my life."

"Well you've had a very easy life in that case. I must go to sleep. Georgie's back tomorrow."

"Lucky you."

Poured a glass of milk. Gave Tilly a tiny morsel of Whiskers.

"Don't be sick," I said and switched off the hall light.

May

May 1st
Yesterday Georgie arrived when she said she would, dead on one o'clock. I'd imagined her driving all the way down from

80

Edinburgh during the night passing through the changing scenery, dawn breaking as she gunned along, desperate to get back. Reality was that she reached Bittlesea Bay the night before and stayed at a hotel on the sea front. Had I been out and about in Bittlesea Bay that evening as Martin was, I might have seen her and her new woman, Stella, walking hand in hand on their way to meet Nic and Simone at *Carlito's Way*, the best Italian style restaurant in town.

Her car was a new one. I was watching through the venetian blinds and as it slid into the parking space outside our house I paid no attention. This was a maroon car – I was looking for Georgie and our navy blue Citroen. Then she got out and carefully locked her door – turned and stared up at the house, a curious expression on her face. Not sad or anxious, resigned. She didn't see me watching. With determination I was thinking, *I've got a fight on my hands but I will win it!*

Georgie didn't use her front door key, she rang the bell. I opened the door and bobbed my head forward to kiss her, she stepped backwards.

"Hello Margaret."

"No kisses?"

"Best not."

The fight drained out of me. I'm not much of a fighter, am I? Instead I welcomed in someone I didn't know very well. Georgie was distant coupled with an old fashioned courtesy as if any argument and discussion was already over and she wanted to show generosity to the losing side – me.

I led her through into our kitchen diner. Coffee percolating away making cheery bubbling noises and filling the room with its seductive aroma, chicken and roast potatoes illuminated in the oven window. Georgie took in the table, table cloth, matching napkins, wine glasses, the bottle of open red wine.

"Ah well Margaret, the thing is …" she said.

"Yes?"

"I didn't expect lunch."

"But one o'clock is lunchtime."

"We never usually have a roast dinner for Saturday lunch."

"But this isn't usual. This is special – a welcome home lunch."

"Margaret, I don't think I can do this."

81

"Do what?"

She waved at the table, "This. I need to be somewhere else in an hour's time. I came because I wanted to clear matters up and felt a letter just wouldn't be fair to you."

"Sit down," I said. Still she hesitated. I pulled out a chair and sat down, "If you want to stand for an hour it's up to you, Georgie."

She sat. I moved away the cutlery and side plates. "Wine?" I asked. She shook her head. I filled my own glass. Tried to drink it but found I couldn't stop my hands from shaking. Put the glass down and hid hands under the table cloth. I looked properly at Georgie. She seemed surprisingly relaxed, was staring past me and out into the garden. She wore a suit I'd never seen before. Georgie rarely wore suits, only for very special occasions. This one was grey linen. Not really warm enough yet for linen. She looked like a visitor from a warmer country. Confident, attractive. In a casual way prosperous. Deirdre would have been impressed. Then she focused her gaze on me.

"Margaret ..."

"Georgie ..."

She smiled at me with genuine pleasure, "You've changed your hair – it looks great."

"Thank you," I smiled back. A compliment when I'd expected a verbal blow undermined me and my eyes filled up. Georgie stopped smiling.

"Please Margaret – I'm sure you'd worked out that I probably wasn't coming back."

"As you can see, I hadn't worked that out. I wouldn't have bothered with this meal."

"But you must have had an inkling. The situation hasn't been perfect between us for a few years. We've been a couple in name only. Both of us deserve something better."

"Have you met someone else?"

"Yes. Her name's Stella."

"When?"

"Two years ago."

"When did you decide to leave me?"

"As you know I've been spending more and more time in Scotland ..."

"So you've been living with both of us," a thought suddenly occurred to me, "and where else apart from Scotland?"

Georgie reached for the bottle of wine and poured herself half a glass, took a gulp not a sip, before answering, "Spain. Stella has a house out there."

"And is that where you've been for the last two months?"

"Stella doesn't like the British winters."

"Does everyone know about you and this Stella?"

"Who's everyone?" she started to sound truculent.

"Friends, your parents, neighbours?"

"Some of them know."

"Deirdre and Martin? Laura?"

"Good heavens no. They're your friends not mi ..."

The timer on the oven buzzed and both of us started. I got up and switched the oven off. Then switched off the percolator.

"So Georgie, what's to discuss?" This time I managed to hold my wine glass steady.

"I felt you needed an explanation. Closure, is it called?"

"I've no idea."

"And also – obviously – although the house is yours I'd like, if it's ok with you, to take my stuff away and maybe some of the furniture."

Later: Deirdre slipped quietly into the kitchen – no mean feat for Deirdre who is usually incapable of arriving anywhere without a fanfare. She'd brought a bottle of wine.

"You can drink it with me or on your own, whichever you prefer. I don't want to be in your way."

"You're not. Sit down. I'll get glasses."

"No, stay where you are – I'll get glasses."

"Did you see them?"

"Yes. I'm sorry, we were watching. Martin spotted them the other evening. They walked past the *Corner Coffee Shop* window. We weren't sure what to do but in the end Martin said, whatever's going on it would be best if you heard it from Georgie."

"Deirdre, I've been such a mug."

Deirdre tentatively patted me on the head – in her words she is not a touchy feely person. She said, "No you haven't. Georgie's the mug."

May 3rd

Didn't go to work. Rang Miriam and told her I wouldn't be in for the next week and to make any excuse.

Not the worst day of my life. Nobody died. But definitely the most painful, bewildering, awkward, embarrassing, demeaning day I've lived through. I should have gone out and left them to take what they wanted, or I should have told Georgie to get lost, and if she wanted anything she'd have to sue me to get it. I was frightened I'd lose my home. That all the money and power seemed to lie with the two of them and I'd get squashed along the way.

Took morning off work. Dressed with care. I'd lost weight so my trousers and shirt looked good on me. So did my red and white blonde hair, unfortunately I couldn't do much about the sad, drawn face under the hair. I found some old makeup and brushed on mascara and blusher, drew in a fuller set of lips because mine seemed to have shrunk to a thin pale line. Earrings to distract from eyes that kept filling with tears.

Again I watched Georgie arrive, watched as she walked round to the passenger side of the car and opened the door for Stella. Stella's legs swinging out, model girl fashion. She wore a pale blue suit, fitted jacket, above the knee length skirt, expensive looking shoes with high heels and viciously pointed toes. Her hair was a tangle of dark brown curls swept up onto the top of her head. She wore sunglasses and she looked over the dark lenses at my house like an estate agent might before making a valuation.

The two of them absolutely matched each other. In all our years together Georgie and I had never been a matched pair. I'd thought superficials didn't matter, that inside we matched up perfectly.

I'd left the front door open and they walked in. Georgie called out, "Margaret," and my name seemed to echo as if the house was already half emptied.

I came out into the hall. "This is Stella," Georgie said. There was pride in her voice, almost as if she wanted to share what she saw as her luck in finding such an attractive woman.

"Hello Stella," I said.

"Hello Margaret," she said with unnecessary warmth, "This is so embarrassing."

"Yes, isn't it? But go ahead, embarrass yourselves," and I went out into the garden.

May 4th
This time did go out while a transit van took away all Georgie's possessions and many of *ours*. Left Tilly with her favourite cushion and litter tray in Deirdre's conservatory for the day. Met Laura in Kew Gardens. Walked amongst blue bells and wild garlic. Saw many squirrels. Laura said, "Why not stay over and go back tomorrow?"

Said, "I'd rather get back. Not fair on Deirdre and Tilly."

"Not fair, not fair. Being so bloody easy going's what's got you into this mess."

She then apologized.

Walk through house. Everywhere there are gaps like missing teeth. The freezer has gone, the tumble drier, two wardrobes, a bed, the leather armchair. Georgie's study is empty and then there are all the small things. It's as if I've been burgled. I keep discovering items that are missing. She's taken the decorative chimney pots from the garden and Georgie doesn't even like gardening or sitting in gardens.

I see that Janice has also been. There's a note saying that if we don't start planting soon, it will be too late. Then *Hope you're ok*. Not ok at all.

May 5th
So much for this diary. It was going to be witty and light hearted. It was going to be hilarious in places. Of course I'm only an amateur diarist. Feel like an amateur in all spheres which is self pitying and I WON'T indulge in THAT! I've read the *Diary of a Provincial Lady* three times. It still makes me smile. I begin with Georgie's inscription, *To dear Margaret, with love from Georgie, Christmas 2003*. That I've read dozens of times and tried to work out how I've got from there to where I am now. Wonder what she bought for Stella, Christmas 2003?

Another thing I wonder about – how E.M. Delafield prevented her real life from creeping in, even if her diary was fictional? There must have been some dark events during the months she was writing the articles and yet the tone of the

85

book remains so consistently cheerful. Or perhaps for her writing and living were two very different occupations.

Georgie has gone. In reality she'd gone two months ago. I expect that everyone who knew us, knew this would be the outcome of our 'trial separation'. To paraphrase Deirdre if I've understood her correctly, I'm the woman who *failed* to smell the coffee.

May 11th
Janice – garden.

May 13th
Sent postcard to Nic and Simone canceling our arrangement.

May 17th
Janice – garden. Am back at work but absolutely hate it. Miriam is on holiday with her mother so there is just me and Tom every day. Can't help myself but I know the office is filled with my misery.

May 19th
Work. Wheeler's Watch.

May 22nd
Tell Mr. Wheeler that I can't continue with WW. He looks disappointed so say I will see how I feel in a month's time.

May 24th
Miriam back from holiday. Says it was a nightmare. Not to be repeated. Says she has aged by at least ten years. Weather and food good though.

May 25th
Janice. 'Meadow' nearly finished. Deirdre itching to see it. I've said a stern, "No peeking". Imagine Deirdre will be a) hugely disappointed as meadow bears no resemblance to Deirdre's idea of a designer garden, b) hugely relieved, because it will be no competition for her 'Italianate courtyard' (Deirdre's title). If this sounds sour it isn't meant to.

May 29th

Went with Miriam to a barbecue near Hove. Miriam very red and hot under the collar when she suggested it. Said firmly, "Absolutely no strings attached Margaret. The two of us are in the same miserable boat so we might as well join forces and prop each other up now and then – as in provide moral support."

I ask, "Who invited you to this barbecue?"

"Woman called Ingrid. Gave her a pound off a man's trench coat the other afternoon."

Took train then walked. Arrived in the middle of what seemed like a private party. Six women who looked surprised and suspicious as we walked up the front path.

"I'm a friend of Ingrid's," Miriam said holding out her carrier bag of wine bottle and packet of Walls Pork Sausages.

Women exchange looks indicating that Ingrid is not a special favourite.

"Better come in then," tall woman in cook's apron says, wipe those feet."

I hand over my bottle of wine and box of organic chocolates. Woman in apron says accusingly, "Are you a Green?"

Sees my bewildered expression and says with slight irritation, "I mean are you one of those women who disapprove of everything: a good cigarette, a fine wine, second home in the Dordogne etc.?"

Answer cautiously that while there are things I disapprove of, nothing on her list particularly incenses me although I'm neither a smoker nor a second home owner.

"Do you like classical music?" she shoots at me.

Feel that our entry to barbecue hangs in the balance. Miriam steps in, "Margaret likes all music, blues, country, classical."

Woman in apron's face breaks into a relieved smile, "Ah classical – how can there be space in one's life for any other? Go on through to the garden. Help yourself to a drink."

We hang up our jackets and walk out into the garden leaving everybody in urgent conversation back in the house. I admire the garden while Miriam commandeers the only deck chair without a proprietorial cardigan, newspaper or bag on it and is arranging her limbs in an attractive and congenial manner.

Women troop out. They are smiling. Have obviously decided to be hospitable. We are introduced. We introduce ourselves. Miriam says emphatically, "Margaret and I, we work together, that's all. There's no hanky panky."

Privately wish Miriam didn't use such terms as 'hanky panky' but it seems to do the trick as she's soon engrossed in conversation with a 'younger woman' about the Bayeux Tapestry. Both seem very knowledgeable. Every one else seems to have a smattering of knowledge re. Tapestry, as there's much head nodding and "Oh I couldn't agree more. Priceless."

I sit on the grass. I say little. Feel I am dull company and that I'm emanating a dull, dark aura. Wonder how long this will persist. Have read that it can take up to two years to recover from a bereavement. Two years of me emanating a dull, dark aura and I'll have no friends left. And what if the dull dark aura becomes an intrinsic part of my personality. *Oh no, let's not invite Margaret, she's a real old misery!*

Try to inconspicuously look at my watch. A woman whose name I don't remember pulls her deck chair closer and says in a good humouredly, aggressive voice, "So which classical composers do you rate?" She waves what looks like one of Miriam's pork sausages in my direction. Try to picture the shelf of unplayed classical CD's gathering dust at home. Think of all those years pretending to Georgie's parents and even a little to Georgie that I loved classical music. Say, "Actually they're all very good."

"Yes, but you must have a favourite."

"Not really."

Woman slaps her knee with free hand, addresses assembled company, "Margaret says all classical composers are very good but she doesn't have a favourite."

Shouts of *Come on now, I don't believe it, not possible.* Miriam says, "You're fond of Strauss."

"Which Strauss? Richard, Johann the elder, the younger?", asks woman with sausage.

"They're both very good."

Woman with sausage looks at me sternly, "I don't think you like classical music at all."

"I didn't say I liked it, I acknowledged that all the composers were very good composers."

"So what *do* you like?"

"Country and jazz. Particularly modern stuff."

Feel I am the focus of all eyes apart from Miriam's – she is staring very hard at a tall conifer.

"Well Margaret," woman says, "I suppose you're old enough and ugly enough to know your own taste but country and jazz wouldn't be my choice."

I get up from the grass and walk back to the house. Behind me I hear woman appealing, "For heaven's sake, what did I say? Surely she is old enough and ugly enough to engage in a spot of lively debate. She should keep out of the kitchen if she can't stand the fire ..."

Retrieve jacket from hall. Miriam has followed me, "Margaret, don't go."

"You stay, but I really do have to go home."

"Would you mind if I stayed? Becky and I seem to have clicked. Timing's crucial – if I rush off now with you, I'll be sending out the wrong messages."

"That's ok. See you Monday."

"See you Tuesday. Bank Holiday, remember?"

On walk back to the station pass woman in trench coat looking very hot and bad tempered – wonder if this is Ingrid?

May 30th

Spend day cleaning drain grilles and drain covers. At the time very satisfying. In retrospect when I find myself considering drain grille and cover cleaning as a possible career move, become deeply depressed.

May 31st

Go with Deirdre to Charleston, home of Bloomsbury set, Vanessa Bell and Duncan Grant. Deirdre finds entire place: house, furnishings, artistic atmosphere, depressing.

In Duncan Bell's studio, which I find moving in its stark simplicity and lack of comfort, Deirdre checks out his paint brush bristles to see whether he washed them properly. She is reprimanded by the female usher for touching the artifacts.

"It's only a lousy cheap brush," she whispers, "No wonder his pics are such daubs."

Also criticizes Charleston's shop for being disorganized, "Whatever happened to good old customer service?"

Also Charleston's tea shop which doesn't open till lunch time.

"What kind of a tea shop is this? Where's the business savvy? Here are visitors, behind those locked doors are cakes and cuppas panting to be sold. Duh?"

Tea shop doors finally open and Deirdre rushes ahead of orderly but slow queue, "Grab seats in the garden, Margaret," she bellows. I choose two chairs out of about twenty unoccupied chairs. After ten minutes Deirdre arrives with carrot cake and tea.

"There's absolutely no sense of urgency in there." she says, sitting down.

"It's a beautiful garden."

She nods, mouth full of cake, "No worthwhile water feature though."

"There's a lake."

"That's not what I call a water feature. A space this size could take a couple of squirting cherubs."

We sit in the sun. After a while I go back into the tea shop and buy delicious sandwiches and more tea. Deirdre relaxes. I relax. Deirdre straightens up and says, "There's that woman who told me off. She likes her food, doesn't she?"

"Deirdre, enough."

June

June 1st

Have washed oven glove twice. Cannot get rid of tinned tomato soup stain. Do not understand how tomato soup got on oven glove although recognise tomato soup's singular propensity to splash. Tomato soup is inclined to rush out of the bowl of the soup spoon and dive back into soup plate with undue force causing soup to splash over front somehow managing to reach clothing even if wearing tea towel. This is only diary-worthy as fresh and singular insight into tomato soup's behavior. Would never have experienced this while living with Georgie as she disapproved of tinned soup and also the wearing of tea towels. Thinks: did I at some low point tuck the oven glove into the neck of my tee shirt while consuming tomato soup?

June 2nd
Went out to do some gardening. Meadow fine, weeds-wild flowers, poppies, fox gloves, cornflowers make a pretty, untidy mix. Rest of garden looks neglected particularly my vegetables. Notice that Lord Dudley since his own back garden has been decked and cobbled, is using the depressions in which I've set my courgettes as a lavatory. Know Lord Dudley is the culprit because even as I survey courgettes he arrives and begins to scrabble the earth. Most dispiriting.

Go back indoors. Sit at the kitchen table and decide to cut a couple of inches off my fringe. Feel much better although fringe looks quite peculiar, a wispy long outer fringe behind which a thicker shorter sub-fringe lurks.

Last week when Laura came down for the afternoon I offered to cut her hair as felt it was beginning to resemble a large ramshackle bird landed at an angle on her head. She was adamant. Said there was something manic and frightening about me with a pair of rusty hairdressing scissors and that in the past when cutting her hair I'd laughed immoderately which she also found unsettling. Said that anyway Iris liked her hair just the way it was, plenty to pull on in moments of frenzied passion. Deirdre with us at the time, wrinkled her nose and said, "Eeugh, much too much information if you don't mind. What about good old love and affection?"

June 3rd
This afternoon read in *Listening Ear* that bogus Electric, Gas and Water Meter readers are roaming Bittlesea Bay on the lookout for vulnerable, lone women. They flash an identity badge before insisting the meter needs urgent reading. In response to "But your lot only read it last week," they reply, "The government requires us to double check – it's in your own interests ma'am."

Apparently the impostors use of 'ma'am' is found to be

reassuring. To illustrate the article was a photo of a 'lone woman' displaying an empty handbag. Cut article out for Mr. Wheeler. He's compiling a Newsletter packed full of grim warnings. Quite apart from burglary, mugging, hit and run (his particular favourite), there are the natural hazards of fork lightning, falling trees, wild dogs, wild cats, also an Uneven Paving Phone-in, the list of dangerous possibilities seems endless.

I suggested I write article about my own badger incident. He suggested he write it up for me as he knows quite a bit about Bittlesea Bay badgers which would make article sound more informed rather than 'hysterical'.

Resent use of word 'hysterical' but do understand that Mr. Wheeler, although a relatively decent chap, does have a chip on his shoulder re. womankind, what with his wife leaving him and him being brought up by an aunt who didn't like boys and never bothered to learn his christian name, just called him "Wheeler".

Apropos to impostor article, I had moved on from this and was dallying in the Property Section when there was a knock on my front door. (It is extraordinary how many visitors choose to clatter my letter box or rap on fragile glass of fanlight rather than use the doorbell.) I opened the door and there stood a woman vicar. She held up her hands and said, "Don't shoot the messenger. I'm not looking for god recruits, just bric-a-brac for our Jumble Sale."

Although impostor article still in the forefront of mind did not like to ask woman vicar for a form of identification. Studied her closely. Dark grey trousers, black V-neck pullover with visible dog collar in V-neck. But could that just be a shirt worn back to front? What did I know of components of genuine dog collar? Studied vicar's face. Pleasant expression. But then had the bogus meter readers worn pleasant expressions? Probably yes.

"I don't have any bric-a-brac," seemed the safest response.

"Surely some bits and bobs, nick knacks, objets d'art, clutter?"

"Not that I can immediately lay my hands on, however if you come back on Monday around this time I could sort something out for you."

92

"Fair enough," she put her hands in her trouser pockets and whistled through her teeth, "In return can I give you a text?"

"No thank you."

"Do you know what a text is?"

"I have some idea."

"Really?" She raised her eyebrows and looked bogusly surprised.

"What if it were a diamond?" she said.

"I still wouldn't want it."

"You're pretty entrenched in your likes and dislikes then?"

"I might be."

Vicar seemed to lose heart in text and looked up the road, "Ok. Is it worth knocking next door?"

Had brainwave. Deirdre had been severely feng-shuied during the previous week. In her gazebo were six boxes of decorative items that the fengshui expert had deemed unconducive to the free flow of Deirdre's yin and yang. I said, "Try number forty two, but don't offer a text. Keep it simple."

Hurried upstairs to front bedroom window to watch possibly bogus vicar's next move. Yes she was going up Deirdre's path. Ringing the bell this time. Not in a position to see Deirdre but did see vicar raising her hands and smiling. I lip read, "Don't shoot the messenger." Then vicar stepped inside.

Half an hour later, passing through the hall found a text pushed through the letter box. Picture of a jolly farming couple leaning on a five barred gate, field of corn in the back ground. MAKE HAY WHILE THE SUN SHINES! printed across a clear blue sky. On the other side of the card was written *Jumble Sale, St. Dunstan's, Saturday 19th, 2pm. 10p admission.*

June 4th

Telephoned Deirdre before I went off to work. For the first time ever, Martin answered.

"Hello, yes, who is that?"

"It's me."

"You. Who are you?"

"Margaret."

"Hello Margaret, Deirdre's not here. She went off at the crack of dawn with a woman vicar."

"What?!"

"What do you mean, 'what?' ", Martin said tetchily, "there's no mystery, they haven't run off together — woman's an antique dealer as well as a vicar. Marriage of god and mammon — anything's possible these days."

"But where have they gone?"

"To her antique shop. I've just paid over two thousand pounds for some flossie with a mystical sounding name to clear out one stack of junk and Deirdre's whizzed off to buy another. Got to go, my cappuccino awaits."

June 4th

Letter from Bank. Did I know I was two hundred pounds over my overdraft limit? Answer, no I didn't. Checked bank statements. Realised pleasing and unexpected surplus cash on previous month's statement was due to Janice not having cashed her cheque. This surplus — inspiration behind a flurry of purchases towards a new, less dispirited look for Margaret. Now bank statement showed Janice's cheque plus my purchases. Considered where money would come from to placate bank. Wondered whether antique dealer vicar might be willing to pay for bric-a-brac. Assembled possible bric-a-brac on kitchen table. Impressive quantity but with exception of aunt's antique broach, each bit almost worthless except in sentimental value. Sat at table and wept. Through tears lined up ornaments, vases, cuddly toys, novelty earrings and saw the development and decline of my relationship. So much stuff from the early years, dribbling away to the diary and the book, as if Georgie had been saying, *Here you are Margaret, something to get on with to stave off loneliness once you're on your own.*

On a sudden thought I went upstairs and into the loft. Georgie and Stella had both been in there rummaging through crates and boxes. There it was, a big, open carton in one corner, the head and arm of a mink coloured teddy bear sticking up. I manhandled the carton back through the trap door and took it down to the kitchen. I sat on the floor and unpacked it piece by piece. All my presents to Georgie. Teddy was the most recent, given that Christmas, still with a piece of tinsel round its waist and a heart shaped card saying ... well something sentimental about strings attached to the hearts of lovers. I thought how she must have squirmed reading that.

94

I would have sat there all afternoon if Janice hadn't disturbed me by banging on the window.

"What's the matter?" she shouted.

I stood up and let her in. Said, "I didn't expect to see you now the garden's finished."

"I was passing. So?", she looked at the chaos that was now my kitchen, "What's all this?"

"Georgie didn't take her mementos with her."

"She wouldn't, would she? Would you like a cup of tea?" and without waiting for an answer she began to fill the kettle.

"Make yourself one as well," I said.

"I intend to."

Which made me laugh a little. Janice was so ... Janice. What you saw was what you got. Her head in the open cupboard helping herself to the biscuit barrel and the tea caddy she said, "Are you up to getting rid of it all?"

I said, "Supposing Georgie comes back?"

"Is that likely?"

"I don't know. What would you do?"

"Doesn't matter what I'd do."

I began to pack it all back into boxes and carrier bags. Took the heart shaped tag off the teddy bear and tore it up. Set the bear aside. Almost to myself I said, "What I'm trying to do is take back my heart," which made me start crying again. Janice didn't hug me like I might have expected her to do. She went on making the tea and setting biscuits out on a plate. Eventually my crying stopped and I blew my nose and wiped my eyes. We took our usual places at the table and she said reasonably, "Don't hang on to that teddy bear if it's going to make you cry."

"I really won't. Perhaps I'll keep it as the representative of my soft side."

"You'd need a giant teddy for *your* soft side. Now tell me, has Deirdre been in to see the garden yet?"

I told her that no, Deirdre had been too preoccupied with her feng shui expert followed closely by a new found interest in antiques. However she and Martin were popping by for drinks and nibbles on Sunday afternoon.

June 6th

Panic stations. Has been raining for three days but now the sun is shining revealing my wild flower meadow to be a weed infested eyesore. The cowslip circle planted for next spring has disappeared beneath the vigorous growth of dandelions, buttercups and common vetch. What were supposed to become lofty pink spires of sorrel to give the smaller plants definition have keeled over. Everywhere there is grass, admittedly not couch grass, a special meadow grass, but to mine, Deirdre's and Martin's untrained eyes, long grass is grass that needs mowing. When Janice arrives again unexpectedly I am manhandling geranium filled flower pots from outside the kitchen door up to adorn the meadow or to distract from the mess.

"Margaret", Janice says, "What are you doing?"

"Trying to make this look better. I'm sorry Janice but Deirdre will take one look at this meadow and her "Eeugh! will ring out across the back gardens."

Janice insists that I stop and come with her to the top of the garden and sit on the bench.

"I haven't got time to sit on the bench."

"Yes you have."

I followed her up the stone steps and sat down. We were high up. Level with my pointed, story book roof. Each side of the roof rows of terraced ice cream coloured houses lay stretched out in front of us as far as the sea. My gaze panned down to my wildflower meadow. It was a circle, diameter of about twenty feet. Glanced at my watch, there was still time to mow it and add terracotta pots around the perimeter. If Janice could be persuaded we could manhandle the stone birdbath up the hillside and set it in a central position.

"Breathe deeply," Janice said.

I breathed.

"Look at Tilly," Janice said, pointing.

Tilly was in the meadow circle, lying on her back, paws in the air. She looked euphoric, rubbing the back of her head against the fresh green leaves of cat mint. Janice said, "Did you know that two dozen species of insect rely on the ox eye daisy?"

"No I didn't."

Scrutinized my own ox eye daisies nodding gently. Know

97

that at least one of two dozen species of insect will be a colony of ants.

Janice interrupts these rueful thoughts, "Margaret what made you decide on a wildflower meadow?"

Which humbled me. Answer: for all the wrong reasons. I muttered, "To be different. To make everyone look at me in a new and admiring light. As a woman with her own ideas for a change."

Cast furtive look at Janice. She didn't look as disappointed in me as I expected. Her eyes half closed. *Don't fall asleep Janice there's still work to do.*

"You love Tilly, don't you?" she asked.

"Of course I do."

"You feed the birds. I've never seen so much stuff put out for them."

"Yes."

"You let trays of seedlings take over your house?"

Uneasy apprehension seeping in that Janice was about to come out with a life changing, *In that case why don't you …*

"You let the badger out. That showed courage and compassion. I remember you said it was trembling."

The more instances Janice found in my favour the more miserable and unworthy I felt.

"What does all that say about you?" Janice asked.

"It says Janice, that you are putting two and two together and coming up with six. I am not a 'nature' person, I'm materialistic. Don't have an original thought in my head. I like nature as long as it's under control and conforms to acceptable standards."

"I don't agree but fair enough. Come on then. What shall I do? Mow the lawn. You bring up the rest of the pots."

She said this absolutely without artifice, as if that was what I wanted then why not just do it? I stared down at the embryonic meadow. Nothing at all in the way of impressive colour yet. Just yellow and white, buttercups and daisies.

"Margaret, this meadow won't ever look beautiful in gardening terms. Yes, in a suburban run of well tended gardens it is an eyesore," she warned.

"It doesn't have to be," I said.

"It does."

Shut my eyes tightly. Opened them again. Saw a small blue butterfly, coming lazily along, gentle swoops, like someone window shopping. It settled, shivering on a blade of grass. Tilly looked up but she was far too old to engage in butterfly chasing.

June 7th

Drinks and nibbles plus tour of meadow passed surprisingly well. Feel Deirdre was under strict instructions from Martin to behave or perhaps it was the other way round. Martin said, "Good god, is that pepper saxifrage – reminds me of my youth?"

"Possibly it is," I said staring down at a minute rosette of leaves.

"Fantastic," said Deirdre, "all this nature. Do you know even the air smells better in your garden."

Then she sniffed and a small frown creased her powdered brow, "Although actually what is that I can smell?"

"Manure," I said apologetically.

"As in 'out of animals' backsides?'"

" 'Fraid so."

"Gross!"

"Deirdre," Martin said briskly, "we all do 'doo-doos'."

"But we don't all spread it on the garden."

The three of us squashed together on the bench, passing dishes of olives and peanuts back and forth along the row. I topped their wine glasses up. Martin lit a cigarette and stretched out his legs, "Well isn't this nice?" he said as if his one wish in life was to be sitting outside on a chilly evening looking at the tiles missing from my roof.

"Golly," Deirdre said, "this garden is going to be unbelievable. I'm envious. Look, there's a dear little white butterfly. I bet it's so rare, only comes to gardens with exotic wild flowers like you're going to have."

"Cabbage white," Martin said, "two a penny. No, fifty a penny. The commonest butterfly in England. Margaret, we don't get butterflies in our garden – Deirdre doesn't allow anything that crawls, squirms or flies. Says first they're in the garden, next they've set up home indoors."

Deirdre shouts Martin down, "That isn't true. I've got an

incy-wincey phobia that's all. I love everything that lives and breathes. Insects don't breathe do they?"

Woman vicar called early evening. Gave her boxes of bric-a-brac. Enquired whether there was anything there of value? No. Vicar asked whether I'd be going to her Jumble Sale as if the weather was fine there would also be a dog show. Said the contestants, human and canine responded well to a good audience. Rather warmed to vicar. Seemed a refreshing innocence to imagine a dog show might be an incentive to give up my Saturday afternoon.

June 8th
Deirdre and Martin so overwhelmed with my garden they've set off for the west of England to see the Eden Project and the Gardens of Heligan. Martin's hoping they can do the lot in a day.

June 9th
Miriam very difficult. Realise she's unhappy but how does she think I feel at the minute?

She broke up with the woman she met at the Hove barbecue within a matter of days. In Miriam's own words, before the *dastardly deed could be accomplished*. Feel Miriam should get out more even if she just stands in the middle of the shopping centre and listens to what's common parlance these days. (Admittedly words 'common parlance' not often heard. Possibly never heard in Bittlesea Bay Shopping Pavilion.) Am inclined to wonder if Miriam's sometimes unfortunate choice of phrasing had anything to do with relationship floundering. *When we ran out of conversation neither of us had the nous to get stuck in*, doesn't sound in any way romantic nor even brutally erotic.

Miriam also talking of chucking her job at the Hospice Shop. She has taken against Mrs. Ferguson. Also says she's met no one under eighty and why should she wear second and third hand togs when own mother shops in *British Home Stores* and *Marks and Spencer? Why indeed?* is my reply which leaves Miriam vaguely dissatisfied.

June 14th
Another letter from Bank this time with red underlining.

Telephoned. After usual security checks the clerical assistant said in a very smug voice, "So you're experiencing financial difficulties Mrs.Charlecote?"

"Miss Charlecote."

"It says Mrs. on your records."

"I didn't have the energy to get it altered after the first twelve attempts."

Pause while clerical assistant decides whether I am being facetious, or amusing. Decides on the latter and chuckles briefly, "Miss Charlecote. Right. Now if you *are* experiencing financial difficulties ..."

He leaves the sentence hanging in the air – sounds almost like a threat. Briskly I said, "So I'd like to increase my overdraft facilities in expectation of substantial funds due in at the end of this month."

"And might I ask where you expect these funds to come from?"

"No you may not. It's a highly personal matter but the funds will be arriving forthwith." Made voice haughty – rather grand dowager talking to impudent whipper snapper.

Overdraft agreed which gives me two and a half weeks to find a well paid part time job to complement my lowly paid part time job.

June 15th

Deirdre returned from her horticultural tour of Devon and Cornwall. Was away five days. Martin livid. Very hot weather and *the nose* has suffered sun burn. Also Martin has been exposed to sight of semi-naked tourist families and found the experience repugnant. Wants to know, *why were clothes invented if nobody's going to wear them?*

Martin information relayed to me via Deirdre as Martin has taken to his bed and is threatening not to get up till it rains.

I said, "But he's never taken against scantily dressed holiday makers in Bittlesea Bay?"

Deirdre explains, "He doesn't have to rub shoulders with tourists here. It's house to car to *Corner Coffee Shop* and back. The metal chairs in the *Coffee Shop* puts the nudies off – chilly on the bum!"

"So what about the Eden Project and the Gardens of Heligan?"

101

"Fabulous! Fantastic! Breathtaking!", waves a wedge of carrot cake up and down in front of her rose bud mouth. (We are sitting at my kitchen table and it is a supplemented Atkins day for Deirdre). "Personally I think they need a bit of a re-think. Small could be beautiful. There's no need to let tropical plants get so big. I mean they're enormous. We both suffered from terrible neck ache. And you can't help looking up because everyone else is looking up and you're worried you're going to miss something. But at the end of the day one green canopy is the same as the next," bites into cake and munches with great enjoyment, "Yum, yum. And not enough benches either. And too many people Oohing and Aahing. You'd think they'd never seen a tree before. I'm glad I went don't get me wrong, but have to admit we had a better time on our detour to Blue Water. I could live in Blue Water. I don't think Martin would go that far but he certainly would spend some quality time in there. Great food, all the major outlets, clean toilets, a multiplex ..."

June 16th

Miriam away with abscess on undisclosed part of body. These days Miriam seems to be away at least two days in each week. Tom Matthews sits on the corner of my desk and begins to tap out a morse code message with my Parker pen.

"I'm worried about Miriam," he says.

"Really?" Move draft letter to the *Listening Ear* re. prevalence of elderly folk joy riding their mobility scooters down the main shopping mall in Marks & Spencer. *How long before a serious accident occurs?*

"I think she's suffering from depression."

Wonder if this might be a good time to ask for a rise or even to suggest that I take over Miriam's afternoon stint as she's proving so unreliable?

"You two are good buddies, would you go and see her?"

"We're not very good buddies," I reply. Memo: Must ask Deirdre if word 'buddies' is becoming popular. Have noticed that it is one of Tom's favourites.

"The pair of you have been chewing the fat on the outside step for years, you must know each other inside out. I'd go myself only ... you know ... boundaries to be observed, etcetera."

"I could telephone," said reluctantly.

"Why not just turn up? En passant."

Tom gets off my desk and seems to be considering seating himself in Miriam's swivel chair, instead he twirls it round, "You know Margaret, I wanted to say, out in the open ..."

Fortunately before Tom can get anything out in the open the telephone rings and he goes back into his office and shuts the door. Makes no further attempt at conversation for which I'm relieved. Wish Miriam would pull her socks up.

Arrive at Miriam's flat and peer through the railings. It is only two pm, a hot and sunny day but the front room curtains are closed. Go down the steps and ring the bell. Hear shuffling footsteps and the door opens about four inches. There is Miriam with a fairisle scarf around her head. She does indeed have an abscess.

"Margaret," she says with some difficulty.

"Hello Miriam. Tom and I thought you might like a visitor."

"I suppose he thinks I'm skiving?"

"Not at all. He's worried. Can I come in?"

Reluctantly steps aside and I walk into the hall.

"Keep the noise down, mother's sleeping."

"I wasn't intending to make any noise," I said.

"You're making quite a bit of noise now. Didn't Georgie ever tell you – you have a very penetrating voice."

"What a horrible thing to say."

"Don't take it to heart. I didn't mean it. Obviously an abscess the size of a ping-pong ball doesn't put me in the best of tempers."

Miriam grips me by the arm and hustles me into the front room. It is in semi-darkness.

"Why are the curtains pulled?"

"I'm depressed. I don't want sunshine, it makes me feel worse."

"When you're depressed you need all the vitamin D you can get," I begin to open the curtains.

"Really Margaret, you are getting very bossy – it's not nice."

"Get me a cold drink," I boss.

"There's nothing in the house."

"Tap. Let it run."

"I don't like you in this mood."

"I don't like you either but I've come to see how you are and I intend to do just that."

While Miriam is getting my water I begin to tidy the room, thump the cushions, stack books and magazines. Miriam comes back with two glasses of water drizzled with orange juice. We sit. Find little to say. Miriam wants to show me her abscess. I refuse to look. Miriam asks me if I will take a photograph of it, I won't have to actually look at abscess, she will position the camera?

"Whatever for?" I ask.

"Posterity."

Again I refuse. "Let's go on the beach," I suggest.

She shakes her head and has to retie her scarf, "I see enough of that damn beach every day as I come in and out of here."

"Fancy a Jumble Sale on Saturday?"

"Margaret I'm looking for La Dolce Vita!"

"Fair enough, but the Jumble Sale is at St. Dunstan's at two o'clock. There's a dog show."

"Whoopee!", Miriam says.

Visit hardly an unmitigated success.

June 17th

Meet Mrs. Ferguson (Hospice Shop) in Morrisons. No chance to avoid her, we are hemmed in by trolleys. Initially think that I am unrecognized then Mrs. Ferguson holds up a tin of Baked Beans in front of my face and asks, "What does the label say about salt content?"

Writing on label far too small to read without magnifying glass but glibly say, "Salt content low."

"Good," and she drops the tin in her trolley, "your would-be pal Miriam's left me high and dry."

"Not my pal," I whinnied a laugh, "very helpful when trying on jackets that one memorable occasion – that was about all."

"Well she's gone. Vamoosed. How's your mother?"

"Amazing recovery. In Scotland now staying with friends. Such a resilient woman."

Mrs. Ferguson goes on to enquire whether I'd like to step into Miriam's shoes? Explained that mother although so resilient might relapse finally at any moment. Say, "In many ways mum's hanging on by the skin of her teeth," which conjures up picture of my old mum in cowgirl outfit dangling by her teeth from an outcrop of the Rockies. Mum's teeth false and about to part company with mum in favour of outcrop.

Suddenly said, "Actually Mrs. Ferguson what I'm looking for is a paid part-time job."

Mrs. Ferguson said, "There's a morning cleaner wanted at Russell's. Six pounds fifty an hour, cash in hand. My granddaughter works there. Ring personnel. Tell them Mrs. Ferguson, Noreen's granny, will give you a reference."

Thank Mrs. Ferguson profusely. Am almost reduced to curt-seying. Barricading trolleys move on and I depart unctuously backwards down the aisle.

Telephone Russell's, a big mail order catalogue outlet similar to Argos only a few minutes walk away. Well ten minutes walk away. *Come in for an interview now*, they say. Do just that. Get job. Start Monday.

June 18th

Postcard from Laura of a 73 Route master Bus. She writes, *Chin up!*

Do not tell Deirdre about cleaning job when she pops in for a cup of Earl Grey because she believes that no matter how poor you are, the trick is to think and behave as if you're rich – says thinking rich automatically draws riches to you. She will advise me not to do cleaning job, that far better to spend my time meditating on cheque for several thousand pounds dropping through letterbox.

June 19th

Go to Jumble Sale. Do not intend to go but somehow find myself in the area of St. Dunstan's Church Hall at ten to two. There is a long queue and many dogs wearing bows, necker-chiefs and natty coats. Everyone is barking or shouting.

Two minutes to two and several women in headscarves at front of queue begin to rap on door with their ten pence piece entrance fee. Someone yells, *Let the bloody dog see the rabbit for gawd's sake!* Queue rocks with laughter. Doors open and we start to run. It all comes back to me. I'd spent the Saturdays of my tens, twenties and thirties at Jumble Sales. I run. I'm a solid woman. In the old days I'd have used my weight and elbows to get to the front. Heart's no longer in it. I'm smiling. I'm running for the fun of it. For the dogs with their leads tangled and their jolly snapping eyes. I wish Georgie was with me and then I don't. She'd hate it. Would not fit in.

There is the vicar behind the White Elephant. She gives me a thumbs up sign and later tells me that sales on my bric-a-brac were magnificent. I see a little girl pouncing on my mink coloured teddy bear, she looks – thrilled!

At refreshment stall buy a cup of tea and a Bounty Bar. Take these outside to where the dog show has already started. Sit on grass at the edge of the Show Area.

"Hello," says Miriam flopping down next to me.

Am quite pleased to see Miriam as for the first time in some weeks she is smiling.

"Just met the vicar," she says. Smile changes to slight smirk reminiscent of Laura recalling Iris. Suddenly feel rather proprietorial about vicar. To forestall any of Miriam's 'phrases', turn my head away and concentrate on Dog Show. Miriam hums irritatingly at my side, pulling the heads off innocent daisies.

There are prizes for the Best Dressed Dog, Dog who looks most like its Owner, most Lugubrious Dog, Longest Tongue, and Waggiest Tail Dog. Everyone claps the winning dog and its owner. Everyone gasps and cheers over the prizes: a giant rubber bone, a box of dog treats, a plastic bowl with DOG written on the side. The afternoon seems to race past. The vicar comes out to give the final prize for Overall Winner. Miriam gasps and cheers the vicar. Prize – a tartan dog blanket goes to a black and tan mongrel wearing a tiny black stetson who has also won the Waggiest Tail contest. It's name is *Sprout*.

June 21st

Dreadful day! Began cleaning job. Met Noreen outside store at seven twenty a.m. She looks nothing like her grandma. Mrs. Ferguson is a big, strong no nonsense woman. Noreen has an intense little face and hands that seem permanently clenched. Look down at her flip flops and see that her toes are also clenched.

As Peter the under manager unlocks the security grilles and

the front doors Noreen says to him, "I bet you hate getting in this early, *he* ought to try it for a change."

Peter replies, *"He* bloody ought to."

Inside the store, Noreen immediately races across the shop floor and round behind the line of counters. I follow hot on her heels trying to look equally intense. We halt in front of a bucket, mop and a strange electrical item that isn't quite a hoover. She shakes its handle at me to take, "Mind, it's heavy."

It is heavy.

"What is it?"

"A floor polisher. Park it behind the counter for now, then fill your bucket from the tap in the men's lavatory."

Want to enquire after possibility of filling bucket from tap in women's lavatory to avoid bursting in on Peter or him bursting in on me but Noreen pointing firmly at Men's lavatory door. Lavatory empty but unpleasant place to loiter. Hurriedly fill bucket. Noreen appears at my shoulder and directs me to put two capfuls of floor cleaner into water and pops a paint scraper in my trouser pocket, this to remove chewing gum or other unknown bodies that have stuck to the floor. She leads me back out into the store.

"Today you have one hour fifteen minutes to wash this floor. Take mop right to left, left to right. Rinse mop frequently. If *he's* about watch your mop head. If it looks dirty, change it otherwise *he'll* make you change it. And *he'll* count that as a black mark against you. Then polish."

"I've never used a polisher before."

"It's not easy. Takes brute strength."

Thinks: if Noreen at half my size can manage the polisher – should be a piece of cake.

"If there's time, wipe the display cabinets down with a damp J. cloth. Once you've got the hang of this there'll be the lavs to do but I'll manage for now. Ok?"

I nodded. Noreen disappeared round back. Swabbed floor. Floor enormous and filthy. Already eight fifteen, judged that there wasn't time to use paint scraper. Rushed back and forth in fear that any moment mysterious and threatening *HE* would turn up.

Noreen puts a streaky mug of coffee on the counter, "Don't stop," she says.

Looks grimly at my floor. "Give us the scraper. You can't ignore chewing gum – it will bugger the polisher."

Bent double, Noreen zig-zags in front of me finding multiple instances of chewing gum which I've taken to be a pattern in the floor tiles. She straightens up, drops scraper plus ball of blackened chewing gum into my pocket and rushes off. Ten minutes later she appears again to whip away my untouched coffee, hisses, "Lose bucket and mop. Get polishing. His lordship's car's arrived."

I race mop and bucket off shop floor, run back to the polisher, plug in. Switch on. It nearly takes my arm off. Careening across the floor (polisher not arm) like … like … like a high speed, enraged giant turtle. Try to bring polisher to heel and it dashes off in the other direction leaving streaks on my still damp floor. The double doors swing open and a trouser suited woman bounds in. Did everyone in Russell's bound or rush? I drag the polisher back towards me and yell, "We're not open yet."

Woman lunges for the handle of my polisher. I fight her off.

"Let go. I'll call security. Help! I'm being attacked." Polisher races up and over my feet causing me excruciating pain, "Ow!" I wail.

"That's not how you do it," woman shouts.

"How I do it is none of your bloody business."

"Give it here."

"No. Clear off. Help!"

Suddenly she lets go and I let go deciding it's not worth being injured in defense of a floor polisher. Liberated, the polisher skids across the floor knocking over my carefully positioned *Danger, Wet Floor* signs. The power dies as woman pulls out the plug. Noreen appears follows by Peter. Noreen shouts, "It's her first day."

Woman shouts back, "God almighty, I'm away a week and come in to mayhem. And you are?" She looks furiously at me.

"Margaret Charlecote."

"Margaret who?"

"Charlecote."

Woman steps back, hands on hips, eyes – malevolent, as if the name *Charlecote* is an absolutely despicable one and not a worthy, historic name brought to England by William the Conquerer.

"Well how *do* you do," she says sarcastically, "I'm Lorraine Carter – the manager. Noreen stop whatever you're doing till you've made sure this *Margaret Charlecote* knows how to use a polisher."

She storms off the shop floor, Peter hurrying in her wake. I hear her say, "Peter in my office. Just who employed that incompetent woman?"

In silence, Noreen demonstrates polisher technique. It is hellishly difficult. Finish floor. No time to use J.cloth. Totter from store at nine o'five. Noreen and I stop at the corner and she explains, "We call her 'he', a. because she doesn't half wear the trousers, and b. because that way she doesn't know we're talking about her."

Continue tottering to T.M. Accountancy. Tom looks critically at me, "Been out on the tiles?" he says.

"Sort of," I reply.

Also wants to know why his most important client *Bristow and Poulson* have received a letter on T.M. Accountancy headed note paper complaining about elderly joy riders in Marks and Spencer. Holds letter up and points to signature, A. Oakley, Accident Prevention Officer.

June 24th
"I've had twins!," Deirdre announces over Earl Grey tea taken at her breakfast bar.

"Really?"

"Follow me quietly and don't look left or right. Or up."

We creep out of kitchen into the garden, me not looking left, right or up but keeping my gaze pinned on Deirdre's Egyptian cotton bottom. Half way down her garden she stops and turns. I stop and turn.

"Now look up. The extension roof."

I see a ramshackle nest, one large seagull and two small bobbing heads.

"If we make a noise, mum or dad go berserk and spatter you."

Do not make noise.

"I think that's the dad on the chimney pot. What a clever boy."

Admire gull family. Whisper (more for something to say), "What does Martin think?"

"He says he's not getting involved. He doesn't follow nature like I do."

"And Lord Dudley?"

"He's absolutely laid back."

June 26th

Have not really studied Lorraine Carter. No time, not even to look up. Keep attention glued on my floor, mop and bucket. Have already been taken to task on state of my mop head. Ms. Carter asks, "Margaret, have you got a particular affection for that mop head? Would it break your heart to change it for a fresh one?"

Would relish answering Ms. Carter back. *Yes it would break my heart. Yes, I am in love with this mop head.*

June 27th

Sunday. I'm exhausted. Spend much of the day in bed accompanied by Tilly. Have completed six days at Russell's.

Yesterday received a cheque for nine hundred pounds from final settlement of mum's estate. Thinks: Could give up cleaning job. Could go back to setting alarm clock for eight o'clock instead of six thirty.

July

July 4th

Tilly is enjoying an Indian summer. She loves my meadow. Watch her make her way through the long grasses and waving stems of meadow buttercup with look on her little round face of absolute sensory delight. And then she flops. And rolls onto her back. And stares at me from this upside down vantage point with a mad good humour. She's happier without Georgie's two cats. Realise now that with all their boisterous health and energy they cramped Tilly's style. Thinks: what is Tilly's style? Tentative and hopeful.

This afternoon went on beach. Initially thought *not a good idea* as being the weekend it was even more crowded than usual. Found a space on one of the dunes. Was prepared for every eventuality. Took a towel, a cushion, a sun umbrella, sun tan lotion, a sarong, sandwiches, a bottle of water and my book. Experience profound sense of satisfaction. This has been my first summer on the beach in years. Georgie never wanted to go on the beach, said beaches abroad had spoiled her.

I snoozed with my book open over my face, then sat up and ate my sandwiches regretting I hadn't made twice as many, surveyed beach as if it were my very own domain. Family parties paddling in the shallows, the real swimmers were further out. I watched one intrepid swimmer, woman with a shocking pink bathing cap, two white rubber daisies over each ear. She had a broad swimmer's back and cut through the water with a powerful crawl powering between a man and a woman who were both doing a sort of sit up breast stroke while chatting to each other. They got a face-full of sea. Choked, flailed and shouted. Strong swimmer pile drives on.

I'm thinking *typical, there's always one who spoils it for everybody else* when woman reaches shallower water and stands up. Instantly I recognise Nic's Simone. She hadn't seen me. She strode out of the water. Behind her the two engulfed swimmers were still remonstrating. Simone shouts back over her shoulder, "Sorry."

Man yells, "Sorry's not good enough."

Simone turns hands on hips, "How about very sorry?"

Man looks disconcerted. His trunks are being tweaked by his woman friend, "Let's leave it John," she says.

He says stiffly, "I suppose it will have to do."

Grinning, Simone came up the beach. I realised that the small heap of clothes and beach bag lying on a rainbow striped towel about six feet away from me were hers. As she reached for her towel I said, "Hello Simone."

Now, she looked disconcerted, "Margaret. Hello."

Dries her face and shoulders, spread her towel out again and lay on her stomach facing me.

"Look, what can I say," she tossed a small sea shell in my direction, "Very sorry?"

I mimic the man in the water, "I suppose it will have to do."

The ice was broken.

111

We chatted about Nic and her garden plans; new patio, an arbour, possibly a folly if Terry their odd job man could put it up in time. Simone said, "It's all double dutch to me but the garden looks great. A winner."

I don't ask about Georgie although I want to but as Simone got dressed she said, "You know Georgie and Stella won't last. That Stella's too high maintenance. Fine to see her one week in three when it's all fresh and lovey dovey – another matter when it's day in, day out. You'll see, Georgie will come crawling back."

"I don't want Georgie crawling back."

She stared at me as if I'm mad, "Why ever not?"

"Georgie finding me a welcome relief because someone else is exhausting or not as great as Georgie thought she was isn't the basis for a good relationship. I want more than that."

"But you've been together ten years – you can't still expect love's young dream?"

I mumbled, "But love has to come into it."

"Oh yeah, love. Different kinds though. Look at me and Nic. Nic waits on me hand and foot and treats me like a goddess. I behave like a goddess. Not to everyone's taste but it works for us," Simone began to rub frosted body lotion over her shoulders which made them sparkle, "Fancy coming over for dinner one evening?"

"Not if Georgie and Stella are there."

"They won't be. As far as I know they're either in Edinburgh or their house in Spain."

"Then I'll come."

July 6th

Noreen feels I'm ready to tackle lavatories. Says, "The GENTS won't bite. Knock loudly when you go in. Once in prop the door open with your bucket. Ok?"

Did this. However within minutes of propping door open with bucket, Peter came along and said he was absolutely desperate. Noreen appeared and told Peter playfully that he was a naughty boy. Then told me to do the LADIES lavs, she'd handle the GENTS today, went in toilet with Peter and shut door.

There is definitely something going on between Peter and Noreen. Miriam would call it *hanky-panky*.

July 7th

Am inundated with tomatoes. Offer dozen to Deirdre. She shakes her head, "More than my life's worth to eat a fresh tomato."

Ask why?

"They're just so ... exposed."

Mr. Wheeler accepts a bag of them. "But that's your lot Margaret," he says as if I'm trying to palm off stolen goods.

July 8th

Much ado about Miriam but first, a first. This morning I cleaned the GENTS urinals. Will enter on my cv.

A two-fold story of Miriam. One o'clock Miriam arrives in dreadful fury carrying a packet of twenty Benson and Hedges and a lighter. Both Tom and I try to persuade her to part with cigarettes. Tom beside himself.

"Miriam, I forbid you to smoke," he thundered which was wrong tack to take. Miriam adopts equally thunderous stance, juts chin forward, eyes flash, shoulders back, "Then I throw in my job," she bellows.

Tom appeals to me as *the voice of reason.*

I say, "Miriam, you've done so well not smoking for so many months."

"What is left to me?" she shouts at the ceiling.

Which is a hard question to answer. Flounder around but Tom is inspired, he says, "Miriam we love you," and puts his arms around her, "Come on Margaret, group hug for Miriam."

Manage tepid hug as find Miriam on occasion bracing rather than huggable. However group hug does the trick and we lower Miriam into her swivel chair. Tom says as if talking to a young and armed first offender, "May I take the cigarettes?"

Miriam snuffles, "All right."

Tom takes cigarettes, says, "Phew, thought we'd lost you there," which seemed a little over the top, not as though Miriam was about to jump out of a sixth floor window. Tom sits down in my chair and I try to find a place to sit on top of the filing cabinet but this impossible without the aid of a step ladder so lean against the filing cabinet. NB. Later find I have bruised my shoulder from constant contact with metal cabinet.

Miriam explains that her mother is going out with Mrs.

Ferguson. Not in any romantic sense but unbeknownst to Miriam they have become close friends with a mutual interest in shopping.

"Tea and biscuits all round might be a good idea," Tom tells me while Miriam is blowing her nose.

Apparently Mrs. Ferguson called at their flat some weeks ago to see if Miriam would reconsider working at the Hospice Shop. Miriam out but mother in. Over sherry and Bombay Mix they'd discussed the lack of attractive clothes for older women.

"What do they want attractive clothes for – who even notices they're alive?" Miriam appeals to us. Tom jerks his head – a movement somewhere between a shake and a nod while I demur.

"I thought you'd demur," Miriam says accusingly.

The previous evening Miriam had arrived home to find her mother kneeling on the carpet, her mouth full of dressmaker pins as she took up the hem of Mrs. Ferguson's 'A' line skirt.

"But surely this is a good thing Miriam?" I said, "gives you an opportunity to get out more and make a life for yourself."

Miriam's brow lowering. Tom says, "I think you're missing the point here, Margaret ..."

Miriam talking to me as if I'm a five year old says, "I may want to get out more and make a life of my own but I don't want to be forced into it, you ... you dumbcluck."

Enter another first on cv. Have never been called a dumbcluck before.

Second fold of 'two fold' Miriam story. About seven o'clock this evening realised that I needed tins of cat food. Tilly although slight cat eats more and more which Deirdre says is a sign of Tilly's worsening physical condition and I choose to see as a sign that Tilly is holding her own.

As I was going into the supermarket spotted woman coming out, head completely hidden by the gigantic mixed bunch of flowers she carried. It was Miriam. Recognised her immediately by the particular type of orthopedic shoes she wears and the fact she treble knots her laces which I'm sure is a sign of something significant.

"Hello Miriam," I said, "Feeling any better?"

Miriam's face wearing embarrassed expression appeared above the flowers,. "Much better," she said gruffly.

"Flowers for your mum?"

"Er yes. Er no."

"So they're not for your mum?"

"Is this some kind of interrogation?"

"Sorry. None of my business."

"Exactly." but then she absolutely beamed at me, "It's funny how life can turn on a sixpence, isn't it?"

Agreed it was and we parted; Miriam walking with the proverbial spring in her step, me mystified.

July 9th

Wake up for once not thinking of Georgie. Instead thinking it's several weeks since I've heard from Janice. Wonder whether to telephone. Did she see our relationship as purely professional or bordering on friendship? Now I'm on my own I realise I've lost all knowledge of where boundaries begin and end, what a lone woman can and can't do. Wouldn't want Janice to imagine I'm attracted to her and be horrified.

A card depicting the Highlands with two highland cattle in forefront of photograph looking stoical from Georgie. Try to see cattle as representation of Georgie and Stella but can't help instead firmly believing that I'm looking at the bovine version of Miriam and myself.

Georgie asks if I could send on the brass fire iron set if I'm not using it. Says if I'm agreeable to request she will forward p & p. Waste ten minutes of my life mulling over how when Georgie and I first got together we used to toast crumpets and buns with the toasting fork appendage. How delicious we imagined the crumpets and buns tasted, even the burnt bits. This at least eight years ago.

Am not using fire iron set. In fact they were rarely used. Consider what sort of fire Stella and Georgie must have to feel the need for them. See an enormous walk-in fireplace, capacious leather armchairs on each side. Carry set into kitchen. Feel obliged to dust them but draw the line at applying Brasso. Send them off with a postcard of Bittlesea Bay under extreme weather conditions, write *Don't bother with p & p. Take care. Margaret.*

Nic rang cock-a-hoop as if there hadn't been any awkwardness between us for the last few months.

"Margaret is that you?," she bellowed down the telephone, "Guess what? I've won it. The Golden Trowel is mine! Well deserved I might say. Seen the competition and frankly some of those gardens were non-starters. How's your patch? Coming along nicely? Plenty of birds and bees?"

Some time later asked me to a celebratory barbecue, would also ask Laura as she was 'a tonic'.

July 10th

Laura telephoned to say she's agreed to celebratory barbecue at Nic and Simone's but hoped Nic wasn't going to drone on about gardening all evening. Asked if she could stay over as she intended to drink as much as her stomach would hold. Says she's in two minds whether to bring Iris.

Go to Deirdre and Martin's for the evening. They are taking me through the *Star Wars Trilogy* so that I'm prepared for something called *Revenge of the Sith* which comes out next year. Deirdre orders three large pizzas because nobody is willing to share. Film for the evening *Episode V1, Return of the Jedi*.

I ask, "How can it be a trilogy when we're already up to number six?"

Deirdre says, "That would take too long to answer – Lord Dudley wants to sit on your lap."

"Lord Dudley wants a piece of my pizza."

"Lord Dudley wants the gas fire on."

"In July?"

"Lord Dudley likes the fire on all year round. Sorry about the film, this isn't one of the best," Deirdre says looking enviously at Martin's pepperoni as does Lord Dudley.

Martin explodes, "Could you all be quiet?," he barks as if addressing an assembly of at least twelve instead of two women and a silent furry cat, "Just because the film's a third rater doesn't mean I want to listen to you lot rabbeting away over complete bloody trivia."

(Martin's bark far worse than his bite. He gets up and switches the gas fire on for Lord Dudley, slaps a slice of his pepperoni pizza on Deirdre's empty plate.)

"Thank you darling," she says. He winces.

I am quite impressed with the *Star Wars* films I've seen round Deirdre and Martin's. Although still confused by the story lines find myself, decades after everyone else, a *Star Wars* aficionado with a yearning to become a Jedi knight. Walk taller as I leave their house and try to adopt a noble expression.

July 11th

Ask Mr. Wheeler if he's ever seen a *Star Wars* film? He says no. Not his cup of tea. Tell him a little of what I've gleaned re. Jedi knights. He says, "Hmmm, not dissimilar to the knights of old but better equipped." Decide Mr. Wheeler has some of Obi-Wan Kenobi's gravitas and wisdom.

Mr. Wheeler asks if I've thought anymore about taking up the mantle of a Wheeler's Watch person. Adds that such a person is also not so far removed from a Jedi knight. Recognise I have walked into a trap of my own making. Say I'm very tired. Mr. Wheeler says the fresh air would do me good. Seeing my un-Jedi like expression Mr. Wheeler says, "Well please yourself." He looks disappointed and old, which is a ploy, because as I say ungraciously, "Oh very well," he straightens up and beams at me. Says, "Good girl, Margaret."

Stomp off home considering whether it is patronizing of Mr. Wheeler to call me a 'good girl' or whether I should be pleased as inside I sometimes still feel at least like a girl if not necessarily a good one.

July 15th

Tom has tried to tell me something he considers important three times now. Today about eleven when I took his tea into his office and placed it on his *Woodpeckers of the Western Hemispheres* coaster, noticed that on stepping into the room, a. Tom began frantically doodling on his note pad and b. his ears turned from white to red.

"Thank you Margaret," he said without looking up from his doodle. NB. nothing special about doodle; square flower pot with rudimentary tulips. I returned to my desk and my own tea. I don't have a coaster I have a blue plastic lid for cat food tins. Within minutes Tom sauntered out of his office carrying his cup, saucer and coaster and sat down in Miriam's chair.

"Well Margaret," he said, "How was your weekend?"

Which was a surprising question seeing it was now Thursday.

"Not too bad," I responded cautiously.

"Margaret can we talk? Really talk?"

"Actually, you said you wanted this set of accounts before one."

"Just stop for a minute."

I stopped typing.

"The thing is ... to get to the point ... cut straight to the chase, none of us are getting any younger. I'm not getting any younger," he clasped his hands around his cup and leant towards me – a slight dampness on his upper lip, "Margaret I'm going to tell you something which nobody else in the whole wide world knows apart from Miriam and a few close others."

"Better not. I'm terrible at keeping secrets."

"Doesn't matter now or it won't. Margaret I'm thinking of coming out."

Said nothing. Waited for Tom to finish sentence; *to play, of my shell, in a rash.* He didn't. He shut his mouth and stared at me hopefully.

"Coming out of what?"

His adam's apple appeared and disappeared back under his shirt collar, "Coming out of the cupboard."

"Do you mean closet?"

"Yes, although I'm happier with cupboard. In my mind's eye I'm stepping out one of those bulky dark Victorian cupboards into daylight. A closet seems too cramped for a big chap like me."

Puzzled I said, "But what about that time you brought in the local paper, complaining that lesbians were taking over Bittlesea Bay?"

"Testing the water. Seeing how the land lay. Funnily enough – well not that funny – Miriam confided in me about the two of you, then I came out to her ..." *Thinks: good buddy Miriam had kept this mighty quiet.* "... sorry to hear about your partner Georgie leaving but as Miriam says at least you've had several bites of life's cherry – we've had sweet fanny adams."

When Miriam comes in at one she looks cheerful. Goes into Tom's office and shuts the door. Is still in there when I go home. Call in at Hospice Shop. Very crowded. Spot Miriam's mother putting price tickets on a pile of men's shirts. Mrs. Ferguson is at the back of the shop sorting through the LP's, "What about an Irving Berlin?" she shouts.

Miriam's mother says, "Isn't there anything more up to date?"

"Matt Monro's Greatest Hits?"

"Oh yes. Put *Born Free* on."

Buy a cracked milk jug just for something to buy. Mrs. Ferguson offers me a reduction but I refuse.

"How are you getting on at Russell's?", she asks.

"Very well," I reply briskly and hurry out. Don't want Miriam's mother telling Miriam where I'm working or what I'm doing. Don't know why or do know why. Am ashamed.

July 17th

Ridiculous phone call from Deirdre. She and Lord Dudley want to go into show biz. Approach this statement with caution as in the past Deirdre has accused me of not taking her seriously.

"What does Martin think?" I ask.

"It's nothing to do with Martin, Lord Dudley's my friend not his."

Cannot imagine what Lord Dudley could do in show biz as his main claim to individuality is that he's always in a tearing hurry and treats seated visitors' stomachs as trampolines.

"So how will you go about getting into show biz?"

Deirdre laughs, a tinkling sound. I can imagine her bobbing blond curls; "Lord Dudley will be the big star, I'll just be his manager."

"But what will he be doing?"

"He'll start with walk-on parts. He's very good at walking on."

"Doesn't he more run on?"

"Run, walk – whatever cats are required to do," she says irritably, "I'm going to get our cleaner to make him a little jacket and a cap."

"A cap?" I squeak.

"Yes a cap. With a feather. In midnight blue velvet."

"Crikey."

"Wherefore 'Crikey'? Obviously he'll need a stage costume."

"You'll have to get him used to it."

"Yes!? I'm not a complete fool."

"Of course not. That's not what I mean. I was trying to make supportive small talk."

"Thank you but in this instance I don't need supportive small talk. However, if you're not too busy with whatever you do that requires you to go out at the crack of dawn Monday to Saturday I would like you to write a couple of short scenes seeing as you've got O Level English Language. Martin said if they're any good he'll video them as part of Lord Dudley's cv."

July 18th

Relationship with Lorraine Carter reaches new low. Have been accused of abusing my bucket. In fact I've actually broken my bucket which Noreen says is unheard of at Russell's. A bucket should last a life time. Noreen is impressed, Ms. Carter icily angry. Refuses to accept it was just an accident.

Incident occurred as follows: washed mop head in LADIES lavatory sink. Had brainwave that instead of leaving mop head soaking wet I'd shake it out of the window. Window very high. Could stand on toilet but no lid or seat so would be standing on the porcelain rim which struck me as dangerous and also unsavoury. Emptied bucket and upended it – stood on bucket. Waved mop head out of window. Mop head flew off wooden mop handle and disappeared. Leaned as far forward out of window as I could – no sign of mop head. Then jumped and looked. Came down hard and split the bucket.

Horrific scenes. It's as if the bucket is a person and I've killed her. Have even offered to replace bucket but that is not good enough. Ms. Carter wants blood. NB. Wet mop head fell on windscreen of her car as she was in the process of parking. Says major accident could have happened. Says I have a frivolous attitude.

July 20th

Begin writing scene for Lord Dudley. Realise it is a complete waste of time but rather enjoy it. Also find myself writing scene for Tilly who sits on the arm of the chair not quite asleep.

"In your hey day Tilly you'd have acted Lord Dudley off the stage."

Ring Janice. Start talking too early as take the answer phone voice to be Janice herself. Think all she'll get by way of message are the words, "... you in weeks. Best Margaret."

This evening read *Listening Ear*. Letter page very dull. People wanting to meet up again with people they'd met in the war, two correspondents writing to congratulate the council on the new parking bays outside the library. Decided to resubmit my article re. joy riders in *Marks and Spencer*. Added inflammatory paragraph for likes of Deirdre's Martin enthusing over the smoke free zone that is now the *Corner Coffee Shop*.

July 24th
Deirdre drops me outside Nic and Simone's house. They have a large hedge of rhododendrum concealing the front garden and house which disappoints Deirdre who likes to check out who has a larger/grander house than she has.

"Will they mind if I ask to use their loo?" she asks.

"Yes. You'd hate a stranger asking to use your loo. It's just an excuse to snoop."

"I'm not a stranger, they met me at your house."

"You haven't been invited this evening."

"But I want to see inside. What about if I shepherd you up the front path. Looks like it might be pretty steep."

"I'm not an invalid."

"You could pretend you were. That you've developed some spinal weakness."

"No Deirdre. Thank you for bringing me, now go home."

"I wanted to say hello to Laura and give Iris the once over."

"Well you can't."

I get out of the car clutching my bottle of wine.

Deirdre leans out of her window, "Shall I collect you about eleven?"

"No."

Laura met me at the front door.

121

"Is Iris with you?" I immediately ask.

"No, she's dancing."

"Where?"

"The London Palladium."

"I don't believe you."

Laura grins, "Well everyone else does so trap shut."

Follow Laura through hall, sitting room, french doors onto patio. Can hear Nic's voice coming from the side of the house saying, "York stone, pea gravel and grasses – sort of Derek Jarman look only no expense spared. The clematis folly was the clincher – they'd never seen anything like it. Gob smacked ..."

Simone lies on a rose patterned sun lounger, between her toes are a pair of turquoise plastic toe dividers, also she wears matching sarong.

"Love kisses," she shouts, "Can't get up – my Raspberry Sorbet not dry yet."

Nic appears leading a party of four women. Nic wearing thorn proof trousers and a khaki shirt with epaulettes. She looks as if she's emerging from the African interior, *This way chaps, better bivouac out in the open tonight.*

Introductions: Sonia and Sammy, a Tess and a Maggie. Thinks: Maggie looks exactly like a Maggie should look, tussled wavy hair, hazel eyes, warm uncomplicated smile. Thinks some more: I look exactly like a Margaret does look, ramrod straight back and desire to please face. Experience unwelcome memory of Georgie's damning *with you everything's either a joke ... or a whimper*, and resolve to be normal for once in my life.

Nic takes me by the elbow and leads me back into the sitting room, we stop in front of the fireplace. "What do you think? Pretty bloody marvelous?"

Above the fireplace in a dark wood frame hangs the Golden Trowel inscribed to *N. Meredith, Bittlesea Bay in Bloom, 2004. First place, Contemporary Garden Category.* Along the bottom of the frame Nic has had inscribed, *Determination, Perspiration, Exultation!*

"Get it?"

"Fabulous Nic."

"Follow the leader Margaret – I'll give you a hand with yours next summer."

Thank Nic profusely. Nic takes Golden Trowel from wall

and I study it from all angles, am convincingly amazed, enthralled, inspired and much more.

Laura comes in and says, "Blimey, what's that worth? Is it hall marked? Can I have a butchers?" and Nic hurriedly replaces Trowel on wall saying, "I think the barbecue should be about hot enough to start cooking." Leads us out. Laura winks at me. I wink back.

Enjoy watching Laura weave and dive as only she can do. One minute she's playfully annoying Nic with crass comment on alternative use for goujons of plaice, next tweaking Simone's big toe, and on to regaling couples with funny dance orientated story about herself and Iris at a ball in Eastbourne.

"We went as Andy Pandy and Luby Lou."

Everyone laughs although later overhear Maggie asking Tess, "Who are Andy Pandy and Luby Lou?"

"Didn't they win the Eurovision Song contest a few years back?"

Simone particularly and surprisingly empathetic. Has Nic move her sun bed next to my chair and says, "Whatever glib guff I came out with on the beach I do know how hellish it must be for you. If me and Nic split up I'd be devastated. Wiped away. So sorry."

An hour passes pleasantly. I talk to Maggie who is also a keen gardener. We discuss at length the possibility of a hose pipe ban along the south coast. Maggie seems to have insider information regarding the depth of water in our reservoirs and it is not enough. We need several inches of rain or one in five people to stop taking baths for at least a year for reservoirs to reach their required levels. I am feeling we have exhausted this subject but no, Maggie has more to say about the water saving methods of our friends in the Netherlands. As I nod and say *Good gracious* for the tenth time the side gate swings open. A woman climbs up the stone steps to the patio. She wears a dark trouser suit and a pink shirt. Blue black hair. Pale face. My mouth drops open. "Hello you," Nic shouts and hurries towards her.

"Never mind *hello you*, I've been ringing your front door bell for at least ten minutes," the woman says crossly. Her voice has a brittle but not unattractive quality. I know that voice well. It has rung in my head for weeks. This very morning it beat out the refrain *Margaret, chewing gum. Can you see it? Yes I know it's black, it's still CHEWING GUM!* Lorraine Carter. I was horrified. I hadn't told a soul, not even Laura about the cleaning job. Cleaning job represented yet another step down the ladder of success: no partner, no money. No house? No friends?

Nic had reached me in the introduction line-up, "And this is our friend Margaret. Lorraine – Margaret."

"Nice to meet you," I say looking Lorraine straight in the left ear.

"Well hello Margaret," her steely eyes narrow.

"Lorraine's the manager at Russell's. She gets us a staff discount on our garden furniture. Might give you one if you play your cards right."

I smile weakly. Lorraine smiles thinly. Laura pops up in between us.

"I'm Laura," she says, "Is it some sort of kismet that our names are so very similar? Blimey!" Laura's head is exactly level with Lorraine's cleavage. Amazingly Lorraine throws back her head and roars with laughter.

Lorraine very much takes to Laura. Apparently they share a mutual passion for golf which is news to me re. Laura. Hear Laura say wistfully, "Unfortunately Iris my better half resents the time I spend out on the links."

Try to recall one instance of Laura out on a link during our twenty year friendship. Fail.

July 26th

Laura and I set off for Laura's mother's flat in Ealing. It is her mother's birthday. Laura has a terrible hangover and is driving carefully as she feels her blood is made up of one part blood and nine parts alcohol.

Decide to come clean re. my cleaning job. Try a Tom Matthews, "Laura I want to tell you something that nobody in the whole world knows about me ..."

"Not now Margaret, I've got a splitting headache."

Say, "Since when did you start playing golf?"

"Please Margaret. My head. Have you no sensitivity?"

Laura's mother is still in her dressing gown. She makes Laura a bacon sandwich as Laura says bacon is the best remedy for hangovers. Also mugs of strong tea. It is now early afternoon and we watch an old *Columbo* on TV with guest star Jack Cassidy as the murderer.

"David Cassidy's dad," Laura observes, "What series was David Cassidy in?"

"Partridge Family," Laura's mum and I shout.

"Jack Cassidy was so handsome," Laura's mum says wistfully. Laura and I both look astounded and bewildered in turn.

I say, "He's weird looking. I don't think the hair on the middle part of his head belongs to him."

Laura's mum is undeterred, "They all wear rugs. I'm all for rugs once a man starts to go bald."

"Dad didn't wear a rug," Laura says.

"We couldn't afford one."

"That wasn't the only reason surely mum? Men don't tend to wear rugs in England."

"Oh in England," Laura's mum says dismissively as if she'd spent all her married life in Hollywood.

We agree that although *Columbo* predictable somehow that makes it even more enjoyable particularly when watched on a Sunday afternoon.

"Look at the time," exclaims Laura's mum and hurries to get changed and apply her makeup. Laura clears away the mugs and plates. In the middle of the coffee table she sets her mum's birthday present, a history of the jigsaw puzzle and the boxed set of *Poldark* videos I'd found in the Hospice Shop some months earlier. Laura's mum thrilled.

After dinner Laura goes into her mum's understair cupboard to telephone Iris on her mobile. Emerges three quarters of an hour later looking anxious.

"What's up?" her mum asks without taking her eyes of Ross Poldark who is very dashing with his sideboards, frilled cuffs and wine coloured velvet jacket. I'm wondering whatever happened to red headed Angharaad Rhees who played Demelsa, his wife? NB. My own mum used to say that red hair tended to fade. Thinks: Have a red headed cousin whose hair has never faded in fact it's got redder and redder when it's not being black or blonde.

"Iris didn't like my surprise present," Laura says.

"What did you get her?" Laura's mum asks.

"Margaret got it at the same time she got yours. Boxed set of *The House of Eliot*. I'll have to go round later," Laura says morosely.

"I wouldn't bother," Laura's mum says.

Laura drops me off at the station before hastening to Iris's side. In the Tesco Garage she'd bought a plastic box of Ferrare Rochas chocolates. I fear that Iris may think these common but Laura won't be told.

"Allow me to be the judge of what Iris likes," she says, "you've caused enough trouble with the videos."

July 27th

Was called into Lorraine Carter's office this morning when I'd finished my shift. "The lion's den," Noreen said with big eyes. Did not know what to expect. Tried to quell that wretched optimism of mine which would invariably produces a scene in which Lorraine shook my hand or clasped my forearm, *From now on Margaret although it may appear that I still wield the iron fist in the iron glove where you're concerned underneath*, taps impressive bosom, *you and I are firm friends*.

No basis to build the above on as after the introduction at Nic and Simone's she'd managed to avoid me for the rest of the evening.

"Sit down Margaret," Lorraine said. She had her back to me and was watering several pots of African Violets on the windowsill. Not much of a lion's den, more a large broom cupboard, almost cozy. I sat. I waited. She took her time. Finally began without turning round, "You've put me in rather a tricky position. Nobody in Russell's knows a thing about my private life."

"Same here," I said agreeably.

She set down the miniature enameled watering can (five pounds ninety nine pence, catalogue no. G65/4368) down on her desk, "But you don't matter," she said.

This came as a surprise. Would have liked to take a five minute break to consider these four words – whether they were unfair or a matter of fact.

"Margaret why did you take this cleaning job?"

"I need the money."

"But it's not well paid."

127

"But there aren't many jobs that are well paid that I'm qualified to do in a small town like Bittlesea Bay."

"From what I gathered on Saturday neither Nic nor Simone know you're working here?"

"Yes. No. That is correct."

"So I could sack you and it wouldn't affect my friendship with them?"

I sat up straight. I may not be a Jedi knight but nor was I willing to be walked over, I said, "You haven't given me a written warning yet."

Unsmilingly she said, "That can be arranged."

"Look I'm not about to tell anyone here about you. Why should I?"

"You might just let the cat out of the bag. You don't strike me as the brightest bulb on the Christmas tree."

Went very quiet. Was so angry. She fiddled with her note pad. I would not break the silence. Finally she said, "You better go now, but I'm warning you another incident like the broken bucket and you're out."

July 30th

Sunday. A Russell's free day. Nic and Simone are on holiday and I have promised to water Nic's garden. Nic lives two miles along the coast. No buses on a Sunday. My own fault. My *Don't worry Nic I've found a new and speedy secret route to your house* was too convincing.

"Yeah? Great," Nic said as if it is accepted that I am an Outward Bound type woman who travels across country, takes the path crows fly and can negotiate uncharted tracks and gullies. Perhaps she thinks I own a small pinto pony, *Giddy up*, and off we trot.

Deirdre has come to the rescue and suddenly my Sunday is handed back to me. Would like to tell her about my run-in with Ms. Carter but Deirdre would order me to leave immediately. I should and could leave – there is mum's money in the bank, I could put a little time and effort into finding a decent job, after all I am the fastest typist in Sussex or I was ten years ago when I entered *The fastest typist in Sussex Competition*. However there is something about being almost sacked that makes me dig my heels in. Thinks; if I'm going to be sacked I'll take

Lorraine Carter down with me. Which is rather dramatic and sounds like something I've seen at the cinema with Deirdre and Martin.

Deirdre collects me at nine thirty a.m. She's dressed in a black linen ensemble worn with pink and white striped tee shirt, big sunglasses, big hair.

"Plant watering outfit," she says, "my idea of casual."

My idea of casual are a pair of pyjama bottoms and a vest. Read in Deirdre's face a desire to say something. She manages to quell this as she is itching to see Nic and Simone's house exterior and garden.

Five minutes later we screech into their drive.

"I see they've got gravel," Deirdre says, in the tone she uses to denounce stone cladding, Austrian blinds and upvc double glazing.

"Gravel's not so bad."

Deirdre takes both hands off the wheel before the car's quite stopped and counts on her fingers, "One bad for tyres, two, bad for shoes, three, cats do their poos in it. I rest my case."

While I'm watering Deirdre holds up her hand to block out the sun's reflection on the glass and peers through Nic and Simone's front room window.

"Not bad," she concedes. I make my way round the back with Deirdre following – *some repointing needed there, says Deirdre* – marches up onto their patio and exclaims, "This is a fabulous garden. Fabulous. Must be fabulous to sit on this terrace and look at the sea in the distance. Oblique sea views," she declares as if practicing for an estate agency exam. I continue watering while Deirdre sizes up the back of their property.

"I like their style; shabby colonial," she shouts head pressed against the glass of their conservatory. Turns her head to an uncomfortable right angle to better see inside, "Oh yes. If I really personally opted for this style, and I don't, their interior is exactly how I'd have it."

I start on Nic's tubs. Deirdre has moved to the kitchen window where she is again craning her neck to see better, "So they've had the dividing wall removed – fab idea. Oh-oh, tut-tut."

She sounds deeply concerned.

"What's up?"

She looks back at me, shakes her head in … disappointment, shock, disgust?

"Very bad fengshui," she says sorrowfully.

"What is?"

"They've put a freezer in front of the kitchen door."

"There wasn't room anywhere else."

"Then don't have the freezer. That is so bad. Really affects the circulation of good vibes. There's a technical word for it but for the moment it eludes me," she smiles.

Her smile was so insincere she could have been speaking to a client. I wave my free hand in front of her face and her eyes flick back into focus.

"You need that hose on 'soak'," she says, "Give it here."

"No really, it's fine like this."

"Give it here," she says firmly and commandeers the hose, "To get the water to penetrate below the surface of the compost you've got to give them a really good drenching."

She points the nozzle into Nic's giant pot of petunias and lobelia followed by Nic's two giant pots of geraniums and buzy lizzie, followed by all the rest of Nic's giant pots. All the flowers are flattened by the time Deirdre finishes with them. I have an unworthy niggle that Deirdre is trying to sabotage Nic's admirable pots. I think, I'll have to come up on the bus tomorrow afternoon and try to salvage some of them.

"There, that should hold them," Deirdre tuns to me with a triumphant beam, "Now I suggest we go to the *Bittlesea Bay Caff* for a cream tea."

"It's only ten thirty. I've just had my muesli."

"By the time we get there it will be ten forty five – we can count this as lunch."

"I'd never dream of having a cream tea for lunch," but Deirdre is already in the car and revving the engine.

August

August 2nd

Deirdre has bought a third garden shed from Argos. We are sitting in the *Corner Coffee Shop* as outside there is a storm raging and waiting for a break in the rain to make a dash for *Evans Outsize* as it is the last day of their sale.

"Where's Martin?" I ask her. It is three pm. and this is one of Martin's usual times to be monopolizing a table at the back of the room.

"Putting up the shed."

"In this weather?"

"I left him in shed number two."

"Why do you need so many sheds?"

"Because I keep filling them up. I am an artistic, creative woman. I crave colour and novelty in my life. Along comes Mrs. Feng Shui and she wants the colour and novelty out. Says I will never have a quiet mind. And I know," here Deirdre holds up her hands as if I've been arguing a feng shui point with her for the last ten minutes, "a quiet mind is the universal goal but it's not easy. Whoever said Feng shui was an easy life choice must have been ..., Deirdre searches the Coffee Shop for inspiration, amazing."

Rain stops and we decamp to *Evans*. Deirdre swoops onto a rack of pale pink, rose pink and fuschia pink tee shirts, "I've lived and died in these, she says holding one up, You can't have too many pink items in your wardrobe."

I head for a pair of black chiffon trousers embroidered with a run of red roses up each leg, a mere seven pounds.

"Unbeatable value," I enthuse.

"Transparent. You'll have problems."

"For the beach."

"You've got to get to the beach first."

We both grin picturing me walking jauntily down our High Street, "They're so pretty."

"Fair enough."

I buy them.

Deirdre drives us home and comes in for a mug of sliced lemon in boiling water to counteract the *Coffee Ice Magnifico* and iced bun. We both bemoan the lack of McVities chocolate biscuits to go with our health drinks. Spend a further enjoyable hour discussing more spiritual matters and what other people do wrong that we get so right. At six she leaves, says she is flirting with Atkins tonight, giving him another chance to shift those pounds.

Upstairs I try on chiffon trousers. Yes they are beautiful and unbeatable value however they are truly transparent. Also there is a strange tie fastening at the front allowing an excess of flesh to peek unalluringly through. Thinks: at least a lover might find me desirable in such trousers. Imagine meeting prospective lover at front door, me in chiffon trousers and swishing the tie fastening suggestively, "Darling, you're just in time to help me get out of these." Realise mistake as my desire narrowed eyes focus on the dropped jaw of Unigate milkman.

August 4th

Dreamt about mum when she was very ill. In dream I did things differently, was not so absorbed in mine and Georgie's life. In dream I was whole heartedly there for her and not wishing myself at home with Georgie and the cats. Woke up heavy headed. Think as Deirdre would put it, "What was that all about?'

Go downstairs to feed Tilly but Tilly not in usual place, i.e. two steps ahead of me on way into kitchen. Find Tilly in the front room lying on the fleece I left on the settee the night before.

"Nood norning Tilly. Grub up."

For first time ever Tilly didn't respond. Her body was in a tight curl. Her green eyes opened slightly. They looked up at me as if I'm far removed from her and no longer the focus of her cat life.

I repeated *nood norning* several times. Her eyes are closed and refuse to open again. Banged on cat food tin with fork. Stood in kitchen feeling very much alone. Made myself cup of tea. Don't manage to take it back as far as the bedroom, instead sit down on stairs. Through the bannisters I keep an eye on Tilly – she seems to be barely breathing.

Deirdre and Martin away at Martin's parents. Nic and Simone still on holiday and Mr. Wheeler doesn't have a car.

132

Thinks: I must get a cab and take Tilly to the vet. But I don't want to do that. I know she's near the end. I've taken cats to the vet before and they know what's going on, that for whatever reason I've wiped my hands of them.

At eight a.m. I telephone Peter at Russell's. Cannot face speaking to Lorraine Carter. Say, "Sorry Peter I can't come in today – my cat's very ill."

He says, "Oh dear that won't go down too well, what about me saying you're laid low with a virus?"

"No. My cat being ill is the truth. It will have to do."

"Well hope kitty gets better soon," he says.

Leave a message for Tom.

Want to make Tilly more comfortable but can't imagine how. She licks cat milk from my fingers and momentarily I'm hopeful. Then her head drops back as if she's quite exhausted. I feel her ears, her nose, her body. She doesn't feel hot in fact she feels quite cool. I whisper, "Please wake up Tilly," but she won't.

At nine o'clock I try Georgie's old mobile number. Surely she'll want to know that Tilly is ill. She'd loved Tilly as much as she'd loved her own cats. On the third ring Georgie answers.

"Hello," she says.

"Georgie, it's Margaret."

There is an infinitesimal pause before she says, "Margaret, what's the matter?"

Thinks: does something have to be the matter? But of course it does.

"I think Tilly's dying."

In Georgie's background someone turns down *Start the Week*.

"Has the vet seen her?"

"Not recently."

"Does she seem in any pain?"

"I don't think so – only worn out."

"Look Margaret, Tilly's an elderly cat. You don't need me to tell you your options," she then tells me my options, "either get her to the vet or let her die at home with you."

There is just a hint of exasperation in her voice.

"Ok," I say, "thank you. You've summed up the situation for me. That's exactly what I needed. Nice to speak to you."

"Nice to speak to you too," she says, her voice now formal.

I replace the receiver. Hearing Georgie's voice, its disinterest has been like a hard blow to my chest. As I return to Tilly my body is hunched over, as if I'm protecting myself, as if there's no reason left to stand up straight. Sit down next to Tilly. She edges towards me so that she's touching my thighs and *I'm* comforted by *her*. I'm thinking so this is what it's really like to be alone. Not the single woman at a club or dinner party, not shoving a trolley round the supermarket with no one to ask, "Shall we give green tea a go?", no it's Margaret seeking comfort from her dying cat.

If this diary were a modern fairytale some woman would arrive unexpectedly. Lorraine Carter nurturing a secret soft spot for animals and for me, or Janice just having an intuition that Margaret needs her as she straightens up from heaving a paving slab in some garden a few miles away. But no. This is only a diary so I write the true bare bones. Nobody came. Georgie did not ring back to see how Tilly was or how I was coping. When Tilly died I was on my own.

August 6th
Lorraine Carter away on golfing holiday till today. This morning she cornered me while I was punctiliously J.Clothing the glass jewelry cabinet. Stood at my shoulder checking quality of my polishing technique for some minutes then said in cutting tone, "How's the cat?"

"She died."

I concentrated on glass blinking back tears. Lorraine walked away. Saw her again as I was leaving. She gave me a long, considered look then I heard her say to Peter, "After all, stuff happens. What's a dead cat in the scheme of things?"

August 9th
It's now or never. I've got to start going out and meeting other women. Love Laura and Deirdre but they have their own lives with me on the periphery. Thinks: well I say 'it's now or never' but not quite sure what I mean. Do I have a fear that if I don't inject some urgency into organizing my life I will drift? Vision of small, battered rowing boat becalmed on a pond.

Have tried to explain my feelings to Deirdre. She nods and smiles but doesn't quite understand the effort I need to make.

"Put yourself out there girl," she said, "I would in your shoes."

Easy to say when not in my shoes.

Even Miriam seems happy. Has taken a week off and was vague when I asked her what she was doing, where she was going and would it entail her mother? Said, "As of now I'm very fluid."

August 10th

Have passion fruit and orange juice in Deirdre's garden. Fledglings now the size of large shopping bags, peer down at us from the extension roof and make hopeful 'peeping' noises.

Deirdre confides in a low voice that Vera and Morag have objected to her feeding the gulls Lord Dudley's left-over cat food. Said this is unhygienic and will encourage rats, foxes etc. plus many hundred more sea gulls.

Deirdre starts laughing and adds, "Actually I hardly have to put cat food out anymore, the parents poke their heads through the cat door and help themselves from Lord Dudley's bowl."

Privately think this is an unsatisfactory state of affairs and the road to ... perdition? Ruin? Regret?

August 11th

Well? Would you believe it? That takes the biscuit! And other phrases indicating complete astonishment. This evening received telephone call. Immediately recognised Lorraine Carter's voice even though it was hidden behind an unfamiliar warm vivacity as if she were speaking to an old and valued friend! Had she got the wrong number, but no she called me Margaret. Perhaps another Margaret? No again – she wanted the Margaret who was the friend of Laura, Nic and Simone. Did she mean Maggie, friend of Nic and Simone? No she didn't. She'd already asked Maggie but *she'd* had to say 'no' as she'd be on the South Downs with Tess celebrating their china anniversary.

"Do try and come Margaret – I'm calling it a supperette club," she said insistently as if trying to tear me away from all the many other social events filling my normal Saturday evening.

Wanted to say, *But what about my written warning? Is that now on a back burner?* Also to ask, *Does 'supperette' mean the same as 'supper', as in there will be food?* Instead gushed back, "Of course I'll come. I'd love to come. Now exactly where are you?"

Rather proud of my tone of voice – I sounded like a successful, busy woman on equal footing to L.C.

August 12th
Re. equal footing with Lorraine Carter. This morning, as usual we were back on unequal footing – my chewing gum scraper has been taken away to be resharpened and I'm having to make do with a knife from the canteen. Ms. Carter said in passing, "Though how your scraper got blunt is beyond me because I've never once seen you using it."

Did not feel this worthy of a reply. Attempted to read L.C's eyes but they were veiled.

Have realised that I hardly enter anything in this diary about T.M. Accountancy anymore. This because very little to report. Miriam and Tom seem to be getting on like the proverbial house on fire and there are no more cozy chit-chats on the back step. Horrid feeling that Miriam now thinks our positions have been reversed – she is on the up and up while I am on the down and down. Have to admit that she seems much better.

And now I know why. Deirdre telephoned to tell me to look out of my front window which I did. Saw Martin flushed of face in charge of several black dustbins. Open window.

"What's going on Martin?"

"Deirdre's antique furniture is due at three. I'm cordoning off our side of the road. Ok if I cordon off your bit?"

"Of course. Want a hand?"

Martin throws withering look, "Only if you can persuade Deirdre to cancel this truck load of second hand furniture and return two thousand pounds to my bank account."

"I don't think I can do that."

"I thought not."

Mr. Wheeler appears wondering what size pantechnicon can warrant the use of so much road? Martin mutters, "There's the unloading to be taken into account," but sulkily withdraws one dustbin from outside Mr. Wheeler's gate before going back indoors. From behind me in the kitchen I hear Deidre's voice coming from the telephone receiver, "The miserable old basket case," she's shouting. Hope Mr. Wheeler can't hear. Return to phone and say quietly, "Deirdre, he has a right."

"He has a right to a torrent of abuse. Exciting isn't it?"

"Very."

Forget about Deirdre's delivery and climb up to my meadow. I'm surprised how good it looks after so short a time. In the centre of its circle I've planted an old fashioned tea rose in memory of Tilly. Not really appropriate but I wanted a shrub that would last for years and years. Sit on bench and think about getting another cat but not ready yet. Think about possibility of meeting a new lover – not ready for that either. Count on my fingers the months that have passed since Georgie left. Count from end of February. Almost six months have gone by. There are still 'firsts' to get through: first birthday without her, first autumn, first Christmas. Think sourly that of course at New Year Georgie was with Stella. Can't bear to go over all those times when Georgie was away 'on business' when she must have been with Stella. Feel spirits dropping. Concentrate on few small clouds scudding across wide stretch of blue sky. In the distance is the sea, a straight green ribbon on the horizon.

Down in the street I hear Deirdre's lorry arriving. There is a crunching sound as the first dustbin goes over and under its wheels. Powerful brakes squeal. Wonder whether the vicar is actually driving lorry and am sufficiently curious to start back down to the house. Suddenly I recognise Miriam's voice sounding rather officious.

"Delivery for Mrs. Deirdre Storm. I need a signature."

Then Deirdre, "I'm not signing anything till I've checked the goods. Where's my Martin got to?"

Spot Martin in an upstairs room in the process of lowering the blind. He mouths, "Keep shtum," and then the blind blots him out. I go round by the back gate. There is Miriam and the vicar. Both are wearing black jeans and black singlets and they are unloading Deirdre's furniture onto the pavement. So far there is a very formal three piece suite covered in a maroon and cream striped shiny fabric, several wobbly occasional tables – spindly legs painted gold, two matching book cases with carved pomegranate detailing, two footstools and several

137

wooden crates. Oh, and a six foot high statue of nude woman holding sheaf of corn or wheat.

Deirdre beaming turns towards me, "Fabulous. All fabulous. A few bits to give the garden an artistic gravitas and the rest for the back sitting room. Sort of Regency Buck chic."

"Fabulous," I enthuse, call out to Miriam, "Hello Miriam – I thought you were on holiday."

Miriam nearly drops the pedestal she's carrying.

"Steady," cautions vicar who's crumpling under the weight of the top half of a full size lamp post.

"Margaret what are you doing here?" Miriam looks flustered. "I live next door."

"Keep it off the pavement Miriam sweetie," vicar says. Miriam sweetie keeps it off the pavement.

"Back garden," Deirdre says as they stagger past.

August 13th
Miriam sporting an air of quiet confidence when she arrived at one o'clock. Says she intended to tell me but wanted the relationship to 'bed in' in more ways than one first.

August 14th
This afternoon bought *Listening Ear* and took it on the beach. Blustery, English seaside kind of day. Set up my striped windbreak, set out towel, sandwiches, yoghurt drink, notepad and biro. Weight newspaper down with large pebbles and browse through: main story, postal van reversing into the bollards outside the cinema at six a.m. in the morning. Headline; **What a difference a day makes!** *Twelve hours later and many innocent cinema goers could so easily have been massacred, fumes local bobby!*

On inside page find article plus indistinct photograph of badgers. There is now a Bittlesea Bay Badger Protection Society which already has five members and its own web site where readers can report sightings. Tear this article out and place inside of notebook. Move on to Letters page and am rewarded by yet another polemic from Martin.

Sir! In reply to A. Oakley, (self styled Accident Prevention Officer), I would like to emphatically state that when I'm ready for a mobility scooter I shall feel free to ride it at maximum speed wherever I like and A. Oakley had better just jump out of my way! This person illustrates

all the worst, small minded traits synonymous with the provinces.
Sometimes I ask myself why the heck did I ever leave London?

Make note to headline my own reply 'Storm in a Teacup.'

August 16th
Re Miriam. Since meeting the vicar she's improved consider-
ably. Says she and the vicar, (Miriam refers to her as 'the
vicar' or 'my vicar'), have long talks about life. Says vicar is
on her wave length and who'd have thought dull old Miriam
(this is Miriam referring to herself in the third person),
would have snaffled such a prize. Says she said this to vicar
and vicar most gratified to be considered a prize worthy of
snaffling.

Ask how Miriam's mother is getting along with Mrs. Ferguson? Very well. Idyllically. And is thrilled that Miriam's new
friend is a vicar. Miriam has to ration amount of conversation
her mother has with vicar as mother continually brings conversation round to whether vicar can categorically vouch for an
after life and give specific details of what Miriam's mother can
expect.

"I mean, my vicar's not a travel agency. She'll be asking next
what the weather's like up there and should she take her winter
coat."

N.B. Believe Miriam is being wryly comic here rather than
her usual sarcastic.

August 17th
Deirdre treats me to lunch at the *Bittlesea Bay Café*. We have
double egg and chips, white bread and butter twice. This is not
an Atkins day in fact her friendship with Atkins seems to have
cooled over recent weeks.

We go outside onto the terrace that looks down over the
cliffs to the sea front. We discuss how this café would be worth
millions if the owners revamped it and opened in the evenings.
Double egg and chips twice arrives and I announce that I am
going to dip my bread into my egg. Deirdre says she is going
to make chip butties out of her bread.

This is something of a special occasion, a saying goodbye to
my deceased cat Tilly occasion. Deirdre says, "No matter how
busy we get in our lives we shouldn't let deaths and births pass

uncelebrated unless you really don't like that person or pet. I had a real soft spot for Tilly."

Deirdre stares dreamily out to sea where a small white sailed yacht is tacking across our field of vision. Suddenly she says, "Do you believe in messages coming through from the dead?"

Say cautiously, "Perhaps messages do come through from the dead but I haven't personally received any."

"I'll tell you something. Don't feel affronted that this happened to me and not to you."

I insist that I wouldn't dream of being affronted.

"Yesterday afternoon there was such a strange smell of sea and flowers in our lounge. Nothing fishy or unpleasant – sort of perfumed yet other worldly. I'm ninety nine point nine five certain that it was your Tilly telling me to tell you that she's absolutely fine where she is."

Am affronted. Can't imagine why Tilly should choose to haunt Deirdre's lounge several weeks after dying asking for messages to be passed on to me. And why would she bring a sea smell in with her? Not as if she drowned or were a fish.

Deirdre continues in her dreamy voice, "Definitely sea and flowers. I looked up the chimney to see if there was anything or anyone up there."

Thinks: why ever should a smell of sea and flowers find their way up or down Deirdre's chimney?

"That smell just made me think of your Tilly."

As Santa Claus?

"Mm. Interesting", I said.

"Ah well," continues Deirdre, "Here's to you Tilly wherever you are," Deirdre raises her half full cup of cold cappuccino in the direction of the sea front.

"To Tilly," I intone. I do not raise my cup which is empty.

"Get 'em out then," Deirdre says and I fish Tilly's box of ashes out of my rucksack. Say hesitantly, "Deirdre the terrace is rather crowded for chucking ashes hither and thither."

Deirdre grabs the cardboard box, "Don't be ridiculous," turns to crowded table on other side of us, "You won't mind if we scatter my friend's cat's ashes will you?"

Woman with stiff grey perm replies, "You will be careful – we don't want it flying back over our salads."

"Of course we'll be careful. These ashes mean a lot to my

140

friend, we want them nestling in mother earth not on your lettuce and tomatoes."

Inside I cannot help starting to shudder with laughter. There is something truly marvelous about Deirdre. At that moment I admire her hugely. Get to my feet, lick my index finger and test the wind's direction. It's in our favour.

"What should we say?" Deirdre asks.

"Nood norning Tilly."

"Oh you and your talking cat. Very well."

We toss the ashes out over the balustrade. They fly forward in a fine grey shower, "Nood norning Tilly," we say together. And then we shout it, we bellow "NOOD NORNING TILLY," so that many feet below us down on the beach people look up and start waving. We wave back.

August 18th

Trawl through *Lonely Hearts* column in local paper. Have never noticed these before. They're slotted in between *Situations Vacant* and *Articles for Sale Under Five Pounds*. No *Women wanting Women* or *Men wanting Men*. Not too many *Women wanting Men*. Most of the column taken up by *Men wanting Women*, Read following:

"Who'll start the bidding? Stunningly attractive man mid forties wants to share his peak of condition with like bodied female. If you've got it, why not flaunt it my way?"

Fight urge to leave a sultry voiced message on advertiser's voicemail.

"I'll start the bidding. One sack of compost over your BIG HEAD."

August 19th

Take in tomatoes and sweetcorn for Miriam and Tom. Both pleased with tomatoes but seem apprehensive re. sweetcorn. "There won't be any beetles in them?" Miriam asks, "In the supermarket they're all clean and yellow."

Reply that there shouldn't be any beetles. Notice that both Miriam and Tom double knot the carrier bags no doubt to prevent escaping beetles.

August 20th

Very late for T.M. Accountancy this morning as Lorraine Carter

141

called an urgent staff meeting which involved not opening Russell's till quarter past nine instead of nine o'clock. Announced that the store would be closed for ten days during September for a re-fit. "Whoopee," I whispered under my breath which LC who has supersonic hearing picked up. Announced with gaze drilling into my forehead, "Staff with employment record of under six months will not receive salary for that period. I think that's just you, Margaret."

Leave store. Make my way through throng of furious customers demanding entry. As sprint to office, imagine scenario where I lure Lorraine Carter into a dark cellar. As she makes her way down chill stone steps, the shadows conceal booby trap of mops, brooms and Lorraine's spare set of golf clubs, positioned half way down. "Aargh!" as L.C. topples forward. Does not die but during several days confinement in cellar reaches an understanding of the more empathetic approach needed with her staff.

Late afternoon set off for my Wheeler's Watch. It's raining. Wear storm proof jacket with the hood up. Do not wear Wheeler's Watch sash as I'm feeling rebellious. Walking down Stirling Avenue – through the rain I see the familiar figure of Janice coming towards me on the same side of the road. Am about to shout *hello* and wave but before I can do this she crosses over, carries on past me without a single glance.

Could, should have called out to her but have uneasy feeling that she was actually avoiding me.

August 21st
Visit Deirdre and Martin. We are not watching a film tonight we are sitting in 'the library'. Late yesterday afternoon Deirdre telephoned an antiquarian book seller and ordered six yards of hard back books with red or green covers and gold lettering. Specification; must be mint condition and no dust. There are four incomplete sets of Dickens and Thackeray, several large tomes by G.K. Chesterton and the abridged works of Shakespeare.

Take in bottle of port as that seems in keeping with Regency Buck chic. Deirdre says, "No, but thank you, I prefer passion fruit but Martin might imbibe."

Martin does.

Actually the room looks ok apart from resembling a stage set. Martin wears his dressing gown over silk pyjamas and leather slippers so he looks exactly the part but Deirdre in a kaftan covered with a pink, red and black circular pattern belongs to another theatrical production – say a play set in the nineteen sixties.

"What you thinking?" she asks.

"I don't know what I'm thinking yet."

"You don't like it?"

"I think I like it. I thought you didn't like books."

"They're not books, they're interior decoration. I intend to get the cleaner to wipe them over with disinfectant before yacht varnishing them – should facilitate dusting."

Martin gets between me and Deirdre with the bottle of port and my glass, he is frowning hugely at me and and dilating the famous nostrils which is a signal that I am on dangerous ground.

"It all looks lovely," I say quickly.

"You don't mean that," says Deirdre.

"I do mean it."

"You don't. Say what you really think. Go on everyone else has had their fourpence worth ..."

"Deirdre, all I was thinking was that the room looked extremely nice in a theatrical way but that you didn't quite match it ..."

Martin pulls the face of one in extreme pain while Deirdre looks furious.

"Please don't get angry," I say.

"Actually I just don't do anger," she says angrily, "why should I have to match?"

"Of course you don't have to ..."

"I don't want to match. If I wanted to match I would match. I'm happy not to match. Other people might want to match, not me!" Flops back in Regency striped chair and stares furiously at a dingy oil painting of a horse and foal.

"Stop it Deirdre," Martin says.

"I will not stop it," she begins to blink rapidly, "It's true. I don't match. I don't match with anything or anybody. Always the odd woman out. The butt of every joke, the fall guy ..."

I stand next to Deirdre's chair (more of a throne), pat her

144

shoulder, "Come on Deirdre, I didn't express myself very well. Why ever should you have to match your furniture? You are you, unique."

"You don't mean that ..." pulls miniscule pink handkerchief from sleeve.

"I do."

Martin pats Deirdre's knee briskly, "You need a Jaffa Cake."

Deirdre looks tremulously at Martin, "I do. I need a Jaffa Cake. Margaret I insist you share our Jaffa Cakes."

August 23rd
Book in with Michelle at *Hair Today*. Watch her in the mirror as she dispiritedly pulls at my lackluster locks. Not much left of the aubergine high lights. Does not appreciate my self styled fringe.

"You have made a mess," Michelle said.

"Won't that be a challenge for you? Rather fun?"

Regret the word 'fun'. Can read in Michelle's grimace that 'fun' is a nasty, uncool word that her nasty, uncool, middle aged clients use.

"Doesn't make my job any easier. What's it to be this time?"

"Same again."

"The copper tint?"

"No, the blonde and aubergine highlights."

This time while she works on my hair I receive a lecture. *What is the point of making me look like a celebrity if I then neglect my hair? Don't I realise that I'm very lucky to have so few lines and wrinkles considering?*

"Considering what?"

"Considering your age. What's your self image like?"

In surprise I look up at Michele and she grins back at me, "I've been on a course. Understanding the client's psyche. I'm not just a hairdresser anymore, I'm a beauty therapist. Premature aging of skin, hair and body can be put down to drink, fags or depression. I reckon you've got depression."

Admit that I have had depression and that at the moment it's not easy to think well of myself. This information galvanizes Michelle.

While my hair is in tin foil she cleanses, tones and moisturizes my face and neck, setting each little product bottle in a row on the shelf in front of me.

"How you feeling?"

"Soothed."

"Want some more?"

"Go on then but no eye makeup."

"Spoilsport. I'll use a bronzante."

"A what?"

"Wait and see. Eyes closed, head back."

An hour later eyes open and face forward I find I look relatively wonderful – I am tanned, I sparkle, I glow from the neck upwards. Michelle looks equally pleased.

"Know who you look like?"

"No tell me." *Sharon Stone, Susan Sarandon?*

"Dame Judy Dench."

"I'm much younger than Judy bloody Dench."

"That's what I meant, a young Dame Judy Dench."

I settle up. Give Michelle a sizable tip. Buy all the beauty products.

Michelle says, "Put that lot on everyday. Look like a star, feel like a star, get treated like a star."

Walk home features carefully positioned. Study new me in hall mirror. Like what I see but how to reconcile young Dame Judy Dench with also being a Jedi knight? Log on to the Bittlesea Bay Badger Protection Society website and become their sixth member. Almost immediately I receive an email welcoming me and offering a chance to *See Badgers at Play!* Am also offered an information pack for the remittance of two pounds fifty which covers printing costs plus tea and biscuits at each meeting.

August 25th
Wear cotton beany hat to *Russell's* as don't want LC to see my particularly attractive hair before Supperette Club on Saturday. Very hot. Head threatens to explode.

August 26th
Ditto.

August 27th
Lorraine Carter's Supperette Club is surprisingly well attended.

146

Seems that women have come from as far as Brighton. Early on I overhear someone say, "I've come all the way from Brighton. Quite a slog to get here."

The club is in a room at the back of the Felgate Arms, a pub tucked away on the outskirts of Bittlesea Bay which Georgie and I passed many times always making a comment on how uninviting the building looked. However, the back room has been transformed ... NB. Realise having never been in back room have no real way of knowing what it looked like before but assume the addition of pink and purple balloons, a banner proclaiming, "Welcome! Women of the South Coast!" and at least twenty candles are down to Lorraine Carter who is wearing a natty striped shirt (plus trousers and shoes) and making introductions in a confident drawl. Sees me and calls out, "Ah Margaret ..." Comes close and murmurs, "You have made an effort, dear."

I have made an effort. Have slapped on all Michelle's unguents including the *bronzante* and wear a pair of black linen trousers and a white shirt which sets off my bronzed face and neck. Notice my hands and wrists look unhealthily pale and resolve to keep these when possible out of sight.

Lorraine takes hold of my arm and uses me as a battering ram to break into an already animated circle.

"This is Margaret. She's a writer. Rather well known in literary circles. Margaret I'm sure these ladies will look after you. Rather shy," she says to ladies before heading towards the open door where more women are arriving.

My arm is grabbed again, "You're Sarah Waters aren't you?"

Admit that I'm not, nor Jackie Kay or Stella Duffy. Someone says, "Perhaps she's the mother of a famous lesbian writer." Someone else states quite aggressively, "Well you're certainly not Jeanette Winterson," as if my next strategy might be to try to pass myself off as Jeanette Winterson. Am about to explain that I am nobody in particular when in my head I hear a chorus of Deirdre's and Michelle's voices, *Big yourself up Margaret, act like a star, get treated like a star* ... Modestly confess to being a diarist in the reportage style of Samuel Pepys. Immediately an expert on Pepys steps forward, face radiant at finding a soul mate. She says, "Can we get away from this crowd and have a really rigorous discussion?"

Respond quickly. Say, "Actually no. At the moment I'm up to here with Samuel Pepys," and pull an expression of intense exhaustion.

"I quite understand. He's so very comprehensive, so detailed, so historically absorbing ..."

I hold up hand, laugh, step backwards, turn on heel and head for supper table.For six pounds I am able to buy a large bowl of salad, a large baked potato and a large plate of vegetable curry plus a raffle ticket that gives me the chance to get in free the following month. As a non-smoker I take my various plates and sit with my non-smoking sisters in the spacious and brightly lit non-smoking section. Find myself staring wistfully across to the darkened, candle-lit, smoke filled smoking area where the women look much more mysterious, sophisticated and the kind of women I might like to know. Find myself thinking of Georgie.

A non-smoker offers to buy me a drink, tapping a plastic bottle of Buxton Spa water tantalizingly, "Thank you," I say, "I'd love one."

Smilingly she brings it back, "One pound twenty."

"That much?" I sympathize.

"No, you owe me one pound twenty."

It may seem as if I'm saying non-smokers are mean and dour which obviously I'm not because I and many of my friends are non-smokers and we/they are very attractive and generous women. It's just that a woman with a cigarette in one hand, glass of wine in the other, open necked shirt with gold jewelry, tanned ankles set off by white socks and some sort of jaunty loafer – well these are just a few of my favourite things!

Decide to go home before the raffle. On my way out I meet Lorraine Carter. Say boldly, "Lorraine why did you tell everyone that I was a writer? It made me look very foolish."

She folded her arms (possible defensive movement), said, "Did you want me to tell them you were my cleaner?"

"You didn't have to tell them anything about me."

She moved closer, pushed her face into mine, "It was a joke Margaret."

"Not a very funny one."

"Oh please," she said and went back inside.

148

August 28th
Spent day debating with myself re. job at Russell's. Have never experienced someone disliking me before. Who to talk to? Deirdre definitely not the right person, nor Laura. Rang Janice although she'd never replied to my cut off phone call weeks earlier. Resolved that I would not leave a message if she didn't answer. She didn't answer.

Spent much of evening feeling sorry for myself, thinking how I was on my own with nobody to rely on for help. Went to bed. Dreadfully missed at least having Tilly to cuddle. Made resolution to be strong, self sufficient – sleepily found myself searching for words beginning with 's'. Last words remembered, sure footed.

August 29th
Caught Lorraine Carter watching me with a smug smirk. Nobody else around so pulled the most horrific face I could manage at her. She looked startled but said nothing.

August 30th
Visit this morning from Deirdre's other neighbours Vera and Morag. I'm still eating croissants and reading the Sunday paper when they arrive, their mission – to sound me out re. light from Deirdre's antique lamp post.

"Honestly Margaret, I've never needed curtains before," Morag says, "Go to bed when I'm tired, wake up with the dawn. I've tried an eye mask but it's left a wavy indentation under my eyes."

Indeed it has.

"Doesn't the light bother you?"

Explain that I sleep in the front bedroom, even so am aware that Deirdre's lamp post is on from dusk till midnight and then off and on triggered by a) burglars, b) a badger, fox, cat, mouse, c) gust of wind, d) Deirdre who is a light sleeper and always on lookout for possible burglar, badger, fox, cat or mouse. At almost any hour of the night our back gardens can be suddenly transformed into a scene from Colditz when an escape attempt has been rumbled. *Englander, we can see you! Give yourself up or take the consequences!* N.B. Know this because I'm often awake during night and looking out of windows. Am not sure why.

149

I ask Vera and Morag in and offer tea. We sit in my front room rather than the kitchen where they would see offending lamp post sticking up above Deirdre's sea blue willow fencing like a prop from Dixon of Dock Green.

"You've got it very nice in here," Vera says approvingly, "I like your faded florals."

This is reference to recently purchased floral cushion covers from Hospice shop, under influence of Deirdre's *Regency Buck chic* look. Find myself regarding these with suddenly critical eye as have been into Morag's and Vera's house and found their clash of floral, stripe, pattern and pictorial to be unrelaxing rather than obviously *RB chic*.

"Very nice," Morag agrees briskly, "Now Margaret, we know Deirdre is a friend of yours so what's to be done?"

I promise I will have a word, murmur the phrase *possible compromise could be reached.*

"*We've* already had to compromise with our panties," Morag says.

NB. Wonder why I react against word 'panties'? Decide word represents too much intimate information about Vera and Morag.

Vera agrees and adds bewilderingly, "I hope it won't escalate into the War of Jenkins Ear."

I say, "It shouldn't come to that."

August 31st
Definitely don't want to speak to Deirdre about lamp post at the moment. Am avoiding her. Just when I thought her hare brained scheme of Lord Dudley going on stage had died a natural death, Deirdre has left a message that on the contrary Lord Dudley's acting career is very much on track. He may get a pantomime booking in one of a possible several small theatres within a fifty mile radius of Bittlesea Bay.

"Margaret, it is imperative that you come up with a vehicle in which Lord Dudley can shine by the weekend as Martin's borrowed a camcorder."

Am wondering if I could just disappear?

Do not disappear. Retrieve playlet that I'd started when Tilly was alive. Complete nonsense but encompasses Lord Dudley's predilection for sitting in box lids and leaping onto visitors' stomachs. Briefly it is an advert for indigestion tablets: family lying prostrate on settees, armchairs, floors etc. after large meal, enter Lord Dudley who leaps from one stomach to another. "Ouf!" recipients of Lord Dudley's leap shout ... Lord Dudley makes final triumphant leap onto table. On table is lidded box. Lord Dudley knocks box to floor retaining box lid. A shower of *Rennies, Eno's, Alka Seltzer* or *Andrews* shoot out of upended box. *That's just what we need*, says senior family member, *What a clever cat!* Lord Dudley sits in box lid looking proud.

Showed script to Deirdre. She is genuinely thrilled. The moment Martin comes back from the *Corner Coffee Shop* she will get him to begin filming, will I be a full-up family member. No! I stop Deirdre from rushing out of my kitchen door clutching script.

"In return Deirdre I want you to do me a favour?"

Deirdre's smiling face closes up like a flower when the sun goes in, she rightly mistrusts friends asking favours, "What do you want?"

"I want you to get Martin to put a timer on your lamp post so that it doesn't come on after ten o'clock at night."

"Those witches have got to you, haven't they?"

"Morag and Vera did call round but they have a point."

Deirdre, as always when crossed, furious. Shouts, "Sod 'em."

I ask her to keep her voice down. She bellows, "There is no way I'm going to expose my soft underbelly to those two!"

Reply that it shouldn't come to that with a little diplomacy.

Deirdre demands, "Why should I have to be the diplomatic patsy?"

"Because you won't get this script otherwise. If I say it myself it's excellent and may launch Lord Dudley on a brilliant career."

Deirdre smiles maternally, "Do you really think so?"

"Anything's possible."

A moment's impasse then, "Oh very well. Actually Martin's been complaining as well, this gives me an honourable way of giving in to him without seeming to give in. Done, but I hate those two old ... crab apples."

September

Go to evening meeting of B.B. Badger Protection Society. Meet in woman called Monica's house. There are five of us, four women and one man. Monica says eagerly that on one occasion eight people came and she ran out of chairs. Did not know what to say so sucked in my breath which seemed to satisfy her. We sat round her round coffee table. The first half hour spent studying a map of Bittlesea Bay and discussing whether a proposed ring road was a good thing or a bad thing. Man said if it got him to B & Q quicker it would get his vote. Monica brought in tea and marshmallows – women had one each, man had four.

"Regarding the badgers ..." I said. So far no badgers mentioned.

Man said, "Not much on the badger front at the minute. It's getting a bit nippy to be hanging about at night."

"When would be a good time for me to come back, badgerwise?"

They all looked nonplussed. Monica said defensively, "We do address many other environmental issues – this ring road being a point in question."

"I don't have a car."

"But that's hardly the attitude ..."

Made my excuses and left. Dusk outside and very pleasant. Walked slowly enjoying the freedom of being out of Monica's sitting room. Became aware that Janice was walking, no loping along at my side.

"Hello stranger," I said.

"Hello," she said sullenly.

"You always seem a little sullen Janice. Is that the real you or is there someone else behind a sullen mask?"

She grinned and slipped my arm through hers which made me, inside, feel quite choked. Couldn't remember the last time anyone had shown me spontaneous physical affection. Such a small gesture, but still.

Janice walked me home. At my gate she stopped, "Any news of Georgie?" she asked the expression on her face closing again.

"None. Coming in for tea, a glass of wine?"

"Better not."

She looked as if she was about to say something, almost a woman torn, "Perhaps we could meet up one afternoon?" she asked hesitantly.

"Great. Yes. Shall I ring you or you ring me?" *Oh Margaret, must you sound so desperate?*

"I'll ring. Take care."

And off she loped, her shoulders hunched.

September 2nd

Write to *Listening Ear* re. lack of sufficient space in town's main meeting place, the *Corner Coffee Shop*. Ask whether it is justifiable for single male customers to monopolize a four person table for anything up to three hours? Quote: *I myself have experienced this selfishness first hand when searching for a seat after a strenuous day's shopping. I have been met with open hostility and actual lies as in, "I'm expecting a party of three." Three who failed to materialize during my hour spent perched on bar stool which is probably the worst form of seating for person with persistent back problems. Sign myself A. Oakley, Orthopedic Practitioner, Four Poster House, Bittlesea Bay.*

September 4th

Go to Odeon with Deirdre and Martin. Film, *Spider man 2*. Martin as always in charge of ice cream tub selection from freezer cabinet while Deirdre buys cinema tickets. As Deirdre is about to part with twenty pound note for three tickets (cinema Deirdre's treat today as she's just had an order for several trillion pounds worth of canned fruit label designs), Martin shouts, "Hold everything – there's no ice cream!"

Cashier says mildly, "You're not wrong."

Martin says heavily, "I know I'm not wrong. Where is it?"

"We're out of ice cream."

"As in today, tomorrow, forever?"

"Beginning of week."

"What kind of cinema runs out of ice cream?" Martin roars.

People queuing behind Deirdre begin to shuffle impatiently.

"Couldn't we buy tubs in Marks & Spencer?" asks Deirdre.

Martin fixes her with his *I'm seeing you in a new light Deirdre and not liking what I see*, says icily, "Are you bonkers? M & S ice cream tubs must be ten times the size of our usual one person tub and I DON'T SHARE!"

"I don't either," Deirdre says appeasingly.

"Me neither," I say agreeably.

"Then what are we going to do with tubs that big – make ourselves sick?"

Woman behind Deirdre says, "If you don't want tickets can you get out of the queue?" which enrages both Deirdre and Martin.

"If I want to stand in this queue for the rest of my life I defend my right to do so," shouts Martin.

"We may be buying tickets, we've not decided yet," Deirdre tosses back her curly mane.

"Decide somewhere else sweetheart – I'm losing my rag," man shouts.

"What?! What did you say?!" Martin roars.

Deirdre and I hustle Martin out of the queue and we reconvene at the popcorn counter. "We'll get popcorn," Deirdre says determinedly cheerful.

"We will not. We're going home. I will not watch a film without my tub," and Martin storms out onto the pavement.

Leave Deirdre and Martin making their way acrimoniously towards the car park. Go back in cinema, buy ticket, buy giant packet of M & M's. Watch *Spider Man 2*. Very enjoyable.

September 6th
Go with Deirdre and Martin to watch *Spider Man 2* as don't like to admit I've seen it without them. Pull face at cashier not to give me away. He ignores me. Plentiful tubs. Multiple flavours. Toffee for me. Even on second viewing an excellent film.

September 7th
Receive email from Tabby, ex-old school chum. Says she may be passing through Bittlesea Bay during the next fortnight and might look me up which will involve her staying two nights. Reply in urgent tone: on no account look me up as am suffering from a highly contagious virus. Delete unnecessary embellishment re. food parcels being left on front step for fear of spreading infection in community.

September 8th

Tom Matthews has given Miriam and myself a ten percent rise plus bonus. He says he's had a brilliant year, that his luck changed when he *came clean about his sexuality*. Miriam tells Tom that she's so glad he did and that the only way to salvation is through the Lord and complete honesty. Miriam beginning to sound more like a vicar than *her* vicar. Have seen her studying the Bible and making notes, believe her to be memorizing appropriate verses including large sections of the Sermon on the Mount.

To celebrate the success of T.M. Accountancy Tom is arranging a small drinks party on Friday, or at least Tom is giving us money to arrange a small drinks party for him. It will be a select few, Miriam and the vicar, Tom and his boyfriend and me.

Reply arrives from Tabby that contagious virus very commonplace at the moment. Several other friends are suffering from it. Says she will be in touch nearer Christmas re. further attempt to link up. Regards to Georgie.

Respond briefly, there is no Georgie. Receive same day reply from Tabby to enquire whether Georgie has succumbed fatally to contagious virus? She hopes not but if so, her deepest condolences. Email Tabby explaining Georgie's defection to Stella.

September 10th

Tom's boyfriend very tall man in his forties. His name is Barry. After several drinks he begins to repeatedly repeat the information that at six foot eight and a half inches he is technically a giant.

"Really?" I say, "Good gracious ... that's astonishing ... well I never ... of all the bars in all the world ... one swallow doesn't make a summer ..."

"Yes I'm technically a giant."

"Well I'll eat my hat ..."

We all sit on the desks with the exception of Barry who stands next to the door frame better to illustrate the problem he has with door frames. I find myself passing round the trays of nibbles: soft cheese and salmon, cheddar cheese and pineapple, mini-quiches, Hula-Hooops, and re-filling glasses.

Miriam says, "Oh Margaret, some wine spilt over here, get a cloth."

Think: *what am I, the bloody waitress?* but keep insincere smile in place. Tom looks smitten and very happy, throws admiring glances Barry's way. Barry reciprocates by touching the ceiling with the palms of his hands, Tom shakes his head in admiring disbelief. Miriam looks smitten and happy. She is tossing Hula-Hoops at vicar and vicar also seems charmed. Rather envy Miriam. Secretly feel that were my heart free I would suit vicar far better than Miriam, imagine myself and vicar nibbling from opposite ends of mini-quiche ... However my eyes do begin to glaze over while half listening to plans for Harvest Festival at St. Dunstans. Tom says although he and Barry are committed atheists they will certainly send a basket of appropriate produce.

Not a bad evening. I get over chip on shoulder at being designated waitress. Only at the very end, as we go our separate ways at the street door of T.M. Accountancy do I feel a real pang. The two couples set off arm in arm while there is solitary me shouting my cheerful 'Goodnight' to their uncaring backs.

September 12th
Heaven. Ten days with no Russell's. Store is closed till Tuesday week. Sunday and lie in bed reading local. Spot, *Sirs, I must remonstrate in the strongest tone regarding your perverse willingness in publishing one A.Oakley's inflammatory, often ludicrous letters. I feel that A.Oakley is pursuing a personal vendetta against myself and many of the male population of Bittlesea Bay. I believe the name A.Oakley to be a pseudonym and the accompanying job titles farcical. If these poison pen letters lurking beneath the flimsy guise of public comment continue I will be forced to forward a dossier of information gleaned re. this contributor to the police. Your servant, Martin J. Storm.*

Immediately begin letter re. *Storm Force 8!*

September 13th
Briefly meet Janice on terrace of *Bittlesea Bay Café* prior to meeting Deirdre. Janice tells me she is away on a hiking holiday with friends for the next two weeks. Says it was all booked months ago. Do not know why this news should feel like a

156

minor bomb shell dropping but it does. My eyes fill with tears and I have to put on my sunglasses even though there is not a hint of sun. Janice awkward rather than sullen. I think that we are both aware ... but of course that's absolute nonsense. Nobody's aware of anything. After a few minutes silence we begin talking at the same time, "I didn't mean ...". "It's none of my business ...".

Janice gets up, shoulders her bulky rucksack as if she is leaving the district that instant.

"Speak when I get back," she says.

"Lovely," I say and hate the sound of my voice.

Deirdre arrived. "Wasn't that Janice I saw going down the hill?"

"Was it?"

"I reckon it was. Now egg and chips twice – I think you're in the chair."

Morosely we both eat our egg and chips. Deirdre admits to having had a small contretemps with her cleaner. She says cleaner has no respect for Dyson and has used an abrasive sponge on Smeg, the recently purchased fridge freezer.

I ask, "Has Smeg taken over from Atkins as your new best friend?"

Deirdre sits back in chair, chip poised inches from rose bud mouth, "Is that supposed to be sarcastic?"

"Sorry, Deirdre."

She smiles and shrugs, "Actually Smeg *has* taken over from Atkins. I just love to fill Smeg with unsuitable food and Atkins doesn't like having his instructions countermanded but Atkins can get stuffed."

A large grey seagull fledgling lands on the terrace wall.

"Chick, chick," Deirdre calls waving a tomato ketchup covered chip at it.

"Peep, peep," I call which is the correct seagull fledgling sound to make. I offer it half a slice of bread. Chick must weigh two stone at least, looks at us with its beak open as if aston-ished. Closes beak. Opens beak. *And another thing ladies ...*

"Cake?" Deirdre asks.

"I don't think baby gulls should eat cake."

"Not the bird. Us."

"Too full."

Deirdre slumps dispiritedly. She'd love a cake but won't eat alone. I rather crave a piece of cake but cake at lunchtime seems decadent and the road to nutritional ruin. Gull chick flies away up onto the cliff top and Deirdre and I sigh heavily.

September 14th

Visit Mr. Wheeler. Have noticed that since his garden has become overgrown there is now a splendid crop of blackberries maturing along his far wall. With St. Dunstan's Harvest Festival in mind have daydream of me arriving at church and enchanting Miriam's vicar with punnets of same. NB. Am not trying to lure vicar away from Miriam but feel in need of womanly admiration from some source. When Georgie lived here at least she complimented me on my wine glass washing technique and always appreciative of my dumplings once the cold nights set in.

Have discussed this problem with Deirdre who says ideally I should be able to confirm my own fabulousness. Says if she can do it, I certainly can. Says, if she waited for Martin to confirm her fabulousness in any department she would … and then can think of nothing 'she would …' so says *It's not going to happen. Savvy?* Which doesn't help so am, in small harvest festival way, fantasizing about vicar a. administering approval, b. blessing me, c. laying hands at least on my head.

Mr. Wheeler says he's sorry but I can't have his blackberries he's promised them to Vera and Morag who are making fruit pies for their *Autumn Bring and Buy.* Am I going? Say, I hope not.

Inspect own vegetable plot. Unfortunately it has peaked too early. All that's left are a few split tomatoes and some desiccated runner beans — nothing that would impress Miriam's vicar.

Tabby quiet for almost a fortnight then today I receive a postcard, postmark Majorca, technicolor photograph of sandy beach and frolicking bronzed holiday makers. Tabby writes: *Am having a fabulous time. Re. break-up do you realise if these were proper marriages Georgie would have been your third? Might have been wiser to settle for Ronald. Sympathy, Tabby*

September 15th
Deirdre arrives absolutely bubbling over with excitement. She's dressed as a bearer of good news in shocking pink trousers and tunic top cinched in at waist with brocade sash. Also brocade shoes and brocade bow in curls which bobs about with every movement Deirdre makes and Deirdre is constantly on the move. Hurtling through my kitchen door she's waving her cheque book and a sheet of note paper.

"Open up the bubbly," she yells.

Admit to not having any bubbly.

"A slice of lemon in a glass of tap will do. Any biscuits?"

Find biscuits. Initially biscuits not to Deirdre's taste but on re-consideration she scoffs half the packet, "Not bad," she says, "Cast your eyes over this you clever little munchkin!"

Sticks piece of paper in front of me on the kitchen table. I gasp and read out, "For the sum of one thousand pounds I renounce all rights to script entitled *Lord Dudley – Indigestion Super Hero!*."

"So?" says Deirdre, her blue eyes sparkling, elbows on the table, "You going to sign on the dotted line?"

"Have you sold the script?"

Deirdre withdraws elbows, "That's insider information. No can divulge."

"Deirdre a thousand pounds is a lot of money."

"I can offer you less."

"Will it be on television?"

"Yours not to reason why…"

"Did you intend to write me a cheque this very minute?"

Deirdre's elbows return to table top, "I did."

"Go on then."

I sign on the dotted line.

September 16th
My birthday tomorrow. Laura rang to say she's sorry she can't make it but she'll be down next week. She and Iris are going camping again in an effort to resuscitate their flagging relationship. Ask if this is a good idea as Laura is never at her best rubbing shoulders with the natural world. Laura says on the contrary, she is Nature's child it is Iris who always insists on pitching herself against the elements. Why can't they just

159

enjoy the tranquility of Nature from a rose covered B & B in a pretty village, why must it always be walking boots at dawn and gruel?

"Have a good birthday," Laura says. "I'll only telephone if I'm suicidal."

September 18th

Yesterday my birthday. Laura did not ring. Miriam remembered. Gave me a card and for the first time ever a present, a small ceramic bowl in the shape of a cat's head.

"Me and my vicar chose it," Miriam said proudly, "It's specifically for used tea bags."

"Thank you. Thank her."

"Doing anything special?"

"I don't think so – not this year."

"Well, try and keep your spirits up."

Felt as if she saw me as an invalid and that was fair enough. I would get better. Another mile stone about to be passed. Went home. Deirdre's and Martin's car not in their drive way, wondered if Deirdre would be home later for perhaps a small celebration up at the *Bittlesea Bay Café*. Let myself in.

The second I opened my front door I knew something was different because suddenly there were elements of the house as it had once been. Ahead of me on the kitchen floor were two cat dishes, bulging supermarket carrier bags waited to be unpacked, the atmosphere felt warmer – more alive. From our front room came the rustle of someone putting down a newspaper. Above me on the landing Samson and Delilah peered down fearfully through the upper bannisters. Georgie was back.

Went into front room. Georgie sitting in the window bay an uncertain expression on her face. She got to her feet, then half sat down again but straightened, "I've left my cases in the car, I've not just moved back in Margaret, only I had to let the cats out, they were going mad in their baskets."

Didn't know what to say or what I felt inside. I hadn't expected this, was unprepared. Many conflicting emotions. Unpacked the groceries she'd brought.

She followed me into the kitchen. "Just a couple of nights Margaret – is that too much to ask?" Felt that it should be but said, "Of course not." Stopped myself from saying, "This is your home as well."

Made up the single bed in the box room that had once been her study. Opened her birthday card. Nothing flowery or personal. Water colour of lone woman looking out to sea, her hands on a white balustrade. *Happy Birthday Margaret. Love Georgie.*

September 20th

At office said nothing to Miriam which was ok as these days she expects me to be quite subdued. In the evening Georgie went to see Nic and Simone. She came back late after I'd gone to bed. I heard her steps on the stairs – very slow as if she was deadly tired. They stopped outside my bedroom door. I almost called out to her but couldn't.

September 21st

This morning started back at Russell's. L.C. away for a few days, fly fishing. Information courtesy of Noreen. Or white water rafting. *He likes his sport*, Noreen says and *Wouldn't suit me*.

Apart from Deirdre and Mr. Wheeler who have seen Georgie out in the garden nobody else knows that she's back. My life feels very precarious. Nothing is definite. It surprises me but I have changed. Have lost my boisterous optimism.

This afternoon we talked properly for the first time. Georgie didn't leave Stella, Stella asked her to go. Apparently it was Stella who couldn't stand the day to day living with the same woman – she called it *the day to day tedium*. Georgie very defensive of her. Said, "She's used to being independent. She actually liked the set-up of me living with you and enjoyed the excitement of our stolen days together. Stella's a woman who thrives on intrigue."

I listened with tight face and chaotic thoughts as Georgie used me as a confidante and not one third of her drama.

"Will you continue seeing her?"

She shook her head, "She's met someone else. Someone more flexible." Then she bowed her head and started crying. At first I

161

was frozen, could not even stretch out my hand to touch her. But she was so sad, so heart broken that her sobs physically hurt me, forced me out of my chair. I put my arms around her and held her head against my breast saying, "I'm so sorry. I'm so sorry Georgie," all the time inside I was crying as well, *Why should I be sorry? Why should I?*

September 22nd
This is all so odd. I can't get a grip on the situation. When I imagined Georgie coming back, and hundreds of times I had imagined it, I'd seen her asking forgiveness, admitting a terrible mistake. Stupid stuff, *You are the only one – it's taken this time apart to make me realise what my true feelings are.* And then a period of adjustment. Perhaps a better relationship built on new knowledge and reawakened emotions. In every daydream I'd never once thought I'd be sharing my home with a woman I hardly knew, who loved someone else but had nowhere to go.

She's in such a fragile state of mind. I watch how she touches the furniture – the corner of the table, the arm of the settee, a book shelf as if reassuring herself that they're solid. She was never a talker, now she's almost silent. She looks beaten down and inside I'm furious with this Stella person for reducing Georgie. It would be easier if I were furious with Georgie as well but I'm not. Which doesn't mean … which doesn't mean my feelings are the same as they were. Every morning I wake with a sinking sense in the pit of my stomach at another difficult, unresolved day to get through. Can't make even the smallest plans.

This evening Janice rang from a call box in the Lake District.

"Margaret I'm thinking of coming back early," she said, "Will you be around at the week-end?"

Told her that Georgie was home, that I couldn't talk. There was a silence apart from what I think was the sound of rain. Then Janice sighed, she said, "Ok. You take care of yourself."

"Yes," I said, "I will", but the line was already dead.

September 23rd
Met Deirdre in Debenhams tea shop. Deirdre surrounded by shopping. Tells me with a wide smile that she can't help being

a Debenhams girl then sees my face and says, "Ok, sit down. I'll get the drinks. Carrot cake or Danish?"

"Carrot cake please," I said dully.

Sit with my head in my hands till Deirdre returns. She has bought hot chocolate to take away and cake in a bag, says, "Come on, we can't talk in here."

I follow her out to the car park. We get in the car and she drives down to the sea front. It is a vile wet day and we have the sea front to ourselves. I sit and stare at the waves pounding the beach only yards away while Deirdre takes the tops off the styrofoam cups.

"Choccy's boiling hot so go steady," she says, "Now spill the beans."

Say, "It's not working. It's an appalling situation."

"Whatcha going to do?"

"What can I do? Can't turn on her while she's so miserable. She needs support, affection, care."

"Oh give it a rest. Are you a prize mug or what? She dumped you Margaret. Georgie was doing the dirty on you. Of course she's miserable – because she can't get what she wants. She's not miserable because she's let you down, made you unhappy for the best part of a year and is still making you unhappy. Let's get a reality check here."

Bow my head over cup. Feel it warm my face and tired eyes.

"Do you still love her?" Deirdre asks.

"I don't know. No I do know. I want to make her happy again ..."

Deirdre interrupts, "You haven't made her happy in years. You can't. You don't have what she wants for her to be happy."

Almost smiled, "Don't pull any punches Deirdre."

"I'm trying to make you see sense. Georgie is bad news. In less than a week she's transformed you from a woman in recovery to a tearful wreck. You're my friend. You're Laura's friend. You're our friend. I want us to go out and have laughs like we've always done. I don't want you doing the anxious chicken bit over a woman who only half knows you're alive. Sorry if that sounds cruel. Do you know, you've completely spoilt my Debenhams Day. I've a good mind to take the stuff back."

Whether I want to or not Deirdre invariably makes me smile, "What did you buy and I'm not a chicken?"

"Hen, chicken. Whatever. I bought jersey bedding in cream and white. Molds to your body or that's what it says on the wrapper. And an autumn raincoat, pea green with a pink and pea tartan lining. Fabulous. Definitely won't see another one like it in Bittlesea Bay. Ready for your cake?"

"Yes."

September 24th

L.C. called me into her office this morning. Didn't ask me to sit so stood hands folded over stomach and fresh packet of J.Cloths.

"Shut the door please," she said.

Closed the door and resumed position. L.C. very interested in inner workings of mini-stapler, said, "Will you be going to my Supperette Club tomorrow? Membership tends to fall off in the autumn and I'm trying to keep the numbers up. If you want to bring anyone with you ..."

This was said in pleasant if distracted voice – obviously mini-stapler of supreme importance.

"I don't think I'll be going and why should I after last time?", I said and then more confidently, "although if I wanted to, there is someone I could bring."

Lorraine puts down stapler and gives me her full attention, "You surprise me. Word on the grapevine was that you'd been left high and dry months ago."

"Perhaps the *word* got it wrong. Look Lorraine why don't you give this Margaret baiting up? Let me just get on with the job I'm paid to do."

She laughed carelessly, "Oh that, well you're a lousy cleaner ..."

"No, I'm an excellent cleaner considering the work I get through in an hour and a half. You're lucky to have me as a cleaner."

Her eyes looked mean, "I don't happen to think so."

My eyes looked reasonable, "That just isn't true. What may be true is that you don't like me, or perhaps you have a suppressed infatuation for me ..."

"Get out of my office!"

164

"Certainly. We'll think about the Supperette Club. Can't make any promises."

The stapler whizzed past my ear.

Laura rang to say she needed to talk about Iris. Camping had not been successful. Should she take 'camping' as a metaphor for life? Told her I didn't have an opinion one way or the other. Laura sounded surprised, "But you must have an opinion. You're my friend."

"Sorry Laura, don't want to talk or think at the moment."

"I'll come down immediately."

"Please don't."

"Please don't? I'm Hurt and Offended of North London. Let me come down, I insist."

"No."

September 25th

Georgie says I must carry on exactly as normal, that I mustn't let her disrupt my newly fashioned life in anyway. Which isn't possible. Feel terrible. Oppressed. Everything I say sounds flat and common place. Sense of humour has gone awol and can't imagine it ever coming back.

Went to Lorraine Carter's Supperette Club with her. I didn't really intend to go but Georgie saw it written on the calendar.

"What's this Margaret?" she asked trying to smile like she'd smile in the old days, "*You* haven't let the grass grow under your feet."

I tried to smile back. Replied in a light carefree voice, "I've only been once – it wasn't too bad."

"Shall we go?"

"Ok. Why not?"

On arriving I was immediately cornered by the Samuel Pepys woman. By the time I got free saw Georgie and Lorraine Carter on the far side of the room, chatting away like old friends. Didn't feel confident enough to join them. Saw a flicker of the old Georgie, how she lights up in the company of attractive women and must admit LC can do attractive with anyone but me. Later asked Georgie, "Do you know Lorraine Carter?"

"Yes. From years ago."

Asked no more questions. Inside felt hot with all the

jealousy of recent months. Caught Lorraine studying me with curiosity. What did I have to partner a woman like Georgie? But we are not partners. We are nothing. Hardly friends.

Realised something or reaffirmed something at the Supperette Club. I was carrying our plates of baked potato topped with chile back to where Georgie was sitting in the smoking section, part of a group of women yet not taking part. She wore one of her lightish coloured suits from her time in Spain and unfamiliar leather loafers without socks. She smoked a cigarette which she'd stopped doing at home.

Although her head was quite still her gaze was moving, sifting the crowd. I thought she was searching for me and I smiled – with pleasure and relief at being sought. She didn't smile back. In fact she hadn't noticed me at all. Her gaze passed over without seeing me – Georgie was searching the room for Stella or a woman who was like Stella. And if she'd seen someone, Margaret with her plates of steaming baked potato would have been forgotten. I doubt if Georgie would have even waited around to explain.

September 27th

Laura telephoned while Georgie was out and I told her what had happened. For once Laura seemed – quietened. Asked me how I felt? Said, *just terrible. I want to go to sleep for a year.*

She told me something interesting that she'd heard a character say in a film she'd seen with Iris. It had made her think about her own relationship. Surprisingly serious for Laura. That you can love somebody but if they always make you feel bad about yourself then you're better off without them. And that is how Georgie makes me feel: like second best or a stop gap or even a retirement home. I've thought back over our recent years together and I was feeling like that then, accepting her self absorption and reserve as the love a long-term relationship shakes down into.

I want to feel exciting, lovable, interesting – I want to feel that there's still lots to find out about me, not as if I'm a book she's read too many times. Am I ungrateful? I've prayed for Georgie to come back. Seen her as the missing piece of my life puzzle. But life isn't a jigsaw with a finished picture at the end of it. The picture can change. Can renew itself. Can't it?

166

Miriam and the vicar called in.

Miriam said, "We're all worried about you Margaret. You may not be aware of this but you missed the Harvest Festival although I specifically reminded you about it on Friday lunch time. Mum and Mrs. Ferguson were hoping to see you. They'd arranged the flowers and they looked terrific. Really we're very disappointed ..."

"Even at their best I couldn't imagine they'd be scintillating."

"Well obviously, not by yours and Stella's standards but then who would be?"

"Don't get annoyed I wasn't including you in with them."

"Well I do include me in with them – Miriam is my friend.

I could tell from Georgie's expression that she was getting

September 28th

Miriam and the vicar called in.

Miriam said, "We're all worried about you Margaret. You may not be aware of this but you missed the Harvest Festival although I specifically reminded you about it on Friday lunch time. Mum and Mrs. Ferguson were hoping to see you. They'd arranged the flowers and they looked terrific. Really we're very disappointed ..."

At this juncture the vicar touched Miriam's arm and Miriam stopped talking.

"What Miriam's trying to express is her concern for you. She says you don't look well and indeed you don't. We were passing by and wondered if you might like a walk in the park with us?"

Outside I heard Georgie's car draw up. I said dully, "Georgie's come back."

"But that's good news, surely?"

"No Miriam, it's not that simple," and then Georgie was opening the front door and calling out, "Margaret, are you in?"

"Front room," I said.

An awkward half hour. I made tea. Produced biscuits. The four of us moved into the kitchen. Miriam, her vicar and myself sat down while Georgie paced restlessly up and down, usually with her back to us so she could stare intently out of the window and patio doors. She didn't join in the conversation which was mostly about St. Dunstan's, T.M. Accountancy or Miriam's mother.

Once the vicar asked her, "Do you have any deeply held beliefs?" and Georgie grinned but not very pleasantly and said, "I don't think I do."

After they'd gone she said, "What a pair of bores those two are."

"I admit they weren't at their best but they'd come to see how I was. They weren't prepared for you."

"Even at their best I couldn't imagine they'd be scintillating."

"Well obviously not by yours and Stella's standards but then who would be?"

"Don't get annoyed I wasn't including you in with them."

"Well I do include me in with them – Miriam is my friend."

I could tell from Georgie's expression that she was getting

168

irritated. She made me think of a wild horse desperate to shake off reins and rider.

"Yes Margaret, boring Miriam is your friend, daft Deirdre is your friend and lecherous Laura is your friend – a fine trio. Hardly one decent working brain between the three of them. Why surround yourself with these ... losers?"

"You're the loser," I said slowly – each word like a drop of freezing water.

Her head jerked back and she stared at me. I held back a bitter laugh. In our ten years together I had never been rude to Georgie, I'd withheld any critical opinion, smoothed over disagreements, gone along with her. She walked out of the kitchen. I heard the front door slam and then the roar of her car engine.

September 29th
Georgie back by the time I got home from work at lunchtime. She'd been away all night. Sitting up in bed waiting for her to come home I read through my diary from the very beginning. Not all painful reading, some of it even made me laugh but not like I laughed over E.M. Delafield's *Diary*.

An interesting discovery. From February 25th, the evening I began to realise that Georgie no longer loved me: I *stared into a rather somber face. Tanned but not like Georgie's tanning booth tan. Tanned like someone gets when they work outdoors. The woman must have been at least ten years my junior. She was my height, brown hair cut short, steady brown eyes. Nothing really distinctive about her and yet the thought sped across my mind that she was quite unique. Not in an immediate physical attraction way, just an observation, a first impression. And I knew absolutely that this first impression was true.*

Janice! All these months I've been puzzling over just why Janice looked so familiar and now I know.

Asked Georgie where'd she'd been all night. She said, "I slept in the car. A bit chilly but I've done it before."

"When you were with Stella?"

"Yes. Towards the end we had some almighty rows."

Now we are polite. We respond to each other over barriers of our own making. Somehow we have set each other free. I don't quite understand how this has happened.

169

September 30th
I've asked Georgie to leave.

October

October 5th
Georgie left today. The third time counting in February, April and now. Each leaving has been very different; shock, despair, miserable relief. She's found a flat in Brighton which is twenty miles away, not far from where she used to live. At this moment I can't imagine we could ever be friends in the future.

Spent some time thinking that these last few weeks – how as miserable as they've been, they've been good for me. I've seen Georgie objectively and realised that the woman I loved was in part a fabrication, part a memory. How I'd held on to the Georgie of our early years, been comforted by rare glimpses. I remember seeing us both reflected in the supermarket window months ago when we'd physically differed so much – see now that our outward differences mimicked our inward differences.

Thinks: in my imagination Georgie grew taller, more attractive, more clever, sophisticated while I dwindled into small, indistinct, boring, unattractive and finally worthless. Discussed this phenomena with Laura rather than Deirdre as Deirdre too blanket dismissive of unpleasant thoughts or considerations. Laura surprised me. Said she was aware that I'd come to see myself negatively in comparison to Georgie and hadn't known how to deal with it. Said I became a shadow or the grey background to the colourful desirable woman I saw Georgie to be, enabled Georgie to become even more colourful and desirable. Laura felt that in the months after Georgie had left, miserable old bat that I was, my old self had started to resurface.

Laura reveals that she is now in therapy and finding it all very interesting, particularly information relevant to herself. Iris is also in therapy and they're getting on better than they ever have before, discussing their mutual self fascination.

170

Generously, Laura brought the conversation back to me saying, "Not laying down any hard and fast law here Margaret but I think with you the key thing is to feel the same size as any future partner, this in the abstract of course. If you feel small and worthless take that as a sign that something's going wrong."

"What about you? How do you think you and Iris suit each other?"

"We are different faces of the same coin."

"Will I ever meet her?"

"Hard to tell. You know me, I like to compartmentalize."

October 7th

Meet Nic and Simone in town late night shopping. This time they don't try to avoid me.

"How you doing?" Nic asks putting her arms round my shoulders.

"Ok."

"It didn't work out then?"

"No."

Simone asked, "For the best perhaps?"

"I think so."

"Will you see her again?"

"Too early to say."

They treat me to Fisherman's Pie and baked beans in Debenhams.

October 9th

Lorraine Carter has been meek and mild to everybody for at least a week. Noreen says that she's probably dating and getting 'it' regularly. Noreen complains that *she's* not getting 'it' at all. She really likes Peter, in fact if he wasn't such a slow coach she thinks she could fall for Peter but in the meantime she's got to fill the vacancy any way she can.

"What do you do when you're frustrated, Margaret?" she asks.

I tell her, "My partner left me recently so I'm not bothering too much about the lack of 'it' at the moment."

"Oh shame!," says Noreen, "Did he go off with another woman?"

"It's painful Noreen."

"Sorry. Must be awful. Did he go off with another woman?"

"*Too* painful to talk about."

October 11th

Feeling a bit better although it is still easy to get shaky when anxious. Also back to normal with Miriam. We have resumed eating our sandwiches on the office step and Tom has retreated behind his closed door.

Miriam tells me that all is not well in the Tom and Barry camp. Tom has developed an aversion to Barry's feet. Says he's been over-exposed to them. Has told Miriam, "They stick out at the end of the bed even though we've got a king size. Every morning I see them, long, white and boney. I've appealed to Barry not to wiggle his toes. His last partner found toe wiggling a turn-on. Believe me Miriam as far as I'm concerned there's nothing worse than white, wiggling toes."

The vicar suggested Barry wear socks in bed of a colour decided by Tom but Tom says, it's too late for socks, his aversion has traveled right up Barry's legs. Leg warmers perhaps?

However Miriam and I are relieved that it's Tom going off Barry rather than the other way round. Miriam said, "I couldn't stand any body else with a bleeding heart in this office," as always her sympathetic self.

October 12th

Prune Tilly's rose bush then stop for boiled eggs and toasted soldiers. From my position at the kitchen table I'm able to watch Deirdre's Lord Dudley entertaining himself with a gigantic caterpillar. At least I think it's a gigantic caterpillar. Very nasty looking, oily black, fat, about four inches long with a sort of hard carapace. Each time it curls up Lord Dudley pokes it open with his paw. This scene depicting nature red in tooth and claw is distracting me from my soft boiled eggs. I go outside and find a plank of wood. Bat the bug behind the plant pots. Have uneasy thought that were Janice with me she would disapprove of my batting bug. Put Janice from mind. Return to eggs. As I settle down the bug crawls back into view. Seems quite chirpy. Sort of 'second round'. Lord Dudley delighted. Out I go again and bat bug firmly back behind the pots while also registering what a fearsomely disgusting bug it is. Could not imagine what it will turn into: something slimy with scales and wings. Not a dragon. A small dragon would be ok. Surround bug with more pots. Return to stone cold eggs. One of my toasted soldiers a little blackened and curled, looks suspiciously like batted bug. Cannot eat any more. Bug again appears. Thinks: if this bug was a human being or a scruffy animal I would not keep batting it. Go out with old tea cup. Upend over bug, slide piece of cardboard underneath. Feel queasy as I meet with invisible resistance. Carry teacup etc. up slope and push cup, cardboard and bug through gap in fence into Mr. Wheeler's garden. Turn round to find Lord Dudley in hot pursuit. He also disappears through gap in fence.

October 14th
Find half finished letter beginning *Storm Force 8!* and can't think what it refers to. Have not read the *Listening Ear* for several weeks. In Deirdre's having tea and muesli bar, (Atkins has been deserted for muesli and okra diet), see this week's issue. Deirdre follows my gaze and says, "Definitely not my kind of newspaper. Martin buys it for the letter page. Some daft correspondence with an A. Oakley. He's convinced she's a spinster, embittered, possibly retired or in part time work."

"Could almost be me."

"That's what I said but you're off the hook. Martin says you're too young and incapable of either base cunning or crass stupidity. Another muesli bar?"

"No thanks. Should you eat five at a time?"

Deirdre nods her head, "Absolutely. I'm dieting but no way am I going to starve myself. Anyway, now A. Oakley's gone silent, Martin says she's running scared or in a looney bin."

Murmur that 'looney bin' rather an unpleasant term and also say, "poor woman".

"Nonsense. It's a fantastic word. I love it. She's in a bin full of looneys. Completely ga-ga!"

Wince internally. Later at home reflect on why and how my letter writing has turned into an issue with Martin who I'm very fond of? Move on to, is Martin secretly enjoying the cut and thrust? Move on to whether I should send one last letter or stop this instant?

October 15th

Peter, the under manager, has asked Noreen, the head cleaner, to marry him. Noreen is *over the moon* although expressed apprehension re. not having done 'it' with Peter. Is concerned that a. Peter won't be up to the job, b. that she has done 'it' with Donald the warehouseman and also the delivery driver whose name she doesn't know and will Peter be disappointed in her if he ever finds out which is on the cards as particularly Donald is a known blabbermouth? Vis a vis Lorraine Carter, Noreen tells me, "*He*, (meaning LC) has advised Peter that *he* (meaning Peter) will be professionally marrying beneath him which is a sure recipe for unhappiness and disastrous vis a vis his, (meaning Peter) career."

Ask what Peter had said in response. Peter said, "My Noreen's not as green as she's cabbage coloured."

Imagined Lorraine Carter's response, "Oh surely she is."

Have reached the conclusion that L.C., although a lesbian, doesn't like women. Of late her animosity towards me has slid beneath the surface. Have no doubt it waits like a drowsing shark.

October 16th

Reluctantly accompany Mr. Wheeler to Vera and Morag's *Autumn Bring and Buy Sale*. Have never walked the streets with Mr. Wheeler before at least not without my Wheeler's Watch sash and on the look out for tom foolery, hooliganry and chicanery. Find myself marching – swinging my arms, head well up, trying to keep my jaw line at his same right angle to neck.

"This is what it's all about," he says.

Assume he's not referring to the same 'it' as Noreen and wait several minutes without Mr. Wheeler elucidating before I ask, "What is it all about?"

"Fresh air. Oxygen. Life."

So we march along, the sea in the distance, today a misty blue. The leaves are turning from green to gold, some are already fluttering down. Nothing on the pavement yet dry enough for a satisfying crackle underfoot. Know exactly what Mr. Wheeler means however personally wish that the afternoon's life destiny didn't end at an *Autumn Bring and Buy Sale* in a Nissen hut behind Morrison's Supermarket.

At door we pay our entrance money and receive free raffle ticket. Mr. Wheeler says ponderously, "Go forth Margaret and buy until the pips squeak."

Thinks: sod that I'm spending two pounds then straight off home. Spend twelve pounds. Hear pips protesting rather than squeaking. Buy one blackberry and apple pie, one oozing Victoria sponge cake, two patchwork cushion covers and an embroidered table cloth. In raffle win bottle of Amontillado Sherry. Am about to take it from raffle organizer (large woman wearing wrap around floral pinafore not seen since the 1950's), when Mr. Wheeler materializes at my side and says, "Why not let them keep the sherry to raffle again?"

"I won it fairly and squarely," retort.

"But charity Margaret."

Let my eager hands fall to my sides. Woman in apron beams at Mr. Wheeler as if he is a greek god or similar heroic figure, "Thank you Mr. Wheeler," she gushes.

Repress own retort of, *Don't thank him, thank me.*

"Well done Margaret."

Feel patronized by everybody. Feel treated like a bloody child. Make resolution to go nowhere in the future with Mr. Wheeler. Someone taps me on the shoulder. It is Morag, "Would you like a kitten?"

Say "No," brusquely.

Immediately imagine thin starving kitten crouching by dustbins and add, "Why?"

"Vera found one crouching by the dustbin last night. It's very thin. Starving. We'd keep it but there's Jenny (budgerigar) to consider."

Say I will let her know this evening. Morag says, "We thought of raffling it off later – to keep *Bring and Buy* interest at fever pitch."

Say sharply, "Under no circumstances will you raffle a poor starving kitten. I'll take the damn cat."

"Oh what a nasty temper," Morag says but slaps her hands together as in a job well done.

Am amazed to spot Deirdre turning over the linen stall. She is literally turning over the stock, heaving up the neatly folded piles and dumping them back down again so she doesn't miss any piece of antique fabric that might be lurking underneath.

Morag who is still with me clicks her tongue and says, "I folded that linen myself. Such an unpleasant go-getting, walk over the poor and needy, type of woman."

Agree wholeheartedly that Deirdre is exactly that and sidle over to linen stall.

"What you after? Not your normal stamping ground?" I say.

Deirdre doesn't look up, intent on fingering material with an expert touch, "Saw you giving up the sherry. You're a daft ninny. Haven't had a sniff of anything decent here – it's just a pile of dog's doo-doos."

"Buy something anyway."

"I've parted with twenty pence just to come in this rat hole. What's in the carrier bags?"

Show Deirdre my purchases. For once she's impressed. Not with cakes with cushion covers and table cloth. Holds them up and scrutinizes carefully, "Not bad. Table cloth maybe eighty years old, cushion covers, early American patchwork. I'll give you a fiver."

"I paid seven."

"Seven then."

"No ten."

"Ten! I'm a friend. By rights you should hand them over as an early Christmas present."

Deirdre gives me a tenner. I give tenner to stall holder. Deirdre's eyebrows disappear into her curls.

"You're mad."

"Cup of tea?"

"Not in here. I'm starting to itch. And don't at any future time offer me that cake or pie. They must be full of germs, ticks, fleas, termites ..."

October 18th

Kitten very plain. About ten weeks old, grey, black and white. Thin. Has bags under her grey eyes. Am smitten. After Morag and Vera leave I sit with her and try to entice her into chasing a piece of string. Finally kitten stretches out tentative paw. Remain on the floor, kitten wakefully asleep next to me. Think that this has not been a bad day. Amend thought to this has been a good day.

Think a bit about Deirdre and the conundrum of me liking

her with all her obvious faults far more than I like Morag and Vera who are decent good women.

Think a lot about Janice. But that is about all I'm good for at the moment: thinking.

October 19th

Caught Deirdre in flagrante kissing Smeg today. She looked slightly embarrassed and said, "I can't help it. I love Smeg."

Smeg powder blue with chrome name plate and very handsome as opposed to Dyson who is yellow and grey and untidy looking, as opposed to Atkins who is invisible and a hard task master, as opposed to Martin who is pale with ruddy cheeks and built on cuddly scale.

Enquire after Deirdre's relationship with newly acquired pink iPod, birthday present from Martin and capable of storing thousands of Deirdre's favourite tunes. Deirdre shakes curls. Says she has no time for iPod. She has not one single favourite tune. Can tolerate three minutes forty five seconds of Barry White under party conditions but that's about it.

"Where is iPod even as we speak?" I ask.

"No idea. Prefer Martin vastly to iPod."

Put the loves of Deirdre's life in preferential order: Lord Dudley, Smeg, Dyson, Martin, Nigella (this brand name of set of tea, coffee and sugar canisters in powder blue to keep company with Smeg), Tom Hanks, Ikea, Bluewater, John Lewis.

October 21st

*"We plough the fields and scatter
the good seed on the ground ..."*

Miriam has impressive baritone. Two seagulls sitting on fence of T.M. Accountancy back yard watch her with look of surprised admiration.

*"And it is fed and wa-atered
by God's almighty hand ..."*

She stops singing and we begin discussion as to whether it is *God Almighty's hand* or god's impressively large hand.

"Will take that one to my vicar".

Gulls cock heads to one side appear to be much enjoying our quasi religious discussion, beady eyes following the progress of our sandwiches to our mouths and away again. Miriam used to say we shouldn't feed them. Said, feed one and there'll be two hundred waiting out here by the end of the week. Now she says she's not so sure as vicar still considering question of whether sea gulls come within the same category as 'little children and lambs'.

Miriam says she is a convert to hymns. Says it's all very well everybody banging on about country, rock and blues having their roots in traditional melodies but what about the poor old hymn? Murmur something about gospel music and she says sharply, "Never mind about gospel music, it's easy to enjoy gospel music, hymns take a bit of hard work, test your vocal chords. What hymns do you know?"

Think hard and come up with "Those in peril on the sea."

"Good one Margaret! And another."

"To be a pilgrim?"

"Excellent. A stirring lyric," bangs fist into palm of other hand and the seagulls take to the sky.

October 22nd

Lit first fire of autumn by accident. Decided to set light to all till and bank receipts crumpled up and thrown into the fireplace. Forgot that underneath accumulated pile Georgie had laid a fire complete with paper spills and fire lighters. Fire started slowly but while I was out in the kitchen suddenly burst into life. Unseasonably warm morning but decided to enjoy flames. Another trace of Georgie eliminated.

New kitten rushed in, stared at flames and rushed out again. As yet new kitten unnamed. Deirdre has suggested *Deirdre* in consideration of kitten's rather regal bearing and fine head. Laura suggested *Tiffany* then *Dolores*, then *Nebuchadnezzer*.

Sat in armchair trying to pinpoint exactly when Georgie laid the fire. It was the week before she went away. Did she know she was going, perhaps thinking, "This is the last fire I'll lay in this house." Was it a relief or a regret? Did she not give it a passing thought? In future, whatever happens, whoever I meet, I'll let no woman get into the habit of laying fires for me.

October 23rd

Miriam, her vicar and *Eeugh!* ex-school chum Tabby arrive on my doorstep en masse. They form an apparently good natured crowd under the overhanging porch roof, jostling and laughing. I watch them from my bedroom window with alarm. Tabby has a large wheeled trolley with many labels of destination flapping from the trolley handle and straps. Trolley appears to be bulging. Tabby definitely not the deliverer of say my local paper, no Tabby looks as if she intends to stay some days. Am about to tiptoe away from window and hide in the back bedroom till my callers have gone away when Deirdre appears in her front garden carrying a designer watering can which from the way she's waving it back and forth, is empty.

"She's in," she shouts over, "Probably playing deaf. Knock and ring – that should rouse her."

Thinks: sometimes wonder whether Deirdre is friend or foe. Hurry downstairs, fling open front door and shout, "Hello and welcome."

All three step back blinking like little owls, "Do come in."

"Can I come in as well?" shouts Deirdre already tucking watering can behind topiarised weigelia and heading down her path. NB. Deirdre hides watering can because she imagines it is a temptation to burglars, which is also why all her terracotta pots, chimney pots and planters are chained to the wall, the lengths of chain concealed under mixture of pea gravel and purple slate chippings.

Tabby offers me the handle of her trolley and says, "You'll have to lift it off the ground. Wheels are muddy. There are pot holes the size of coal mine entrances along your road."

Carry trolley into kitchen. Guests divest themselves of coats etc. laying scarves and gloves on radiator, Deirdre divests herself of her lilac pashmina but keeps it close to hand as mistrusts guests. Hard to imagine Miriam, vicar or Tabby in lilac pashmina.

"I'll be mum," Deirdre says, "Earl Grey for everybody?"

Everybody disputes Earl Grey. Tabby would like hot water and a little full fat milk, Miriam wouldn't say no to Echinacea or Peppermint tea and the vicar wants tea strong enough to stand a teaspoon up in.

"Builder's bottom tea," Miriam says jocularly. Tabby whose still wearing her overcoat shudders and purses her lips but says nothing silenced by presence of woman vicar with arm draped affectionately round *Builder's bottom tea* woman. In a low voice Miriam says to vicar, At least I didn't say 'arse'.

Tabby and Deirdre flinch. Deirdre says, "And I'm so glad you didn't dude."

Ask for my tea just as it comes while opening a new packet of chocolate digestives.

"It comes as Earl Grey tea," Deirdre answers briskly and carries tray to table, "Now you've got milky Earl Grey, you've got watery Earl Grey and you," she plonks a mug in front of vicar, tea bag still bobbing on surface, "have got Builder's Bottom Earl Grey. Margaret, your Earl Grey's next to the kettle and mine's the cup and saucer. I'm not much of a 'mug' woman."

Deirdre takes her rightful place at the head of my kitchen table and looks brightly at everyone, "I don't think I know your gaggle of friends."

Make introductions. On reaching Tabby, Tabby says firmly, "I'm not a lesbian. I'm a single woman rather partial to her own company."

"Me too," says Deirdre through chocolate biscuit, "I live with Martin who's also partial to his own company. We come together for blissful moments."

Vicar nods wearing expression of great understanding and appreciation, says, "What more can we hope for than such a coming together?"

Miriam nudges her, "And of course god's love."

"Goes without saying. God's love is omnipresent," vicar says.

Deirdre looks baffled. Tabby strokes her chin and says heavily, "In your opinion, vicar."

Vicar spreads hands in multi-faith type of gesture and Deirdre says, "Whatever turns you on."

Feel it is time that I make my presence felt so ask Tabby, "So where are you en route to?"

"Here of course. I assume you received my emails."

Assert sorrowfully that I have no knowledge of emails even as the image of Tabby's two emails float in front of my inner eye, the two emails I'd instantly deleted without reading.

"How long were you intending to stay?"

"A week, ten days. Now you're sans Georgie I thought you could do with some company."

Am aghast. "Not possible," I blurt out, "Impossible."

Questioning faces turn in my direction. I play for time by dropping my biscuit on the floor and then scrabbling for it. Under the table retrieving biscuit look at four pairs of feet, Deirdre's blue suede bootees, Miriam and the vicar's matching brown leather walking boots and Tabby's black lace-ups. They are laced so tightly the top of her feet must bear a criss-cross pattern for some hours after shoe removal. I look at her shoes and hate them. She cannot stay in my house even for a night. Truly not possible.

Deirdre's face appears at an odd angle, "What are you doing down there?"

Chairs are pushed back, Miriam and the vicar are also peering at me. Not Tabby. I can see from her shoes that she's standing up. Above me I hear the rustle of the biscuit packet, she's helping herself to another while I am in torment! Pleadingly I stare meaningfully first at Miriam, then at Deirdre, finally at the vicar who suddenly grins lopsidedly at me and says, "I don't think you're in any fit state for visitors Margaret."

"I'm not," I say in a meek, mad voice.

Heads are withdrawn.

Hear vicar say authoritatively, "Obviously we've all arrived at Margaret's house at a difficult time, the best thing would be for us to leave quietly."

Tabby expostulates, munching as she does so, "I'm going nowhere. This represents my autumn break."

Miriam says, "If you refuse to leave I will stand here and repeat the word 'arse' or worse."

Deirdre queries, "Is that absolutely necessary? Now come along – Tabby is it? I'll drive you back to the station."

"As I said before I'm going nowhere."

From under the table I call out, "Please make her go away."

Tabby's face comes into view, to one side and furious, "Is this any way to treat an old and valued friend?"

Miriam's walking boots approach Tabby's black lace-ups and Tabby's head shoots upwards and out of sight, "I must protest ..." she protests.

Vicar grabs coats, scarves and gloves and she and Miriam frog-march Tabby from my kitchen, "What about my trolley?" she shouts.

Vicar says, "Deirdre bring the trolley."

"I'm not strong enough to carry her trolley."

"Of course you are. Bring it!"

Deirdre's head drops back below table level, "You owe me, you daft munchkin."

Trolley rises off the floor. Deirdre's blue suede bootees pad out of kitchen. Front door slams. All is quiet. Kitten bounces in through cat flap and joins me under the table. Sits watching me eagerly, waiting for play or affection.

October 26th

Feel much better. Initially awkward when next see Miriam and Deirdre but not a problem. Miriam robustly kind and Deirdre amused. Says Martin roared and it's not easy to make Martin roar. On telephone Laura diagnoses a mini-breakdown.

October 27th

Receive Postcard from Janice. A field of scarlet poppies. She writes, "Hope all's well with you and Georgie." Then two words heavily inked out. "Love Janice". Inspect inked over words under halogen light plus torch, am certain they are *miss* and *you*.

October 28th

By way of recompense agree to go with Miriam's mother to visit Mrs. Ferguson who is in hospital after being mugged. Miriam and vicar had already booked ten days in Venice, the City of Romance and so were not available.

In taxi Miriam's mother said the very thought of hospitals gave her palpitations and she doesn't know how she'll get on if she was ever really ill. Said *it would be better if Miriam took her out and shot her*. Murmured, "Surely not?" However once inside the hospital Miriam's mother becomes energized, sends me off in search of a wheelchair for Mrs. Ferguson and makes herself unwelcome with the flower seller by using the Latin names for the flowers she wants: I'll take a dozen *Lathyrus odoratus*, a few *solidago canadensis* and a bunch of *Matthiola incana*.

"We've come to see Mary Ferguson," Miriam's mother tells the ward sister.

The ward sister eyes the wheelchair which I've purloined

from outside Intensive Care and says, "You won't need that wheelchair, Mrs. Ferguson can't be moved."

Miriam's mother ignores this, "We thought we'd take her for a turn around the gardens – she's used to plenty of fresh air."

"We don't have a garden, just a car park and as I said before, she can't be moved."

"We've come a very long way haven't we Margaret?"

I agree that we have. The ward sister sits down and opens a file. We wait. After a few minutes the ward sister looks up from the file and says, "Yes?"

Miriam's mother leans over her desk, "Are you going to tell us something more from that file?"

"No this is an entirely different patient's file," and she waves her hand dismissively at us.

We find Mrs. Ferguson with her leg hoisted high in the air. She seems to be asleep. Miriam's mother sidles up next to the bed, "Mary, Mary Ferguson, it's Veronica and also Margaret, Miriam's little friend."

Mrs. Ferguson opens her eyes, "Veronica?"

"Yes."

"And Margaret, Miriam's little friend?"

"Yes."

"How delightful."

"Yes isn't it? Look I'm wearing that red coat you set aside the other week," and Miriam's mother moves to the foot of bed and raises both arms so that Mrs. Ferguson's vision is full of her and the red coat.

"It suits you. Red's your colour." She closes her eyes and says, "I've had the hell of a time."

"You poor thing. Don't talk about it if it's painful," Miriam's mother scampers back to Mrs. Ferguson's side and begins to stroke her forehead.

"I want to talk about it. Doctor says it's therapeutic. Don't bottle things up he says."

"There, there," says Miriam's mother, "Margaret be a lovey and get a vase. See the flowers Veronica, all your favourite pastels."

"Yes very nice but can I tell my tale or not?"

184

"In your own good time. No apples or grapes?"

Found vase and filled it with water. Mrs. Ferguson just embarking on story.

"... standing at the bus stop outside Barclays Bank just tucking my money into my inner sanctum," Mrs. Ferguson pats an area between her breasts, "and this old chap, he must have been at least my age, raced past me on one of those mobility scooter's and grabbed the money out of my hand, hared off at top speed with it."

"And the blighter knocked you down?" Miriam's mother asks moving the Golden Rod to the back of the vase.

"No, I waved my walking stick at him and yelled, "Stop thief", and as I raised my stick the bus came up behind me and knocked it out of my hand."

"And you with it I've no doubt?" Miriam's mother says opening Mrs. Ferguson's bedside cabinet and peering inside.

"No. I bent to retrieve my stick. I should know better than to bend down with cataracts because then would you believe it, I fell over?"

"Oh I'd believe anything. This is a very nice bed jacket – new or Hospice?"

"New. Toppled into the gap between the pavement and the bus. I could have been killed. Luckily the doors closed on my coat which meant only my leg was trapped. If I'd gone headfirst I wouldn't be here to tell the tale."

"Well," said Miriam's mother, "there's a grand adventure. What do we do for refreshments?"

October 29th

While Miriam away I'm working full time. Am almost in a secure financial position. Will consider giving up Russell's cleaning job nearer Christmas. Wonder why I'm so reluctant to leave? Possible masochistic fascination with Lorraine Carter who now completely ignores me. Left mop head very dirty for five days in hope of tempting an outburst. Nothing. I am beneath her contempt at the moment. Might even consider breaking bucket. Did not go to October's Supperette Club but may go to November's.

October 30th

Met Deirdre at *Bittlesea Bay Café*. Said she'd also received a post card from Janice. Found myself asking, "Did she mention my name?"

Deirdre looked surprised, "No. The card was for me, nothing to do with you. Why would she mention you?"

Own post uninspiring. Autumn bulb catalogue offering me a free cuckoo clock with every order over fifty pounds and a leaflet for Damart nightwear. Feel I must be getting old as actually toyed with ordering two pairs of long johns and matching vests. Thought that if I ordered, the day I put on Damart long john underwear would be the day I would meet the new love of my life who would then be sadly disappointed as I slipped seductively out of outer clothes and began struggling with tight fitting long johns, however if I didn't tempt fate then I would never meet the new love of my life and get that opportunity to be embarrassed. Filled in form and cheque. Destroyed form and cheque. Destroyed Damart leaflet.

November

November 2nd

Check e-mails. Friends Reunited telling me I now have seven school friends waiting to speak to me. Who are these people? Have never had seven school friends. Check before deleting. Weed, weed, bully, big head, unknown, weed. Delete. Am always hopeful that Linda Hughes from Primary School might want to get in touch. I was never a great friend of hers nor even a minor one, I admired her from afar. Have hopes that one day Linda H. might look back over the years and wonder what happened to cheery Margaret Charlecote. But not today. Also a message from the Bittlesea Bay Badger etc. announcing a talk by Mr. Raymond Wheeler on December 1st. Says talk will be advertised in the *What's On* section of the *Listening Ear*.

November 3rd

Visited Mrs. Ferguson in hospital without Miriam's mother.

Mrs. Ferguson asleep but Mr. Ferguson was there, a white haired chap. Distinguished looking. Talk was of Noreen and Peter's Christmas wedding. Peter has been promoted to manager and Noreen is starting a word processing course at the local college.

Mr. Ferguson said, "What about you Margaret, you're leaving it a bit late?"

Explained evasively that I had once been engaged to Ronald but I'd lost him.

"Falklands War?," he asked sympathetically.

"To another."

"Bad luck. Plenty more fish in the sea. You should join a club."

Mrs. Ferguson's eyelids fluttered open, "Margaret's a lesbian, you fool," she said.

"A what?"

"A lesbian. It's all the fashion these days."

Gave Mr. Ferguson a sickly smile. Mr. Ferguson looked very disappointed in me, looked about to make a citizen's arrest, "Good Grief. Dear oh dear oh dear. Ladylike woman like you."

November 5th

Bonfire night. Firework display on cliff top overlooking *Bittlesea Bay Café*. Went en masse with Miriam and her vicar, Deirdre and Martin. Martin protested that he hated crowds, hated children, hated babies, push chairs, fresh air and found the night sky infinitely depressing.

Vicar prompted to expound on God's infinity, likening it to a night sky or any sky for that matter.

"God's what?" Martin roars. (Not from anger only to be heard over the shouting voices of about five hundred people.)

"His infinity. It's enormous. Limitless. Without end."

"I know what infinity means vicar ..."

"Infinity, infinitely. These long words make you think, don't they?" Deirdre interjects, scenting a possible locking of Martin's horns with vicar's dog collar.

Whoosh! Goes the first rocket exploding into a fountain of red stars.

"Quick," Deirdre shouts, "We're not in place yet."

She dashes at the crowd. The crowd although standing with

its back to Deirdre senses her rapid approach and parts like the Red Sea. We rush through in Deirdre's jet stream to arrive breathless at the very front of the crowd and perilously near to the cliff edge.

"Should we be pushing in?" Miriam asks of anyone.

"Yes," says Martin, "otherwise I'd be forced to go home immediately."

"Bad feng shui to stand behind people," which I know Deirdre has just made up.

Whoosh! Whoosh! Crackle! Crackle! Phizz! More fireworks. The infinitely depressing night sky is lit up by brilliant shining stars falling in the shapes of flowers, palm trees and more stars. We the crowd lift up our faces as if the stars are magical drops of rain.

"Ooh!" we chorus, "Aah." Some "Bravos". From Deirdre, "Fan-bloody-tastic!"

Miriam and the vicar are grinning like children, their faces, transfixed, transported.

"Don't look at them, look at the fireworks you ninny," Deirdre says.

A good evening. Pub after. No arguments. All mellow. Martin tells his Mussolini joke. We laugh. Me and Deirdre find it even more side-splitting now that we've heard it at least fifteen times.

November 7th

Phone call from Mr. Wheeler. There is something he'd like to discuss. Whenever convenient. Seven thirty pm this evening would suit him very well. Have become quite at home in Mr. Wheeler's kitchen but for the first time ever he invites me into *the lounge*. There is a roaring log fire, two comfortable armchairs on either side and a tray with two sherry glasses and a decanter sitting on a circular coffee table.

"I don't hold with crisps," he said.

"Me neither," I replied just to be affable.

"Well sit down. I could offer you a plain digestive biscuit – that's rather nice with sherry."

Say no, a sherry on its own would be … just the ticket. Could see from Mr. Wheeler's expression he approved of this phrase.

"It's Harvey's," he says.

"Excellent." Refrained from smacking lips but did manage to look thrilled. Seated in armchairs, sherries poured, we paused. Mr. Wheeler scrutinized the carpet pattern as if pattern held answer to esoteric mysteries. I also looked. Pattern so old fashioned as to be almost cutting edge, orange and yellow autumn leaves on an olive green background. In process of formulating an admiring comment when Mr. Wheeler said, "I suppose you know I'm doing this talk."

"I wasn't sure if it was you."

He shrugged his shoulders irritably, "Yes it is me although why they had to use my first name – I can't stand Raymond."

"It's not a bad name ..."

"It's not a name I'd have chosen." Steely glint in Mr. Wheeler's eyes. Felt this was not the time to express my own aversion to name of Margaret, "What I wanted to know Margaret, was whether you'd mind if I used your badger anecdote in my talk? Also I'd like to take a snap of your back gate. Show the kind of damage badgers are capable of when desperate."

"This is going to be a positive talk about badgers isn't it?" I gulped sherry. Did not want to fall out with Mr. Wheeler but had realised over past months that there can be a hard nosed, unsentimental side to him.

"Of course it will be a positive talk," he barked, "Why ever would I give a negative talk? I like badgers god damnit!" He put his glass down with quite a bang on the tray and rubbed his forehead.

"Are you all right Mr. Wheeler?"

"Not really. To be frank preparing for this talk has brought back memories." He vigorously attacked the fire with a poker. Didn't know what to say so sipped sherry and waited.

"Years ago, in my wife's time there was a badger run through all our back gardens. This was before the gardens were fenced off. The badgers were something the two of us had in common. We'd sit in the kitchen with the house lights off and watch them. Badgers are very playful and affectionate with each other, it was a pleasure, almost an honour to be allowed to watch," he pulled out a large check handkerchief and blew his nose, said, "Oh heck Margaret, I'm sorry about this. Look all I wanted to know was whether you minded me

189

using your anecdote, I didn't intend to give you my life history."

"Please go on," I said gently.

"Not much to tell," he said brusquely, "nothing that makes me look very decent. After she left I was the first one in this block of six houses to put up a fence. You see I didn't care about badgers anymore. I didn't want to sit and look at them on my own. They broke through those fences. Do you know what I did next?"

I shook my head.

"I lined the fences at the point where they were breaking through with sheet metal. That stopped them."

"I've never noticed any metal on my side."

"It's there. On *my* side. Going right down into the earth."

"Well we must remove it ... if that's ok with you?"

"That won't bring the badgers back."

"But it's the principal, so if they wanted to come back they could."

He said, "You are a wooly minded liberal Margaret."

"There are worse things to be."

Mr. Wheeler and his badger story has upset me. Here I am writing sad tales again when I'd somehow hoped for a better run up to Christmas. Have spent some time thinking about Mr. Wheeler and the parallels if any that can be drawn. Actually hope there won't be any parallels. Am determined not to box myself in like he did. I *will* move on from Georgie!

Put badger talk in diary. Wednesday 1st of December. Thinks: might make a party of it. Wonder whether to ask Janice. Pick up telephone and dial half her number. Replace the receiver.

November 9th
Good news! Lorraine Carter is leaving.

November 10th
Miriam tells me in strictest confidence that she and the vicar plan to buy a house next year. Do not immediately say, "What about your mother?" as this might diminish Miriam's recently discovered enthusiasm for life.

Say, "What a fabulous idea. Whereabouts?"

"Nowhere in particular as yet, first we need funds."

Nod sympathetically. Encouraged, Miriam asks me to a clothing party which the vicar is holding. A clothing party? Vicar will have a rail of women's clothes, a brochure, a size chart and a video. I as one of the fortunate customers who will have *the opportunity to buy at cost price plus vicar's commission various spring outfits in the latest fashion styles.*

Explain that though happy to support clothing party *latest fashion styles* may not be my own personal style.

"Oh don't be such a kill-joy Margaret, your image could do with some updating."

On way home mull over Miriam's personal style, adjectives spring to mind: dowdy, rugged and washed-out.

November 12th

Miriam says vicar investigating possibilities of pyramid selling scheme and kruger rands. Do not want to be accused of being a kill-joy so look animated. Miriam says vicar has a first class financial head on her shoulders. Respond with strange whistling sound.

November 13th

Meet Deirdre at *Bittlesea Bay Cafe* at Deirdre's request. Not her usual cheery tone of voice more peremptory order to one of her many subordinates as in cleaner, Morag and Vera, Mr. Wheeler. When I arrive she is already ensconced her back to the view, hands folded over a lime green raffia handbag. Looks up at me unsmilingly and says, "You're in the chair. Earl Grey as per usual … and a scone … with jam … and cream."

"What about the muesli and okra diet?"

Gives me a cool stare, "What about it? You forgot that one didn't you? Constant dieters or inconstant dieters?"

Express bewilderment while experiencing slight queasiness in stomach. Consider option of collapsing gracefully on floor with recurrence of mini-breakdown but caff floor is very muddy and I'm wearing my new fleece lined denim jacket. By the time I return to the table with the tray Deirdre has unfolded a copy of the *Listening Ear* and opened it at the Letters page. One letter is ringed in red.

Dear Listening Ear, skateboarders, train spotters, surf boarders,

191

cyclists, mobile phone users, mobility scooter users, Baby on Boarders, table monopolizers, dog owners, Pot Noodle eaters, Martin J. Storm troopers, four wheel drive drivers, electric blanketeers, Uncle Tom Cobbley and all – I would be interested to know your opinions re. the decision to turn our one cinema into a multi-plex and Pizzeria? Surely corporate business money would be better spent in providing a Wild Life Park or a Wild West Rodeo? May the Force be with you A. Oakley, Jedi Knight.

"It is you, isn't it?" she says as I pour her tea.

"What makes you think that?"

"Mobile phone users and Pot Noodle eaters. You are the only person I know without a mobile and we are the only couple you know who were on a Pot Noodle diet for the best part of the Millennium year."

"That doesn't mean it's me."

"Jedi Knight?"

"*That* doesn't mean it's me."

"I think it does."

"What does Martin think?"

"He thinks it's the librarian who turned nasty when he left our car parked across the library disabled bays while we were on holiday."

"It was just a bit of fun, Deirdre, that got out of hand."

"I'm not laughing," and indeed she wasn't. Had never seen Deirdre's rosebud lips in such a tiny pinched dot.

"Can I make amends?'

"I want you to stop writing letters to the paper. If you don't I'll be forced to tell Martin and he will be very angry. He's built the librarian up into an adversary on the scale of *The Riddler* in *Batman*. It's given him a new lease of life. Instead of just the *Corner Coffee Shop* he's spending two hours in the library every day reading the newspapers and making notes of her suspicious behavior. Finding out that it's only you, would be a huge disappointment."

"Couldn't I start writing with a librarian bias?"

"Definitely not."

"Won't he be disappointed if A. Oakley disappears?"

"He'll get over it. He's found he rather likes the library – they've got a little garden where he can have a coffee and a cigarette."

"Are we still friends?"

"I don't think I can ever be friends with you again after this."

"What about another jam and cream scone washed down with fresh Earl Grey?"

Deirdre folded up the newspaper, appeared deep in thought, "That might go some way towards mending our rift."

November 16th

Meet Vera in the street. She wants to know what my opinion is on Deirdre's newly planted Norwegian Maple? Admit to having no opinion. Vera says, "Not even if it grows to eighty foot, blocks out all the light and undermines our foundations?"

Murmur, "Surely not?"

Vera says, "Morag's writing to the local paper and the council. She says there are laws."

"Indeed there are."

"So you'll back us up?"

Say briskly, "At the minute it's only four foot high, when it reaches twenty feet then I'll back you up."

Leave Vera going on about *people who sit on fences.*

November 18th

L.C's leaving party in Russell's canteen a damp squib. Twelve people including me, LC, Peter, Noreen and a man from Head Office. Whip round during previous week produced enough money (with staff discount) to buy catalogue number SLBE/8721 or Side Light in Bronze Effect, 8721. Bronze Effect lamp base in the shape of a golfer wearing plus fours and a flat cap. Could almost have represented Lorraine Carter in plus fours and flat cap apart from handle bar moustache. Also sufficient cash left over for bunch of forced Sunflowers from Morrisons. L.C. said she was *quite overwhelmed by our generosity.* Man from Head Office presented a cheque, a funereal bouquet of lilies and white chrysanths, and a kiss. L.C. bobbed appreciative curtsey as if in presence of a royal personage. We clapped. Then Avis from the canteen directed us to two tables of nibbles. Best part of the evening. As I heaped crab sticks, profiteroles, mini-quiches and pickled onions onto paper plate, L.C. nudged my elbow and said in a low voice, "Can we talk?"

Retrieved pickled onions from fruit salad bowl before replying in truculent tone, "What now?" Suddenly no longer felt the need to kowtow.

"Perhaps tomorrow? Say nine o'clock in the Felgate Arms."

"Past my bed time," I quipped, "but ok."

November 19th

Lounge Bar, Felgate Arms. Got there dead on nine. LC. already ensconced in curve of horse shoe shaped cubicle, a bottle of wine poking out of an ice bucket and two glasses. She was smoking a cigarette and looked ... nervous?

Took off jacket and sat down. Left some distance between me and her. Noticed her sharp face looked tired. Suppressed that thought. Not the time to start softening. She rested her cigarette in the ashtray and poured the wine.

"I hope you don't mind if I smoke?"

I shrugged. "Whatever." (Thank you Deirdre for all the casual words and phrases I've picked up from you.)

"Cheers," we said and tapped glasses.

"Margaret I owe you an apology."

Crumbs! "Yes you do."

"But first can I tell you a story? I promise to keep it short."

Shrugged again. No way was Lorraine Carter going to win me over after months of rudeness and intimidation.

"This happened a long time ago. I was in my late twenties. I lived with a woman who ... I loved very much. I thought – I believed she felt the same way about me," she took a deep drag on her cigarette before continuing, "we'd been together eight years – seemed like we had something special and long lasting. I could see that getting old together stuff happening to us. How long did your relationship last?"

For the first time she looked directly at me, straight into my eyes. Was I seeing the real Lorraine Carter behind the hard bitten bully or was this just another mask?

"Nearly ten years," I said.

"You did better than I did."

"So what happened?"

"She changed. I can't quite pinpoint where or when. I thought I was imagining her withdrawal, the way she no longer quite focused on me or our life together. Took her a whole year to absent herself completely. One weekend she stage managed an argument. Brought it out of the blue yet made it my fault and symptomatic of all that was wrong between us. That evening she left and never came back. Some friends who I'd thought were *our* friends came and took away her stuff."

"Was she seeing someone else?"

Lorraine poured herself more wine, my own glass sat still untouched.

"Of course she was. I saw them together a few times, they didn't see me. I still can't get over how they could look happy and carefree when they'd just destroyed someone. You see I found out where the woman lived. Had to hire a car to get there. When Georgie left she took my car, said I was lucky ..."

"Georgie?"

"Georgie. And of course the other woman was you. Our world is quite small isn't it?"

November 20th

Thinking back to the beginning of me and Georgie. I remember there was a woman called Lorrie. She was giving Georgie a tough time. I recall Georgie saying, "Lorrie's like a clinging vine. If I let her, she'd choke me."

Had Georgie said that about me to Stella? The awful thing was I could imagine myself metaphorically 'choking' Georgie. It's the obvious reaction when you think someone you love is pulling away from you – to hold them tighter.

Georgie seems to have the ability to move on, leaving distraught partners in her wake ... stuck, bewildered. Believing they were inadequate and responsible for Georgie stopping loving them. Except Stella. Stella must have hurt Georgie a lot. She was no clinging vine.

I think about Georgie more analytically now and with curiosity. How she never lied only withheld the truth or side stepped it. All those years living with each other, yet I didn't understand her at all. What had she got out of being the way she was? So cool and aloof. Always seeming to possess the right answers. She must have been special but I can't remember how she was special.

195

Georgie, Georgie, Georgie. You've caused me so much pain. Oh dear, it is so sore, this hidden thing I know to be my heart.

November 21st
See A4 poster for Miriam's *Clothing Party* in the Hospice Shop window. In lilac script it says, *Fab Clothing offers YOU a chance to Try and Buy at genuine rock bottom prices!* Then a drawing of blonde woman reminiscent of Doris Day at start of comedic film career marching across A4 with smart carrier bag. Doris Day look-a-like wearing box jacket and knee length skirt. Have Miriam and vicar gone mad?

November 22nd
Janice rang. Speaking very quickly she said she'd bumped into Deirdre in the shopping precinct and been told that Georgie and I had split up for good. If I wasn't ready to speak to her she quite understood but she needed to know that I was ok. Speaking equally quickly I said that I was surprisingly ok and very glad to hear her voice. Janice said she was very glad to hear my voice.

November 23rd
Wake up with horrible feeling of panic. Kitten jumps first on bed then on me.

"In a minute Kitten," which Kitten who is proving highly intelligent immediately understands, she curls up against my knees and purrs.

I'd woken from dreams of Janice. Thinks: there is nothing between us (Janice and me), apart from possibly an imagined (on my part) rapport — but if there was — once again I know nothing about her apart from spurious details, she likes tea not coffee, likes face painting and is a druid party goer, also an excellent landscape gardener. She has a courageous face, can look sullen which doesn't mean she is — everything else, that she is kind, sensitive, I've taken on trust. Can't bear to go through a year like this again yet don't want to spend the rest of my life loveless. Inside I have this miserable certainty that it will always be me that is left behind. Abandoned.

Feed Kitten, ring Laura. Have never cried on the telephone before. Laura appalled. Starts crying as well. Says she is desperately unhappy because Iris has started running for an hour every morning. I stop crying and tell her that running for an hour in the morning doesn't need to be threatening. Laura says Iris has a running partner who has perfect muscle tone which she could never aspire to as it would mean making huge personal sacrifices as in giving up smoking, drinking and late nights. Suddenly says, "Oh oh, they're back," and rings off.

November 25th
It's official Tom and Barry have split up. Tom says *more in sorrow than anger*. He asks Miriam and I out for a drink. Also vicar but she can't come as there is a church meeting to discuss forthcoming Carol Service.

We go to pub that is rumoured to be gay. Tom clocks two elderly gentlemen playing *Shove Halfpenny* and whispers, "What do you think?"

Miriam says, *Possibly*. I look unconvinced. However, when one claps the other on the shoulder Tom takes that as incontrovertible proof that they're a long term couple and there's hope for him yet. Seem always to be avoiding kill-joy accusation – nod agreement. A low key evening.

November 26th
Arrive at small room off St. Dunstan's church hall. Miriam's mother is seated behind a table of cups and saucers, Mrs. Ferguson and the vicar are manhandling a dress rail of brightly coloured garments out of an alcove. Both wear tape measures round their necks. Spot Miriam. She is in charge of video and portable television. There are five other women and one man with a leatherette shopping bag.

We have all paid two pounds to get in which includes as much tea and biscuits as we can consume. We sit on a row of wooden chairs. Miriam closes the door.

"Ah, thank you," says vicar, "Lights please."

Miriam switches off light and stumbles back to her place at video control. Television screen – perhaps ten inches wide? Assembled audience peers at Fab Clothing sales video. Camera pans across large hall seemingly packed with lady mayoresses, all smiling and clapping gloved hands. Pan back to catwalk. Young women dressed as lady mayoresses slouch up and down drawing attention to braiding on cuff, button detail, ingenious kick pleat in back of skirt.

One lady mayoress model in close up demonstrates six different ways with an elasticated flower bracelet – bracelet, necklace, pony tail scrunch, bandeau, belt and hippy head band. Video finishes. Miriam switches light back on. I clap.

In front of us vicar stands beaming confidently hands clasped in front of her. Will she start the sale with a prayer? No. Says to man with shopping bag, "I'm afraid I'm going to have to ask you to step outside as us ladies will be trying on."

"I've come on behalf of my wife," man blusters.

"I'm sure you have and here's a brochure to take back to her."

Exit man looking miffed.

Vicar says, "The secret to *Fab Clothing*'s success is versatility which means to you and me, i.e. women on limited budgets – economy."

NB. Should have said vicar is wearing black tights, leotard over dog collar. Mrs. Ferguson hands vicar a tube of emerald green cloth. Like a magician, vicar demonstrates how tube can take her from the office – tube becomes a knee length skirt with useful pockets, to a cocktail bar – pulls tube up to under her armpits and it is a skin tight dress – to a grand ball. Wow! Turns out that tube is double layered. Vicar peels top layer down to make skin tight ankle length skirt again with useful pockets. Miriam's mother and I clap.

"Hold it folks," says vicar, "You ain't seen nothin' yet."

Takes off tube. Turns pockets inside out. Undoes two invisible rows of poppers in pockets and hey presto tube has become a hooded short sleeved top ideal to combat light spring showers. Everyone claps.

Vicar shows us more wonders none as impressive as tube. Vicar could sell ice cubes to Eskimos. Everyone buys tube. I buy three in emerald, scarlet and black.

At home find I can make skirt, long skirt and cocktail frock but not hooded top. Almost asphyxiate myself trying to free my head from useful pocket. Realise tubes are made of a horrid polyester jersey which may not breathe. Have spent ninety pounds. Hugely resent Miriam and vicar.

November 27th

Just when I'm thinking that Margaret of *Bittlesea Bay* must have dropped off the map, Laura rings back re. her running opponent. She's ringing from her mother's understair cupboard so her voice is slightly muffled due to winter coats and general lack of oxygen. Conversation interrupted with, "Fags mum. And ashtray. Chop chop," and later when I hear a burst of the frantic opening music to *Hawaii 50*, "Mum can you turn it down?"

"Another boxed set?" I ask.

"Given up jigsaws – is boxed set mad."

Laura says the reason she's stopped worrying about Iris's running partner is that she's seen running partner's romantic partner and the woman's stupendous.

Ask, "Isn't Iris stupendous?"

Laura pauses then says, "Iris is an acquired taste. Now what about you? Still suicidal?"

Explain that I was never suicidal more very depressed. Also there is someone I rather like who I think might rather like me but frankly I'm frightened of falling in love and being hurt again.

"Hmm," said Laura, "Yes I will have a Guinness. Aren't you rather jumping the gun – you might get several years happiness in before being hurt again? Thanks mum. Cheers."

"Cheers. But how can I believe that someone really cares about me?"

"Because nobody's going to put up with you for several years if they're not at least fond of you."

Change tack slightly while I have Laura's attention, "So what am I doing wrong that makes them stop being fond of me?"

"You're not doing anything wrong. Anyone can get tired of their favourite meal if they have it every night and mum says some relationships aren't meant to last forever. Thank you mum."

"Is your mum listening in?"

"She was just dusting the extension."

November 29th

Spot Janice's white lorry parked outside my house as I walk up

199

hill. She must have seen me because she suddenly leapt out of the cab. Janice does not look sullen – she looks happy. Immediately imagine she's about to tell me that she's met a fabulous new woman in the last few days. Steel myself for bad news.

However, Janice starts whistling self-consciously and wipes wing mirror with her sleeve as I approach. Just somehow know that in this instance, I am the reason she looks happy.

Our faces move unfamiliarly together. I kiss her ear, she kisses a strand of my hair. We go indoors and I say, "Should we get started, there's not much daylight left?"

Janice blinks and looks confused. Instantly we both become scarlet faced. Quickly explain that I am talking about digging up sheet metal from Mr. Wheeler's side of the fence. Janice nods and grins. Goes back out to her lorry for her pickax. I hear her chuckling to herself. Get two spades from my shed.

Mr. Wheeler out on Watch but his back gate was open. It proves very hard job. He'd dug the sheet metal into the ground with a vengeance, it went down at least two foot. Felt sad while digging thinking of Mr. Wheeler then only middle aged blocking out any reminder of good times. Said as much to Janice.

She said, "Never mind Mr. Wheeler, what about you Margaret?"

We both paused for a breather. Very cold afternoon but hot work. Told her I was still pretty miserable about myself. Said, I'd lost confidence and felt it was hard to look forward to my future. Muttered the word *trust*. Said it wasn't easy to believe in a happy future when I seemed to have a prescribed life pattern that started with high hopes and ended with someone, (me) feeling like a dropped stitch. Laughed weakly. Janice didn't laugh at all.

"You have to take risks sometimes. We all have to," she said.
"I know."

"I think we're there," she said, "The metal sheets. I can get my pickax underneath and lever them up if you hold them steady."

We worked together. At first the sheets wouldn't budge, seemed determinedly stuck in the mud. I had a fleeting thought that Georgie would have done this on her own or got

Nic or Mr. Wheeler's help. Where would I have been? Making tea for the workers. On the periphery.

At last they came out. We refilled the deep holes but left a little space between the ground and the bottom of the fence. Just in case.

It was dark, too dark to read Janice's face. I said, "Do you remember us meeting months ago at the Glass Bar?"

Janice bent forward patting the earth with the back of her spade, "Yes," she said.

"You made quite an impression on me, I wrote about you in my diary."

"Yet you didn't recognise me when you met me again."

"No, but you were familiar."

"I recognised you straight away. It was," she said straightening up, "like fate."

November 30th

Go with Martin and Deirdre to see *Meatloaf-The Story*. None of us were ever fans of *Meatloaf* but Martin has been given free tickets by someone who did the theatre lighting and Deirdre felt this would give her a chance to air her new 'Rock Chick' leather jacket. Martin seems unsure of this leather jacket – it is a step in a new fashion direction for Deirdre. Jacket petrol blue. On back is an arrow piercing a silver heart and the words, *Born to be Very Bad!*

Martin tells us sternly in the foyer, "Now understand you two, this isn't the real *Meatloaf*, so when the chap comes on I don't want to hear groans of disappointment – you'll show me up."

Apparently the real *Meatloaf* is about six foot two and this chap is about a foot shorter and square shaped. We troop in. Deirdre is surprised that we don't have a box and that we have to share our row with other members of the audience. She keeps shuddering and fiddling with her hair.

"Sit still," Martin hisses.

Mini-Meatloaf bounces on with wonderful, glorious, fantastic, incredibly beautiful woman pretending to be Cher and Bonnie Tyler. The *Bittlesea Bay* audience goes wild apart from me, Martin and Deirdre. Martin at least nods his head to the music. Glance at Deirdre. She wears a strange fixed smile which I know means she's thinking, "This is no place for a Debenhams girl."

In the interval, old style ice cream usherettes march in front of the stage and I'm the first one in the queue. Bring back the tubs. Martin in great good humour, Deirdre icily quiet. Accepts tub between thumb and index finger as if it is a specimen and a poor one.

"Surprisingly good," says Martin.

I agree, Mini-Meatloaf is surprisingly good also ice cream tub, "And what about Bonnie Tyler look-alike?" I say with enthusiasm.

"I think they both stink," Deirdre says succinctly tapping away with her wooden spoon at the rock hard ice cream. However, when the finale comes, even Deirdre is swept up in the excitement. We, the whole audience, are on our feet singing along to *Bat out of Hell*.

December

December 1st
Go with Janice to *BBBP Society* talk held at the *Palm Court Hotel* on the sea front. Not really a hotel more a bed and breakfast. We are directed into the dining room where tables have been folded up and leant against the wall. We sit down on a variety of chairs.

I recognise Monica and other members. Also Morag and Vera. There are at least twelve more people. These Mr. Wheeler refers to in a loud undertone as *Jo Public*. Man in trilby hat introduces himself to Mr. Wheeler and says he's from the *Listening Ear* and does Mr. Wheeler object to being photographed? Mr. Wheeler doesn't mind at all, in fact directs *Listening Ear* man to his best side. NB. Mr. Wheeler's best side gives the impression that he has a full head of hair, Mr. Wheeler's worst side gives the impression that all hair is trying to escape over a domed hillock.

Vera who is Mr. Wheeler's assistant for the evening hands out photo copies with blurred black and white photograph at the top, possibly of a badger, possibly a bulky black bin bag. Mr. Wheeler coughs and we settle down into attentive silence. He explains that he'd hoped to give a slide show but had been unable to lay his hands on the relevant equipment. However he had put together a series of twelve slides and his neighbour Vera had donated her plastic slide viewer for the evening – could we pass these around while he proceeds with his talk?

"Please do return both box and slides to me at the end," he said.

Feel rather proud of slide depicting the splintered lower section of my back gate.

At some point during the talk Janice takes my hand.

December 2nd
Met Janice in rumoured to be gay pub.

December 3rd
Met Janice in pub.

December 4th
Janice to dinner. Janice tells me that she and her gardening team have a three week job hard landscaping a big garden in the Midlands. Felt physically sick. So reminiscent of Georgie's excuses.

We talked. Janice said gently, "I'll telephone you and you can telephone me any time of day or night. I can't make up for how Georgie treated you, you have to learn to trust me."

Promises to be back by Christmas. I take gulp of air and say, "Look, I won't telephone or expect you to telephone me, I want to get over this fear and make a fresh start."

Janice lopes off into the night. So far she hasn't stayed over. I'm waiting for some imaginary green light to proceed. Sit up late with Kitten on my knee. Realise that one of the things I most like about Janice is that she's so straightforward, treats me as a friend yet we seem to be much more than friends. Georgie was never straightforward. And I recognise that never knowing what Georgie was thinking, doing, feeling was what had undermined me, made me the puppy or the whimperer. I had knowledge now. I wasn't just … loving in the dark. Oh sod it. Must stop writing and get to bed.

December 6th
Receive Christmas card from Tabby. Picture of a horse looking philosophical. Inside Tabby's written, *Where our friendship goes from here is up to you. Season's greetings.*

Send card to Tabby. Choose cheerful, cheeky robin. Enclose short note suggesting that perhaps in New Year we might meet up say half way between each other's house for lunch.

December 8th
Go Christmas shopping with Deirdre. First stop is – Ikea. Mildly quibble as Deirdre starts measuring the length, height and depth of a linen cushioned sofa, "Christmas shopping Deirdre? Gifts for other people?"

She ignores me, "Write this down," she says. I scrabble in my bag for paper and pen. She dictates, I write. She double checks my writing.

"What do you think of the colour?"

"Off white?"

"Yes."

"What about your white leather settees?"

"Sofas," she corrects me, "Look, they're fine for *Bittlesea Bay* but they do not yell London Town."

"But we live in *Bittlesea Bay*."

Patiently as if I'm a small child, "We – not you – me and Martin, want our living space including garden area to replicate cutting edge London."

Squeak, "Reproduction Victorian lamp post?"

"That's an ironic statement. Can we get on?"

We get on to coffee tables and shelving. Time passes. For lunch we retire to the car park as Deirdre doesn't care for Ikea food. She's packed a hamper. Replete we tilt the car seats back as far as they'll go and snooze. After half an hour we make our way to John Lewis. Deirdre points me in the direction of a set of geometric wine glasses for her and matching pair of carafes for Martin.

"There. Satisfied? Two presents off your list."

December 10th
Deirdre incandescent waves the local paper in my face as I enter her kitchen carrying two jars of home-made mince meat.

"Don't think you'll get round me with that," she bellows.

"Calm down Deirdre ..."

"You're a fifth columnist."

"I'm a what?"

Put down jam jars and take paper from her. Headline: *Not so neighbourly dispute. Dear Editor, what has happened to the community spirit so prevalent in our little town during the nineteen fifties? Everyone is out for themselves. Only recently our neighbour planted a Norwegian Maple a mere fifteen feet away from our bay window. These trees grow to eighty feet and more! We feel powerless in our efforts to persuade her to move it before the foundations of our property are undermined. This neighbour represents one of the new breed of incomers, brash, moneyed and beyond reason.*

"Is that you?"

"I'm not brash, moneyed and beyond reason."

"You know what I mean – did you write this letter?"

"Of course I didn't. Your tree's at least twenty five feet away from my bay window and note the use of 'we' and 'our'."

"Then it's the ugly sisters."

Martin appears in the kitchen doorway, frowning.

"Martin, I've whittled the culprits down to those interfering busy bodies next door."

He ignores her and picks up the newspaper, frown increasing.

"What's the matter, darling?"

"Is this true?" he asks, "Will it grow to eighty feet?"

"I have no idea. I thought it was a Japanese Maple. Six foot after ten years."

"Deirdre," Martin says sternly, (she quails slightly), "I want the correct facts about that spindly little runt of a tree in our front garden. What is it and how big will it grow?"

"Japanese, Norwegian, what does it matter?"

"It matters about seventy foot worth. I don't want a bloody tree dwarfing my house and cutting out the light in the library."

Leave Martin and Deirdre arguing. Martin saying tree must go, Deirdre saying over her dead body.

In morning tree gone. Assume Deirdre is dead but see her getting into her car wearing huge sun glasses and a wide brimmed hat looking like an Italian film star. Do not know why I think this as I don't know any Italian film stars apart from Sophia Loren who looks nothing like Deirdre.

December 11th
Leafless Japanese Maple shivering out in Deirdre's front garden. Looks as if it needs at least a warm cardigan.

December 12th
Go to London. Am staying in Laura's flat for two nights. Believe her to be at Iris's flat. Saturday evening follow directions to a party Laura has told me about. Dress with care as I want to make an excellent impression. Wear a red tee shirt with "Some Girls have all the Luck!" written across the front – lucky recent find from Hospice Shop. Am not so sure of my *Fab Clothing* emerald green tubular long skirt even while appreciating useful pockets for keys, loose change and small torch. Legs constricted so can only take minute steps. Walk down several dark and empty roads recalling Wheeler's Watch advice to dress in clothes suitable for a fast sprint.

Arrive at party to find that I'm the only woman wearing a skirt. Predominant colours worn by party goers black with a smattering of gold lurex.

Laura bounces up and says, "Blimey you look like a Christmas cracker."

Stand on dignity. Ask stiffly whether that is good or bad?

She scratches her head in affected perplexed manner and says, "Your guess is as good as mine. Look I want to tell you – you haven't seen me in months."

"But I saw you a week ago."

"You didn't …"

Handsome woman wearing black jeans and tee shirt appears at Laura's side and takes her arm affectionately, looks inquiringly at me.

"You must be Iris," I said holding out my hand. Notice Laura is trying to cross her eyes and wink at the same time. I falter.

"This is Pam," Laura says.

"Ah Pam. I've heard so much about you," I gush. Pam takes my hand, returns it to me with at least two fingers broken.

"I'm Margaret."

"Yeah, I guessed."

Laura says, "I haven't heard from Margaret in eons. How long has it been, six months? She's way behind with my life history."

Agree weakly that I *am* way behind. Pam kisses Laura, grins at me and drifts away towards the kitchen. Laura says quickly and furtively, "Pam thinks I stopped seeing Iris at least four months ago."

"Why would she think that?"

"Because it's what I've told her."

"Why would you do that?"

"Because it's what Pam wants to hear. She wouldn't be happy with the truth."

"Which is?"

"Oh questions, questions. We split up last weekend and I didn't want to come to this party on my own."

"What about me? I'm your oldest friend."

"Precisely and anyway you don't dance."

"I can jig around."

"Not the same thing at all."

"Aren't you even upset?"

"Of course I'm upset but I'm not about to wallow in it. Here comes Pam. Say as little as possible. Treat all questions as incriminatory. You know nothing about anything to do with me – Pam, you're an angel. How did you know I was gasping for a drink?"

Enjoyed party. Met many women I knew through Georgie. Was surprised and pleased that they all wanted to talk to me. Did dance. Regretted telling Laura that I could 'jig around'. Actually danced rather well.

December 14th

Have been roped in by Miriam's vicar for 'Christmas Carol Parade' duties. Miriam has surprised me by disclosing that she plays an accordion. Brings accordion in to the office while Tom is away delivering festive bottles of whisky to his clients and rattles through her repertoire. At the end of an hour begin to find all tunes sounding remarkably similar to one of mum's old favourites, *South of the Border down Mexico way*, apart from *The Sailor's Hornpipe* and *If I had a Hammer*. Try to sing "Away in a

Manger" to tune of *South of Border* etc. This works surprisingly well. Miriam very excited! Says her vicar will be pleased as she's always trying to put a contemporary slant on old hymns. Vicar says it *helps to get the punters in.*

We try others. Find almost every carol with the exception of *Hark the Herald Angels Sing*, can be fitted into *South of the Border*. Miriam muses on whether she should wear a sombrero and a false moustache. Maybe a poncho. She owns several ponchos she'd crocheted herself during the nineteen sixties.

"Crocheted ponchos don't sound very Mexican," I tell her.

Receive scornful look. Miriam says I don't know what I'm talking about and that I'm on very dodgy ground criticizing her crocheting. Explain patiently that no way am I criticizing her crocheting, on the contrary her crocheting is of first class quality but a) a crocheted poncho doesn't sound very Mexican and b) in any case is dressing up as a stereotypical Mexican appropriate for a Christmas Carol Parade?

Miriam looks most annoyed. Says, "I'll be the judge of that," and packs away her accordion.

December 15th

Laura telephoned. Said sorry about the mix-up at party. Said, if you're making an omelette you have to crack eggs. Replied that I did not wish to be a part of her egg cracking activities.

Laura said impatiently, "Can we move on? I want to talk about Christmas."

"Go on."

"Nic and Simone have invited me to their house for Christmas dinner."

"They've invited me as well."

"Did you know they'd invited your neighbour Deirdre?"

Was most surprised, "But they hardly know Deirdre."

"They do now. She called in to offer Nic belated congratulations on her Golden Trowel win. Asked if she could see Nic's famous clematis folly. Said she knew they wouldn't mind as she was such a dear friend of yours. Had seen you through your recent bereavement."

Could not be annoyed with Deirdre. She is unstoppable. In fact during the afternoon in she bounced carrying a small bunch of red roses. "Saw these and thought of you," she said, "Kettle on. I know you'll be livid but I wangled an invite to your mates in the posh house. Throw me out on the street if you're furious."

Switched on kettle. Found vase for roses. "Biscuits Deirdre?"

"Not today. We're on a spiritual biscuit fast between now and Christmas Eve. It's hell but we're taking it one day at a time."

December 16th

Tom offers us the choice of a festive get-together in the office, a meal at Carlito's Way or a fifty pound bonus. Miriam and I opt for the bonus then offer to treat Tom to Carlito's Way as he is partnerless and spending Christmas with his mum – *Absolutely no problemo, adore the ground she walks on, she's one in a million.* Tom quite overcome by our generosity.

December 17th

Miriam is wearing a sombrero and a false moustache, also a poncho but not crocheted. It's made of a piece of grey blanket to which she's appliquéd felt holly leaves and berries. Everyone else including me and the vicar are wearing sensible coats, scarves and hats. 'Parade' consists of the three of us, several small children from the Sunday School and their parents. The plan is to march on the shopping precinct and mingle with the Christmas shoppers.

Miriam very much in her element. NB. Would have never thought at the beginning of the year that Miriam would be in her element dressing up in pseudo Mexican garb and playing an accordion in public. She sets off at our head hailing passers by with "Season's greeting amigos."

We march in twos. I partner a small boy called Simon who is listing all the Christmas presents he hopes to get. "The computer's a cert., the scooter's a cert., the golf clubs are a cert., the ..."

"How old are you?"

"Eight."

"What do you want with golf clubs?"

Gives me a withering look and continues with list.

Miriam now about fifteen yards ahead of us playing *All you need is love*. Vicar sprints after her and orders her to stand still so we can all catch up.

"We'll start with *In the bleak mid-winter* to the traditional tune please Miriam?"

"What about *South of the Border*?"

"We'll reserve that for *Come all ye faithful*."

Miriam twiddles her moustache and says, "Certainment, mon Capitaine."

Vicar looks about to lose her temper. Miriam deflates. Our small parade of carolers proceeds singing weakly.

Shopping precinct packed. No immediately evident Christmas spirit. We are pushed and shoved. I find myself isolated, pressed up against the window of Marks and Spencer. Spot vicar waving hymn sheet above the heads of the crowd, "Sing up," I hear her bellow.

"Snow was falling snow on snow," I shout.

"Snow was doing what darling?" man asks.

"Falling snow on snow," my voice is lost in the noise. Elbows, shopping bags, other hard, indiscernible implements press into me. No sign of vicar, no sign of Miriam's sombrero, no sign of children and their parents, experience feelings of intense panic, I am going to be crushed against this glass window, will slither to the ground and my body will be discovered completely flattened at eight o'clock when the precinct closes. Actually begin to slither but suddenly my scarf is gripped, my arm is gripped. I hear the distinct words, "Yes it is Margaret," as my body is wrested past the window, in through Marks & Spencer's double doors and deposited in the relative quiet at the back of a stack of wire baskets.

"We nearly lost you there," Martin says, "Whose stupid idea was it to go singing carols in that mob?"

Deirdre said, "We saw you from the Coffee Shop. Come on, our coffee's getting cold."

Return with them to Coffee Shop. Martin orders a *Coffee Ice Magnifico* for me and a Danish Pastry. Says if I don't want it, they'll probably manage to get it down. Feel very grateful. Sit quietly listening to their shopping exploits only rousing myself to duck sideways as Carol Parade passes our window looking completely unscathed although Miriam's sombrero now at an odd angle.

December 18th
Telephone call from Laura.
   "You're a dark horse," she started with.
   "Am I?"
   "You kept that one close to your chest."
   "Did I?"
   "I expected you to be in mourning over the fair Georgie for at least a decade."
   "Laura, what are you talking about?"
   "Janice, the galloping gardener."
   Went cold, then hot, then cold again.
   "I'm not sure what you mean."
   "I think you do. Pam told me that a friend of hers knew a woman at work who was best mates with this other woman who worked with a landscape gardener called Janice. And this Janice was, *sick, puke, yuck*, potty about a friend of mine who lived in a twee sounding outpost in Sussex. I said, "No way, my friend not out of mourning for her last partner." Then Pam said 'Her name's Margaret Charlecote.' And there can't be that many Margaret Charlecote's in your twee sounding outpost."
   Found nothing to say.
   "Well?" Laura prompted.
   "Could you repeat that?"
   "What, 'her name's Margaret Charlecote'?"
   "No, the bit that came after *sick, puke, yuck.*"
   Walked on the beach for an hour. Even in winter, the first break in the weather and the beach gets busy. I noticed lots of couples, admittedly most of them straight but all holding hands. Began to calm down. Looked for things that might interest Janice if she were with me, the dogs chasing sticks and discarded plastic bottles, the late seagull fledglings, fat and brown feathered sitting feathers ruffled on the pebbles, the kids and adults bouncing stones on the waves.
   Sit on a bench and think of Janice, how she lightly touches my elbow when I'm crossing the road, picture her face and that rare smile. *Margaret, keep the faith*, I tell myself.

December 20th
Go with Miriam to now definitely gay friendly pub. Have seen advertisement in *What's On* in the local. Small rainbow banner

proclaiming Delicious Home Cooked Food, Fine Wines, Local Beers, Live Music before 9pm and in tiny italics, *Gay Friendly*.

Pub dressed for Christmas: in corner twinkling tree, much tinsel looped above the bar and posters wishing us all a *Very Happy Christmas*.

"This is nice," I said to Miriam when she came back with our drinks.

"What about the rest of the lgbt community?"

Respond mildly, "It's a step in the right direction."

"Right direction be damned, I've a good mind to write to the *List* ..."

Now I've stopped writing it seems everyone else has started. This afternoon Deirdre showed me her long list of complaints about *Bittlesea Bay*'s populace which she intends to send after the christmas postal rush. Final paragraph: *Why can't we ship fifty percent of this town's population including children under twenty abroad and import sophisticated continental types who will start wine bars, restaurants and create a cosmopolitan ambiance?*

Back at table in gay friendly pub I smile warmly at the landlord who looks a little concerned by Miriam's lowering brow and brusque manner.

"Don't do that," Miriam says sharply.

"Do what?"

"Grin at matey over there."

"Why not? No good encouraging us to come to his pub and then finding out we're miserable and aggressive."

"There's a principal at stake."

"Oh for goodness sake Miriam can we just have a pleasant evening?"

Miriam relaxes and actually smiles at me, "Ok. It's great, isn't it? Feeling cheerful."

"Yes."

"You'll notice I'm not asking why. I'm giving you space. I've learnt a bit about human nature spending time with my caring, sharing vicar."

"I'm very pleased."

"So anything doing? Any action? Hanky panky afoot?"

"Nothing to report as yet."

"At least Georgie's a dim and distant memory."

"Yes, just about."

Miriam fidgets with her watch strap then says, "I wanted to say that since the two of you split up I feel we've become proper friends. All the years we've worked together – you always seemed completely absorbed in yours and Georgie's life, there wasn't much room for anyone else."

Study Miriam in yellow light of pub which not kind to her and surely not kind to me either. Realise I like Miriam.

"I know," I said, "I'm glad we're friends. It's odd, only a matter of months since she left for good yet I feel so different. I *was* complacent and set in my domestic couple routines. In a way I don't blame her for leaving, only the dishonesty."

Later in the evening when both of us had settled into a mellow good humour the landlord brought over two free drinks. Miriam managed to get in a few words with him about the lgbt community as a whole but pleasantly, her words slightly slurred. On the way home she told me that the vicar has advised her to replace irritability with compassion which she finds much easier to do after a meal of scampi and chips washed down with several glasses of wine.

December 22nd
My last day at Russell's. Receive a Russell's gift voucher for thirty pounds, a very large poinsettia, and a biscuit barrel. "Don't be a stranger," Peter tells me. "No way," I respond with great enthusiasm as if wild horses wouldn't keep me away.

December 23rd
In Deirdre's gazebo. Quite warm as she's lit her oil powered outside heater. In fact almost too warm. Deirdre resentful as she feels that she has been forced out of the house by Martin. He's playing the electric guitar he's just given himself as an early Christmas present. He has been out first thing to buy the Jerry Lee Lewis Songbook from a local music shop.

"I've had *Your Cheating Heart* up to here," Deirdre said and, "Who is Jerry Lee Lewis? Wasn't he an American comedian? Why can't Martin have someone contemporary and quiet for an idol?"

Admit that although I did used to like *Your Cheating Heart*, (also one of mum's favourites), Martin's bangra treatment had rather overwhelmed the poignancy of the lyrics.

213

Sudden cessation of sound from Martin and we enjoy the tranquility of the low hum of her outdoor heater. Slowly become aware of tap-tapping sound coming from the kitchen. It continues. Deirdre seems unaware of the noise. I notice Lord Dudley in kitchen window which means he's journeyed over several work surfaces to reach this spot. He flattens his relatively flat face against the glass and stares meaningfully at Deirdre.

I said, "Deirdre, I think Lord Dudley's trying to tell you something."

"Oh blast it," she says but good humouredly. Raises her voice, "Come out of there you little devil," she shouts.

No response from Lord Dudley. Tapping sound ceases abruptly then after thirty seconds begins again only more frantically. Lord Dudley makes a silent miaow.

Deirdre shouts, "I mean it. You're in trouble if I have to leave my gazebo …"

Lord Dudley peers back over his shoulder into kitchen. Hear an annoyed squawk and then a large sea gull marches out of the kitchen onto the decking. It riffles its feathers irritably. Deirdre beams. "Clever boy," she says and then to me, "I speak the language of animals."

December 24th
Determined to keep cheerful although there's been no word from Janice. Laura has arrived and says, "You've got her mobile number – ring the woman."

But I won't. Laura in over-excitable mood and spending much time on the telephone to Iris, Pam and her mother.

December 25th
Laura and I trudged up the hill towards the twinkling lights of Simone and Nic's festive front garden singing, *Last Christmas you gave me your heart* at the top of our voices as Laura said she couldn't stand the peace and tranquility that descended on the earth at this time of year.

"Actually last Christmas you gave me your hat," Laura said cheerfully.

It was a misty Christmas morning, about eleven. We'd been asked over for mince pies and rum punch before dinner. Laura and I agreed that as we'd individually been eating mince pies since they'd appeared in the shops at the end of September that we'd make straight for the punch.

"But we mustn't overdo it," Laura said.

"You mustn't. Moderation in all things, that's my motto."

"It would be."

Looking up we could see that several women were already packed into Nic and Simone's loggia. Nic calls it her 'ship's prow' after several whiskies when she imagines herself to have been a ship's captain in a previous life.

The front door flew open and Deirdre streamed out, "Where have you been? I'm feeling very isolated being the only straight woman at this gathering. You didn't walk did you?"

"Yes, it's a lovely morning," we marched briskly between the two inflated reindeer tied to the gate posts.

"Is it?" Deirdre wrinkled her nose, "I'd have driven you – you should have rung."

"We did."

"Or left a message on the answer phone."

"We did."

"C'est la vie," Deirdre shrugged her diamonté shoulders, "Martin bought me this jumper – he has immaculate taste."

"It's very you," I said diplomatically.

"Happy Christmas. Merry Xmas. Season's Greetings. Yuletide smackers," Simone shouted edging Deirdre aside, grabbing me by the shoulders and kissing me loudly on both cheeks.

"Like my earrings?" she swung a large plastic christmas tree earring into my face.

"They're very you," I said diplomatically.

Behind me Laura prodded my back, "They're vile," she shouted, "They look like they came out of a cracker."

"Actually they did. Come here you little devil," and Laura's head disappeared between Simone's big and bouncy breasts.

"Did you-know-what arrive?" Laura asked when she came up for air.

"She did."

"Oh you mean ..." Deirdre said then clamped her hand over her mouth.

"Will you lot stop letting in the cold air and get up here," Nic yelled from the top of the house steps.

215

We trouped inside, cramped ourselves into the loggia. Everyone was shouting, five women making a huge, boisterous, happy noise.

"Ter-rah!" yelled Laura.

"Surprise, surprise!," shouted everyone else.

A sixth woman, Janice stood silent and sullen pressed between the window and Simone's gigantic Art Nouveau jardiniere.

"Happy Christmas Margaret," she said and started coughing.

"Happy Christmas Janice."

And then she smiled and I smiled. I pushed my way through to her. "Why are you here? I didn't know you'd be here," I burbled.

"Deirdre organized it. I asked her to. As a surprise and then I thought, oh bloody hell suppose she doesn't want to see me after three weeks."

"Of course I want to see you."

Nic stood in the doorway wearing a plastic apron, a gravy boat in one hand and a whisky glass in the other. Above the noise she roared, "Mince pies and rum punch being served now in the dining room. Any spills on my new maple effect laminate must be reported immediately to the chef, i.e. me!"

We explode out into the hall. I want to talk to Janice but feel inexplicably shy.

Laura is ahead of me talking to Nic, "I thought Janice would be more of a live wire," she says.

"Bronchitis. Every time she talks she coughs."

"Shouldn't she be in bed?"

"She wanted to see Margaret?"

"She hasn't wanted to see Margaret for at least three weeks, why would she want to see her now that she's got bronchitis?"

"Who's got bronchitis?" Deirdre asked.

"I have," Janice said and started to cough.

We assemble in the dining room. Deirdre starts telling Simone about her new approach to life for the coming year, "Chicken salad or chicken shit – we all have a choice."

"What about vegetarians?" Laura asked.

"Fruit salad or fruit …"

"Cake?" Simone swallows a chunk of cake and wipes her hands fondly on Laura's head, "Deirdre, where's your Martin?"

"Watching television."

"He's not in the front room. Nic got in Hellraiser 1 to 20 to keep him occupied while we all have a laugh."

"He's watching television at home. He says women en masse get up his nose."

"That's not very festive spirited of him," Laura said dipping a stray cup into the rum punch, "This is lovely stuff Margaret, you should have a slurp."

"I'll get you a glass Margaret," Janice said quietly stifling a cough.

Deirdre, who doesn't drink but does eat, tucks into the mince pies tossing her blonde hair tells everyone, "Martin believes Christmas is a Capitalist plot to keep the proletariat content while they're being crushed under the government's boot heel. Martin's very clever. Almost a genius. When he was in his teens he won Mensa."

"Crikey," I said.

Laura says, "Deirdre are you sure he didn't say, "When I was in my teens I wore Menswear?""

Deirdre looks perplexed. Crumbs drop amongst the diamanté. I hug her, "Take no notice, Laura's teasing you. Martin's a smashing chap."

"He is. Not sociable but very generous. Take this jumper ..."

Laura, "No you take it, diamanté is bad for my sinuses ..."

Janice said, "That's enough now, Laura."

Simone rapped on the table with a spoon, "Can we have a toast?"

"Toast! Not after six mince pies and a bucket of grog ..."

Quite amiably yet firmly Janice put her hand over Laura's mouth. Laura subsides.

We all shut up. Nic fills our glasses. Deirdre murmurs that an orange and passion fruit drink might be nice but is satisfied with a Diet Coke. Finally Nic stands at the head of the table and raises her glass, "A toast to Christmas and all our friends, present and ... Simone what's the opposite of present?"

"Departed? Dead? Not present?"

"Whatever, whatever," says Nic, "Merry Christmas to everyone."

"Merry Christmas," we shout, swig back our drinks.

Janice takes me by the elbow and leads me out to the loggia. Suddenly with only the two of us it does feel a bit like standing on the prow of a ship. We face each other and Janice says, "Phew!."

I say, "Phew indeed," and for once don't feel like a prim and proper school mistress.

"I bought you this."

From her rucksack behind the jardiniere she produces a heart shaped, red velvet box. Inside is a tiny silver broach in the shape of a teddy bear. I am speechless. Near to tears. Janice is smiling. Then she starts coughing. Everyone is trooping back up the hall towards the loggia. I hear Deirdre telling someone, "What that woman wants is a tincture of hypericum mixed with echinacea."

"Merry Christmas Janice," I lean across and kiss her.

"Hold it right there," Laura shouts, "That woman's infectious."

We all start laughing.

December 27th

Laura telephones to apologize if she'd seemed unusually boisterous over Christmas but she was finding the reality of no girlfriend unsettling. I asked, "What happened to Pam then?"

"It was not to be."

"Yes, but what happened?"

"She said I was unreliable, Machiavellian, and a real pain in the butt."

"Are you upset?"

"Not about Pam."

"About Iris?"

Long pause then, "Actually I do rather miss her. I can't believe she doesn't like me anymore, can you?"

Loyally reply, "No I can't. Why not ring her?"

"I have rung her."

"Go round. Make her laugh. Push a photograph of the two of you through her letterbox."

"Would that work?"

"It might."

December 28th
Janice on course of antibiotics and much improved. Laura reports that she and Iris are back together although Iris has threatened, *One false move and it's curtains!*

December 30th
See Mr. Wheeler out with Vera. They are in the Hospice Shop holding between them a pair of olive green velvet curtains. They both see me, look embarrassed. Vera hurriedly replaces the curtains on the rail while Mr. Wheeler breaks away and begins to inspect a fine display of tupperware.

December 31st
Janice coming later. We are seeing in our first New Year.

Sat with Kitten on bench overlooking the garden. Everything as it should be. The meadow which I'd mown in early November lies dormant and flattened after the recent torrential rain. Today the sky has cleared and is a cold blue. Most of the gulls are either down on the beach or riding the waves but every now and then I see a white chevron soaring high above me.

Next door I can see Deirdre at her computer, Lord Dudley sits in his box lid next to her elbow. Just now she waved and mouthed *Cuppa at two o'clock.* I nodded.

I feel so very different from this time last year when Georgie was away in Scotland. It's as if I've shed many layers: clothes, loves, likes, dislikes, all routines. This is a ludicrous image but in my mind I am a naked middle aged woman stepping out into unknown territory. A fresh start. How my life turns out doesn't depend even on Janice ... or my friends ... or circumstance. It depends on me.